"THIS DU... ...IS IT?"

"Vital, so far as you people are concerned," said Wilson. He demonstrated with his own right hand. "When she first struggled, she clawed at her throat to try and grip the ligature. Natural reflex. But then, as she began to lose consciousness her arms would have flailed everywhere, trying to get a purchase on something. Then, in the moment of death—" Wilson closed his fist dramatically, ivory knuckled, his fingertips grinding into the palm "—but even tighter than that. That's the cadaveric spasm I mentioned this morning.

"I had to open that poor young woman's fist with a dental retractor. That dust is the last thing Vera Jackman got hold of. Find the source, and that's where she was strangled."

Roper felt his skin prickling, his pulse quickening.

"English village atmosphere and vivid characterization..." —*Publishers Weekly*

A PRETTY PLACE FOR A MURDER

ROY HART

WORLDWIDE.

TORONTO • NEW YORK • LONDON
AMSTERDAM • PARIS • SYDNEY • HAMBURG
STOCKHOLM • ATHENS • TOKYO • MILAN
MADRID • WARSAW • BUDAPEST • AUCKLAND

A PRETTY PLACE FOR A MURDER

A Worldwide Mystery/October 1994

First published by St. Martin's Press, Incorporated.

ISBN 0-373-28021-1

Printed in U.S.A.

For June—at last

ONE

IT WAS CLOSING TIME at the Cort Arms and Vera Jackman had only some twenty minutes of her young life left to her. Although if Vera herself had been told that she was soon to die, she would have poured withering contempt upon the teller in no uncertain terms.

'Me?' she would have retorted, between spitefully gritted but otherwise pretty teeth. 'Not me, old darling. But I can tell you who pretty soon will be. Oh, yes, *indeed* I can.' And with a flick of her long red hair—last year she had been a brunette—Vera would have continued to dry the pots and glasses and stand them upended on the towel beside the beer pumps.

All in all, it had not been one of Vera's better days. At nine-thirty this very morning, Dr Pedlar had informed her that her recent test at the cottage hospital was positive. She was pregnant. At midday she had accepted a dubious £20 note in exchange for ten gallons of petrol at her brother's garage. Sergeant Jollyboy had driven over and gone through the motions of asking questions, but Vera, who was usually an expert on expensive motorcars—and their drivers, if they were male—had only noticed that the car was a Jaguar. A white one, with grey upholstery. She had not looked at its number plate. Since leaving Dr Pedlar's surgery she had had too much on her mind to worry about a number plate—or a fake £20 note for that matter.

Jack Crosby bolted the saloon-bar door behind the last customer. In the public bar Wally Tupper was already emptying the ashtrays and swabbing the tables. Tuesday was always a quiet night at the Cort Arms.

'Is it OK if I blow now, Mr Crosby?' said Vera, draping the towel she had been using over the beer-pump handles. She smiled winsomely. 'I'll make the time up tomorrow. Get here a bit earlier if you like.'

'Yes, sure,' said Crosby, as he came back through the counter-flap. Like most men, Jack Crosby was willing prey to Vera's charms. He *could* have pointed out to her that her contracted hours were seven to eleven, for which he paid her £3.50 a night—there were tips too—and that she was rarely here after ten-forty-five on any night, but he did not. Vera was the main attraction here at the Cort Arms. The boys came from miles to flirt with Vera. 'Like a drink before you go?'

'No, thanks, Mr Crosby,' said Vera. 'I've still got some ironing to do when I get back home.'

'Come on,' wheedled Crosby. 'A G and T, eh? Just a quickie.'

Jack Crosby had a soft spot for her, she knew that. He had been a widower for almost a year now and was starting to send out unmistakable signals. But Vera, especially just lately, had set her sights on far higher stakes.

'Well . . . OK. I will have a G and T. Thanks.' Five minutes one way or the other would make little difference. And, besides, a drink would fortify her for the battle ahead; although it had been a drink too many that had led her into her present predicament. Not that she had been a virgin before that, but she had always seen to it that her boyfriends had used what she called 'precautions.' Vera's blood had been running hotly since she was fourteen and she had soon learned that sex—and even the false promise of it—could turn even the most sensible of men to putty in her hands. It was a power she intended to put to good use when she finally arrived in the Big City.

But what she was not intending to do was to arrive in London pregnant. An abortion was the first thing. And for that she wanted money. Money enough to have it done privately in a *proper* clinic; not on the National Health where you had to sit in the outpatients' waiting room of the local cottage hospital where everyone could see you—and perhaps even recognise you. Old Dr Pedlar—that stupid old fool—had told her huffily that *he* wouldn't sanction an abortion on demand at any price. There would have to be a proper reason... Was she on good terms with the father? There was always marriage...

Such advice smattered of the quaint. Vera was up-to-date, a free spirit of the late twentieth century, a young woman with her head full of plans for a future career that would see her financially independent before she was twenty-one. And her name, at least metaphorically, in bright lights. She'd read how those girls who posed topless for the tabloid newspapers could earn a fortune in just a year. An absolute *fortune*.

'Not your usual self tonight, Vera,' said Crosby concernedly, handing her her gin and tonic with ice and a slice of lemon floating in it. 'I suppose you're still cut up about that twenty-quid note.'

'Yes,' said Vera, not altogether truthfully. 'Sort of, Mr Crosby.'

Crosby sipped at his tankard of best bitter; the best in the county, some said. 'This Mr Crosby stuff,' he chided hopefully, 'let's forget it, shall we? I reckon it's about time you called me Jack, don't you?'

'OK,' she said, hitching one near naked shoulder and smiling flirtatiously at him. 'Sure. Why not... Jack?'

All she had to do was click her fingers. And *zap*! Jack Crosby was well into his forties, but he was steady and, as he had made a point of telling her several times, had more than a fair few shillings tucked away. So, for the time being, Jack Crosby was a boat it was better not to burn. At least, not until she had found someone less sinkable.

'Look,' Crosby said helpfully, 'if you're worried about that twenty... well, you know where to come, don't you? I mean, I'm not short of a few bob.'

'No,' said Vera, over her gin and tonic. 'It's OK, Mr Crosby... Jack... really. But thanks all the same.'

'I was only saying you know where to come.'

'Yes,' said Vera. 'Sure. And thanks.'

But Vera herself, at the moment, was not exactly poverty-stricken. She had £1850 in the building society. Her target was £2000, which seemed a nice round sum with which to launch herself upon London. She would have saved it by now, only three weeks ago, at that time unaware that she was pregnant, she had gone along to Bournemouth and blued nearly £100 on having a set of pictures taken of herself by a professional photographer. Bound into an expensive red-leather album, they were presently secreted at the back of her wardrobe. If Fred were to see them he'd practically go through the roof and not just because of what it had cost either.

Wally Tupper shambled through the arch that connected the counter of the public bar to the counter of the saloon. He carried a plastic bottle of disinfectant. Without a word, he continued through the open counter-flap towards the saloon-bar toilets. Vera tried not to look at him. Wally Tupper gave her the creeps, made her flesh crawl. Vera abhorred anything that wasn't quite normal.

She tipped down the last of her gin and tonic. Time for the fray. She'd got it all rehearsed. Pay up, she was going to say, or I'll make your name stink all over the village. And it was only a small place, Cort Abbas. The right gossip fed in at one end could reappear, luridly garnished, at the other within the hour.

'Well ... Jack ... I'd better be off.'

'Course,' said Crosby with a smile, but with a tinge of disappointment in his voice and his eyes licking all over her like a devoted puppy. 'See you tomorrow then, eh?'

'And I'll try to be early,' said Vera winningly. 'Promise.'

'Don't worry about it,' said Crosby. He followed her through the counter-flap, his eyes fondly taking in the bouncing red hair, the seductive—and much-practised—walk, the lissom legs in impossibly high heels. He had, after all, been a widower for a long time now and he was still only forty-eight, wasn't he? And there was still a lot of life in him, and needs, too, and he was only human, wasn't he? And if he didn't make *some* kind of move soon it was likely that one of the local young bucks might beat him to it; so he summoned up the proposition he had been preparing and polishing for many weeks and, at long last, the nerve to utter it, opened his mouth to frame it... but then snapped it shut again like a frustrated goldfish as Wally Tupper reappeared from the toilets. Perhaps tomorrow... definitely tomorrow.

When Crosby at last let her out into the street, Vera's mortal term had been reduced to fourteen minutes.

The night sky was pricked with stars and the ground underfoot was still exhaling the heat of the day. Vera noticed neither. As a rule, upon leaving the Arms she turned to the right, towards Jackman's Service Station. Tonight her ultimate folly was to turn to the left, her face set, her heels clacking purposefully on the warm pavement.

TWO

THE LINE OF white police vehicles shimmered in the heat of the quiet country lane. At ten o'clock in the morning it was already hot enough to turn all the bodily juices to a sluggishly flowing treacle.

Two duckboards spanned the drainage ditch at the back of the grass verge. Roper crouched on one, Sergeant Jollyboy, the local village bobby, on the other, while beneath them in the dry, leaf-filled ditch Dr Pedlar, the village GP, went through the necessary procedures to pronounce the body lifeless. About this group a couple of cadets were setting up a canvas screen. Another was setting up traffic cones and a blue-and-white diversion sign.

She was—or rather had been—an exceptionally pretty girl. A redhead, although perhaps more by dint of the tinting brush than by any intent of nature. Her face was tinged blue, her eyes filmed and vacant and staring. It was, Roper recognised all too well, clearly the face of a young woman who had spent her last few seconds fighting for air. Her lips and ears were purple, her tongue had been forced outward between her teeth, and about her throat was the unmistakable circle of bruising caused by a ruthlessly applied cord—or whatever.

She lay on her back, her pale limbs slackly spread, dead leaves caught in her disordered but otherwise shiny hair, one black shoe on her right foot, the other a yard or so away along the bottom of the ditch. Her clothes were stylish but cheap—a loose white shirt, cinched in at the waist with a shiny black belt, over a short black skirt. Presently rucked higher still, the skirt revealed a pair of flimsy red knickers, which hopefully disposed of rape as a motive.

'Her name's Vera Jackman,' said Jollyboy, a plump, middle-aged and usually jovial policeman; the sort, Roper knew, who would know this patch like other men know their faces in their shaving mirrors. 'Her brother owns the service station across the village. Fred Jackman. Born and brought up here, both of 'em.'

'Nice-looking girl,' observed Roper. 'Or was.'

'Smart too,' said Jollyboy. 'Too smart for this place.'

'Meaning what?'

Jollyboy shrugged glumly. Murder had never visited Cort Abbas before and he remembered Vera Jackman when she was still in her pram. 'Small village,' he said. 'Sparky girl. Couldn't wait to get out. Had her mind on bigger things. That's the feeling I always had about young Vera.'

Down in the ditch, Dr Pedlar was putting away his stethoscope. 'She's well into rigor, Superintendent,' he said. He was an elderly man and, like Sergeant Jollyboy, murder was something he had never had to deal with before. 'I'd say she'd been dead for about twelve hours. I can't be exact, of course, but that's my guess.'

He passed up his black case and one of the cadets held the aluminum ladder while he climbed out of the ditch with some assistance from Sergeant Jollyboy.

'The poor child was strangled,' he said. 'A cord—certainly not manually.' With a tremulous hand Dr Pedlar took off his spectacles and slipped them into their case. Doctor or not, he was a man clearly disturbed. 'I think, frankly, that you should get one of your own medical people down here, Superintendent. I'm simply not competent, you see.'

'There's one on his way, Dr Pedlar,' said Roper. 'But thanks for your help.'

Behind Pedlar, the scene-of-crime photographer was taking his gruesome pictures again.

Pedlar started across the grass verge towards his car, but only for a couple of paces before he stopped and half turned. 'Oh, yes, Superintendent—there *is* something else I can tell you. Miss Jackman was pregnant—seven weeks. I had her results through from the cottage hospital yesterday... If that's any help.'

In Roper's book, all was grist. There was no such thing as useless information. 'Thanks, Doctor. Any ideas about the father?'

'Sorry. She never told me and I didn't ask her.'

'Pity,' said Roper.

ROPER AND JOLLYBOY drove slowly down the lane, a smallholding on one side, the cemetery of St Christopher's church on the other. According to Jollyboy, the present population of Cort Abbas was down to 400 souls—and falling. The young people could hardly wait to get out.

'It's dying on its feet,' said Jollyboy. 'In summer we get the tourists come to see the church and the old cottages—and take their cream teas at Cort Place. In

winter, it all folds up. The youngsters get bored, so
they hoppit. Can't say I blame 'em really.'

To their right, over a low brick wall, the cemetery
petered out and gave way to the grounds of the church.
The present incumbent, according to Jollyboy, was the
Reverend Smallways. Beside the lych gate a noticeboard bore a few hand-written notices. The church itself was a rugged Norman box with a square central
tower and was surrounded by yew trees. In its shad-
owed porch Mr Smallways himself was parking his
bicycle and taking off his trouser clips.

Jollyboy ratcheted on the handbrake at the end of
the lane where it opened out on to the several acres of
the village green. On its far side, from due north to due
south, ran the only road of any size through the village. Driving down in haste from County Headquarters, scarcely half an hour ago, Roper had almost
driven past it. The green was the hub of the village. On
this side the church, the war memorial, a few thatched
cottages, and what was obviously the village school.
On the far side more cottages, some thatched, some
tiled, a sprinkling of small shops, a Post Office with a
red mail van outside it.

'And that's Fred Jackman's place,' said Jollyboy,
pointing across the green directly into the morning
sun.

Roper tipped down his sun-visor. The garage stood
on a corner, a converted barn with a tin roof, a small
turn-of-the-century cottage beside it. Just the two
pumps. To its right, on the opposite corner, was a
public house.

'And that's the Cort Arms,' said Jollyboy. 'Vera
Jackman worked there evenings. And what I don't

know about this neck of the woods, old Jack Crosby does. He might be worth a chat.'

Jollyboy drove around the north side of the green, crossed the main street and pulled the white Metro in behind Jackman's petrol pumps. He reached over to the back seat for his cap. 'Would you rather I broke the news, sir?'

'It's down to me, Sergeant,' said Roper. 'But thanks for the offer.'

Both swung their legs out of the Metro and quietly closed its doors behind them. Jollyboy put on his cap and squared it. From the tin-roofed workshop came the high-pitched squeal of an electric drill.

Roper braced himself. Like Dr Pedlar a few minutes ago, he regarded certain of his duties as being more onerous than others. This one, the reporting of a death, the turning of a man from a brother into a mere next of kin, was the one he dreaded most.

They entered the workshop. Jackman had his broad blue-overalled back to them. He was working on the radiator of an elderly Massey-Ferguson tractor. Perhaps he had heard them or perhaps he had only sensed a presence behind him, but abruptly the drill was switched off and he was looking over his shoulder at them. Smart clean overalls, safety goggles, fair-haired. At a guess he was about twenty-eight, give or take a couple of years.

'Mr Jackman?' said Roper.

He regarded them warily. 'Yes,' he said, 'that's me.' He laid the drill on the floor of the tractor beneath the seat and raised his safety goggles. 'What can I do for you?'

Roper proffered his warrant card. 'Detective Superintendent Roper, sir. County CID.'

Jackman's glance at the card was only cursory. He reached into his overall pocket for a ball of cotton-waste and began to wipe his hands on it.

'If it's about the duff twenty-pound note,' he said, 'you can forget about it. I've already written it down to bad luck.' The ball of cotton-waste went back into his pocket. 'And you'll probably think I'm bloody ungrateful, but it could cost me more than twenty-quid just standing here talking about it.'

'It's rather more serious than that, Mr Jackman,' said Roper. 'Is there somewhere we can talk more privately?'

Jackman shrugged. He clearly ran a one-man operation, and was reliable enough at his job to be trusted with someone's new white Range Rover which stood a couple of yards to one side of the battered Massey-Ferguson. He led the way past Jollyboy's Metro to the cottage. Immediately inside the front door, the small room on the right had been smartly fitted out with a counter and racks of shelving filled with car-sundries. The cash register was Japanese. Electronic. Like Jackman himself, it was all very organised, all very tidy, and perhaps it was even a moderately prosperous little business.

'Perhaps you ought to sit down, Fred,' said Jollyboy. He had taken his cap off again.

Jackman went behind his counter and perched himself on the high stool. He clasped his big powerful hands beside the Japanese till. 'I don't make number plates to order and I don't do midnight re-sprays,' he said. 'It's all on the up and up here.'

'Yes, I'm sure it is, Mr Jackman,' said Roper. 'In fact we're here about your sister.' He paused to give Jackman a few seconds to come to terms with what was to follow. 'There's been an accident, sir.' Then, after the euphemism, the harsh cold fact: 'I'm afraid she's dead, Mr Jackman ... I'm sorry.'

Disbelief. Horror. Bewilderment. These were the several expressions that chased each other across Jackman's plump, tanned face. He hadn't known; that much was certain. Roper had been a policeman for long enough to know the difference between the expression of shock and the expression of a man found out.

'That right, Ted?' Jackman asked dazedly of Jollyboy; and when Jollyboy nodded sombrely and said: 'Yes, I'm sorry, old lad,' Jackman slumped back against the wall behind him and let his hands fall to his lap. He murmured softly: 'Jesus.' And, after that, nothing at all for the time he needed for his disbelief to give way to unwilling acceptance. Under his healthy tan he had paled perceptibly.

'What kind of accident?' he said, at last. The question had been asked of Jollyboy, the known, rather than Roper, the unknown. Jollyboy glanced questioningly at Roper who replied with a nod which Jackman probably didn't notice; Roper had already settled on Jollyboy as being the most useful aide he was likely to recruit on this job, the archetypal country copper all the way up from his shoelaces.

'What kind of accident, Ted?' asked Jackman again, now with a soft and dangerous edge to his voice.

'The Super reckons it's foul play, old lad,' said Jollyboy. 'Wally Tupper found Vera in the ditch up Church Lane about twenty past nine this morning.'

Jackman's massive knuckles went white and tight on his knee. He was a big lad, Roper thought, and woe betide anyone who chose to upset him.

'Wally Tupper?' he retorted angrily. 'Perhaps Wally Tupper put her there, too, eh?'

'Now come on, Fred,' cautioned Jollyboy. 'You ought to know better than to say that.'

'Why?' spat Jackman, his pale blue eyes suddenly taking fire. 'Why the hell shouldn't I? The man's a bloody nutter, isn't he? The whole bloody village knows it. Ought to have been bloody locked up years ago.'

'You're out of order, Fred,' warned Jollyboy. 'Remarks like that won't get any of us anywhere.'

For a moment there was an awful silence, and Roper only hoped that Jollyboy had not overstepped the mark. But clearly the sergeant knew this man. Jackman relaxed again.

'When did you last see your sister, Mr Jackman?' asked Roper.

Jackman at last peeled off his safety glasses and dropped them wearily on the counter. He pushed splayed fingers through his hair to tidy it again. 'Last night,' he said. 'About five past seven.'

'You left her in the house?'

'No. She went out. The Cort Arms, across the way. She does—did—five nights a week there.'

'Did you hear her come home?'

'I wouldn't have,' said Jackman. 'I was across with my girlfriend. Wareham way. I didn't get home myself till gone one-thirty.'

'And how about this morning? Did you know she was missing?'

Jackman shook his head. Apparently his sister had been an early riser. She was up and out of the cottage every morning by seven o'clock, except on Sundays. Between then and two o'clock or so she had a rota of cleaning jobs about the village: Creed's Farm, the Vicarage, the Post Office, Blattner—the vet—his waiting room and surgery...

'I don't remember all of 'em,' said Jackman. He had hunched forward morosely over his counter. 'But afternoons she helped out along at Cort Place. Every day except Sundays, that was.'

'A busy young woman then,' said Roper.

'Aye,' said Jackman. 'But only lately. Before that she was a lazy little cow.' Slowly, then, he looked up and fixed Roper with a cold hard stare. 'But lazy cow or not, you'd better find out who did her in. Because if you bloody don't then I bloody will.'

'Don't fret yourself, Mr Jackman,' said Roper. 'We'll get the bastard, believe me.'

'Yes,' retorted Jackman softly, 'you do that.'

'There'll be the question of formal identification, Fred,' said Jollyboy. 'Perhaps this afternoon, along at the cottage hospital. Do you think you can manage that?'

Jackman drew the palm of his hand down his face like a man not sure if he was waking from a nightmare or into one. 'Yes,' he said tiredly. 'Sure. I'll be there.'

'The Sergeant and I will call for you,' said Roper. 'About two-thirty. Meanwhile, I'd rather you didn't touch your sister's room—and perhaps keep the matter to yourself until we've had a chance to make a few enquiries.'

'Right,' said Jackman. '... And Ted'—one of his hands rose from his lap and a finger was levelled at Jollyboy like a cocked pistol—'Wally Tupper—until you find out that bugger didn't kill Vera, you keep the bastard out of my sight. If you don't, I'll kill him. Get me?'

'I know how you feel, Mr Jackman,' said Roper grimly. 'But a word from the wise, sir: Don't.'

ROPER AND JOLLYBOY, out in the sunshine again, crossed the end of the lane towards the Cort Arms on the opposite corner. Its roof was newly thatched and the flowering honeysuckle around its saloon-bar doorway was probably plastic, but other than that there seemed no reason to doubt the year 1724 incised into the oak door-lintel. Two cars were already parked on its small forecourt.

'This Wally Tupper,' said Roper. 'Where is he now?'

'I sent him home,' said Jollyboy. Wally, it seemed, was not overly bright and finding Vera Jackman in Church Lane this morning had completely unnerved him.

They turned into the saloon bar, blessedly cool after the blistering heat outside. Two couples, obviously touring, the owners of the cars on the forecourt, were sitting in a corner by the open back door and taking morning coffee.

Jack Crosby, the landlord, was holding a freshly drawn sample of his best bitter up to the light. He was in his middle to late forties, short and sturdy. White-trousered, red-shirted and wearing rope-soled shoes, he looked as if he was dressed for a regatta. He smiled circumspectly at them, knowing Jollyboy for what he was and guessing Roper's profession as soon as he had come through the doorway. As far as Jack Crosby was concerned, when insurance salesmen, brewery area supervisors and policemen travelled in pairs it invariably meant trouble.

'Morning, gents,' he said, switching on his professional bonhomie as he tipped the sample into the drip-tray beneath the pumps.

'Morning, Jack,' said Jollyboy.

Still cautious, and a time-serving student of human nature by way of his trade, Crosby looked from one to the other of them.

'Business, is it, gents? Or pleasure?'

'Business, Jack,' said Jollyboy. A sideways tilt of his head took in Roper. 'This gentleman is Superintendent Roper. He's from County CID.'

The four coffee-sipping tourists in the corner all glanced up at once, like marionettes suddenly jerked to life by the same string.

Roper moved away to the far end of the bar, out of their sight and out of their hearing. Jollyboy and Crosby followed him. Roper settled himself on a wooden stool and formally showed Crosby his warrant card across the counter.

'I'll try not to keep you long, Mr Crosby,' he said. 'You've got a young woman works evenings for you— Vera Jackman.'

'Yes, that's right,' said Crosby. 'Good girl, good worker. Not so hot on her punctuality, mind. Why? What's she done?'

'Nothing, Mr Crosby,' said Roper, tucking his card back into his jacket. 'Miss Jackman's dead, sir.'

Silence. A steel shutter might have fallen between them. One side of Crosby's mouth dropped fractionally so that his jaw suddenly looked lopsided.

'God! She's not what all that business going on across the green is about, is she? All those coppers rushing about?'

'I'm afraid she is, Mr Crosby,' said Roper. 'Can you tell me when you last saw her?'

It took a few moments for Crosby to gather himself again. He swept a hand up through his thinning dark hair. It looked an honest gesture of bewilderment. 'Er... last night,' he said at last. 'Just after closing time. About ten to eleven.'

'About?'

Crosby reconsidered. 'Well... perhaps a couple of minutes before.'

'And how was she? Normal? Upset? Anything you might have noticed particularly about her?'

Crosby drew a thumb and forefinger together across his eyebrows. No, he thought not—although she had not been her usual cheery self. And she *had* made a couple of silly mistakes on the public-bar till... 'But only pennies,' he added hastily. 'She always told me. Dead honest, that girl.'

'Tell us what happened at closing time,' said Roper. 'Whatever you remember.'

'Well... nothing really,' said Crosby. 'Certainly nothing out of the ordinary.'

Like most potential witnesses, Crosby had to have every last detail elicited from him. It was not that he was unintelligent, merely that he thought his observations unimportant.

From remembering nothing, Roper got him to remember everything. Vera Jackman had been standing there, by the pumps. Rough-drying the glasses. At about twenty minutes to eleven Crosby had bolted the saloon-bar door behind the last customer. Wally Tupper had already been emptying the ashtrays and sweeping the floor in the public bar. As he had returned towards the counter-flap, Crosby had asked Vera if she fancied a drink. She had settled for a gin and tonic. She and Crosby had talked for a few minutes. About nothing in particular. At a couple of minutes before ten to eleven, she had sluiced her gin glass under the hot tap and stood it upended with the other washed glasses beside the beer pumps. She had crossed the saloon bar. Crosby had followed her and seen her off the premises. Wally Tupper had left some ten minutes afterwards, having swept the saloon-bar floor and poured some disinfectant down the toilets.

'When Miss Jackman left, Mr Crosby, did you happen to notice which way she went?'

'That way.' Crosby jerked a thumb over his shoulder. Southward along the main street.

'Not towards Jackman's garage, then?'

'No.' Crosby was absolutely sure about that. The floodlights that lit his forecourt and swinging sign had shown Vera's silhouette passing the far window. She had definitely been walking south. Towards the shops and Cort Place.

'Did she usually go that way?'

'No,' said Crosby. 'Just lately, she'd taken to going straight home.'

'Just lately?'

Apparently, during the course of the last couple of months, Vera Jackman had undergone some kind of sea-change. There seemed to have been no boy-friends, no fast cars, no motorcycles.

'And that was her usual scene, was it, Mr Crosby?'

'Yes, but she's—' Crosby broke off, recalled his tenses. 'She was young, wasn't she? Pretty girl, plenty of life in her—' He broke off again at this other un-fortunate phrase. 'Well, you know what I mean. Look, all these questions—there's something wrong, isn't there?' He glanced, frowning, across at Jolly-boy, then back again to Roper. 'She didn't *just* die, did she?' The frown slowly gave way to an expression of dawning realisation. 'Christ, don't tell me somebody did the poor kid in?'

'She was murdered, Mr Crosby,' said Roper. 'Her body was found in the ditch beside the churchyard about an hour ago. It had been there all night. She was strangled—a cord, a rope. We're not sure yet.'

Crosby's face had gone the grey of wood-ash. 'Do you mind if I get myself a drink?'

'Whatever you like, Mr Crosby.'

Crosby walked unsteadily back along the bar and shakily offered up a glass twice to his Bell's whisky optic. As he topped it up with water from a covered jug on the counter, Roper heard the jug rattle against the rim of the glass. Crosby seemed to have taken the news worse than the girl's brother had.

'How about yourselves?'

Roper shook his head. Crosby took down half his Scotch at a gulp before coming slowly back to the end of the bar. He was plainly upset, and perhaps even more upset than a mere employer might have been, even given the circumstances. Under the blood-red shirt was a powerful chest and a broad pair of shoulders. Men murdered for many reasons, and the unrequited love for a girl less than half their age was not the least of them.

'Did any of her boyfriends ever come in here as customers, Mr Crosby?'

'Not that I know of,' said Crosby. 'Mind you, since she started working here I'm not sure she had a regular boyfriend at all. Odd, that, I always thought, a pretty kid like that. But she flirted, mind. Led the lads on a bit. Good for trade, that, a good-looking barmaid.'

'And how long was she working here?'

'A couple of days after her eighteenth birthday,' said Crosby. 'End of January. She'd tried to get me to give her a job before—but I told her she had to be eighteen, told her it was the law. She was pretty anxious to get a job too, it seemed to me.'

'How do you mean anxious?'

Crosby took another swallow and set his glass down on the counter. 'Well . . . she made it seem urgent,' he said. 'She pestered me for weeks. Every time we met in the street. I suppose it was down to money really. Kids these days just can't get enough cash, can they?'

'Can you remember what she was wearing last night, Mr Crosby?'

Crosby puckered his forehead.

'A white shirt—outside her skirt . . . A belt, a shiny black one. A black skirt . . . Black shoes, high-heeled ones. A gold cross—well, a sort of cross.' Crosby drew a cross with a looped top on his counter with a finger-tip. 'Oh, yes; and a wristwatch.'

'You're sure about the cross and the wristwatch?' asked Roper. As he recalled, Vera Jackman hadn't been wearing either.

'Certain,' said Crosby. 'The wristwatch was a little gilt thing on a bracelet.' He shifted uncomfortably. 'Only a cheap one. I—er—well, I bought it for her m'self. A chap came in here one day with a case full of 'em. You know how it is in pubs. She fancied one, and I treated her. Only a fiver, so you needn't get the wrong idea.'

'Did she have a handbag with her?' asked Roper. That was something else he hadn't seen, either in or near the ditch, and few women went anywhere with-out a handbag.

'No,' said Crosby. 'At least, not a proper handbag. It was a sort of purse; a little white thing on a wrist strap.'

'You're sure she was carrying it last night?'

'Yes,' said Crosby. 'Certain.'

Roper took out his notebook and made a few jot-tings:

VJ left Cort Arms at 10.48 p.m. (approx). Walked south. White purse? See WT.

The notebook was tucked away again. 'Thanks, Mr Crosby. Greatly obliged.'

Crosby picked up his tumbler and drained it. 'If I think of anything else, I'll let you know,' he said.

'Yes, Mr Crosby,' said Roper. 'You do that, please.' Then with Jollyboy close behind he started for the door.

'Superintendent,' Crosby called after them. Roper stopped, turned. Crosby had moved along behind the counter and was sluicing his tumbler in the sink. 'If he's a local man, you shouldn't have to look too far. It's only a little place, this.'

Roper stretched a smile. 'Yes, Mr Crosby,' he said. 'How right you are.'

HE BUCKLED HIMSELF into the seat beside Jollyboy as the sergeant drove the Metro out of Jackman's forecourt. A sign on Jackman's pumps read CLOSED.

Another murder enquiry was under way. As yet there was no apparent pattern, no feeling of order to it. For a few more hours chaos would reign supreme. There would be a lot of grubbing about in dark corners, stones to be lifted in the hope of something nasty crawling out. Intuition too would play no small part. And luck.

But, as Crosby had said, Cort Abbas was a very small place to hide a murderer.

THREE

TO AN UNTUTORED EYE, Church Lane did indeed look like a forcing-bed for chaos. It was, in fact, a model of painstaking and methodical activity.

The lane had now been taped off at each end and only residents' vehicles were being allowed up it. The church hall was in the throes of being annexed for a temporary incident room and a British Telecom crew was at present running a line to it from the telegraph pole beside the church lych gate. From each end of the lane a line of blue-overalled and gumbooted cadets were slowly advancing towards the canvas screens behind which Vera Jackman's body still lay. Each held a polythene bag into which he placed anything that looked recently dropped either on the road or on the two grass verges: cigarette ends, matches, the occasional buckled beer can—anything that might be evidential—even though most of it would turn out in the end to be inconsequential rubbish.

Closer to the tent, DI Price was mouthing into a hand-held walkie-talkie. Tall, fair-haired and very Welsh, DI Price was originally from Pontypool and these days was in the fast lane for promotion. Like Roper, he was County CID, but unlike Roper, for whom thoughts of promotion had long since given way to pleasanter thoughts of retirement, Price was still in the necessary business of making a name for himself.

'How's it going, Dave?' asked Roper.

'Almost organised, sir,' said Price. The young inspector prided himself on being a logistician and had all his facts to hand. The pathologist had arrived some ten minutes ago. Twelve cadets were scouring the lane, working in from opposite ends. Six more cadets, a detective sergeant, two detective constables and three uniformed constables were ready to begin house-to-house enquiries as soon as Roper had briefed them. Two more cadets were setting up trestle tables in the church hall. A WPC and an audio-typist were on their way with typewriters and tape recorders, and the temporary telephone switchboard would be installed by noon. And the vicar's wife had turned up trumps with a lady from the WI: there was now an operational tea urn in the church hall.

'Who's the path man?'

'His name's Wilson, sir. Says you and he did a case together earlier in the year. Down at Redbury Sands.'

'I know him.' In Roper's book Wilson was a good 'un, a professional. And so was DI Price. It all augured well for a quick result.

Inside the canvas screen Wilson, greenly masked and in his shirtsleeves, was already at work; the scene-of-crime photographer crouched above him recording at the pathologist's instructions. Into an incision in Vera Jackman's upper right abdomen Wilson was easing a knife-tipped thermometer to take her liver-temperature. On the opposite side of the ditch, taking notes, squatted the coroner's officer.

'Morning, Mr Wilson.'

'Morning, Superintendent,' said Wilson cheerily, through his mask. 'Bad do, this one. Got anything yourself yet?'

'Missing handbag, missing jewellery. How about you?'

'Only a guess or two as yet,' said Wilson. 'Strangulation, of course; that goes without saying. The ligature had a smooth surface, so it definitely wasn't anything like a rope or a cord. And it was done from behind.' Wilson shuffled a few inches to one side to give Roper a better view of Vera Jackman's head and throat. 'The ligature-bruising is continuous at the front here. When we turn her over, I've no doubt that we'll find the crossover point at the nape of her neck.'

'And how about those scratches on her throat?'

'Her own fingernails,' said Wilson. 'I've no doubt about that either. Her instinct would have been to try and claw at whatever the ligature was to try and get it off. But of course, the poor child couldn't.'

'Could the ligature have been applied after she was dead—to put us off the track?'

'Doubt it,' said Wilson. 'This is a classic case of ligature-strangulation: cyanosis of the skin—this blueness above the ligature depression, congestion of the facial arteries; and if you look closely, you'll see several burst blood capillaries in the eyes.'

She might, suggested Wilson, have taken up to five minutes to die. There were several factors: the physical strength of her murderer, the physical strength of Vera Jackman herself, whether the position of the ligature and the pressure applied to it might have triggered a swift vagal inhibition—in which case Vera might have been dead inside of a minute. Strangulation was rarely quick, however, and whoever had done this had either been desperate or cold-bloodedly tenacious.

'How about rape?'

'Mm...don't think so,' said Wilson. 'All her clothing is intact. But the interesting things are her hands: look.' Wilson lifted one of Vera Jackman's hands a couple of inches from the dry leaf-mould in which she lay. 'I can't open that fist, Mr Roper—nor the other one.'

'Rigor mortis?' said Roper.

'No, *sir,*' said Wilson. 'Cadaveric spasm. Nothing at all to do with rigor. We call it the "death grasp". Nobody understands the mechanism, but it's always associated with death by violence. The victim reaches out for something—anything—sometimes only air. See? The nails have bitten right into the flesh of her palm.'

Wilson shuffled back to where he had been and began to carefully withdraw the thermometer from Vera Jackman's liver. He tipped it towards the light. 'Twenty-five centigrade,' he said over his shoulder to the coroner's officer. 'So she's been dead for somewhere between—say—ten to thirteen hours.'

'Is that as close as you can get?' asked Roper. He pulled back his cuff and looked at his wristwatch. It wanted twenty minutes to eleven o'clock. 'I can tell you for a fact that she was definitely alive at ten to eleven last night.'

'I'm still only guessing,' said Wilson. 'I'll be able to tell you more accurately when I've had her on the table.' Strangulation, he explained, as he continued about his macabre business, raised the body temperature. Another phenomenon, like the cadaveric spasm, for which no one as yet had provided a rational explanation. It was this immeasureable temperature rise which led to his vagueness about the time of death. And, also, it had been a hot muggy night last night, which would have helped the body retain its core temperature. He would have to get the mean of the night air-temperatures from the Meteorological Office and feed that, together with the various temperatures of Vera Jackman's internal organs, into his computer. He would not have a reasonably accurate time until perhaps late this evening—after he had concluded his autopsy. He pressed a plaster over the incision he had made to insert his thermometer, and drew a circle around it with a red, felt-tipped pen to avoid confusing it with any other incisions he might have to make during the course of his later examinations.

'May we turn her over?'

'Have you got plenty of pictures?' Roper asked the photographer.

'Yes, sir—I'm on my third cassette of film.'

Vera Jackman's belt was unclasped and she was rolled over. Because of the soft bed of leaves upon which she had lain, there had been little upward pressure to dapple the patches of post-mortem lividity on the back of her legs and behind. They were consistently bright pink, where her unpumped blood had been drawn downward under the influence of gravity.

Wilson passed the belt up to Roper and drew up the back of Jackman's shirt.

'Hello—what's this?' he said, plucking up whatever had fallen from inside the shirt on to the leaves beside Jackman's waist. 'Could this be the jewellery you're looking for?'

He handed it up to Roper, holding the glittering object fastidiously by the two ends of broken gold chain between plastic-sheathed finger and thumb.

It was the cross that Crosby had mentioned seeing Jackman wearing last night; although strictly speaking it was not a cross but a more pagan symbol. An *ankh*. Egyptian. Given as a wish for eternal life. A love token. Like a key, with a loop at the top, the way Crosby had drawn it on his bar counter.

Roper decided that it couldn't be gold. Dangling it by its chain, he decided that it was too heavy, too ornately patterned to be anything but costume-jewellery. A girl who had to work in a bar at night to make a few shillings was too unlikely a possessor, and besides, it wasn't hallmarked. It was a decision made too hastily and one that he would later regret. He passed it up to Price for noting and bagging.

'Did she die here, Mr Wilson?'

'Can't say yet, Superintendent. Sorry. Tell you tonight, perhaps.'

THE HUBBUB in the church hall ceased as Roper came in.

'Right,' he called. 'Gather round. Tea down. Notebooks out.' He sat himself behind the trestle table nearest the door and took out his own notebook and opened it in front of him. Cigarette smoke floated in the shafts of sunlight streaming in at the windows. Someone thoughtfully set a mug of tea in front of him.

'Victim's name: Vera Jackman. Eighteen years old. Death by strangulation. Body found in Church Lane, by one Wally Tupper, at nine-twenty this morning. She was pregnant—six weeks—that could be important; but for the time being we'll keep that information to ourselves.' Pens and pencils raced over opened notebooks.

Roper took a sip of his tea, almost black, and thick with sugar, but tasting like nectar in the heat of the morning. 'Vera Jackman was last seen leaving the Cort Arms—that's the local boozer—at approximately ten-fifty last night. The landlord is pretty sure she was walking south—which is that way.' Roper pointed to his right. 'She lived with her brother, at his garage— that's straight across the green: that way. That's all we know.' He took another mouthful of tea while the pens and pencils caught up with him.

'Now, this is what we *want* to know: Where did she go after she left the Cort Arms? Who was she going to see—if anybody? Did anyone else see her after, say, ten-forty-five last night? Where? You also ask everybody where they were last night—and get them to substantiate it, perhaps with a witness. Right?'

A few officers nodded, a few still scribbled.

'And if anyone did see Jackman after ten-forty-five last night, what sort of state was she in? Was she running or walking? Did anyone see anything unusual? A new face in the village? An unfamiliar car parked somewhere? According to her brother, she did a few morning jobs round about. Find out where. Get opinions about her. Facts where you can, opinions where you can't. Find out who her boyfriends were, where they live...'

They all knew what to do, Roper knew that, but they had to be hustled along and given direction. Some of them were ridiculously young, uncut boys, scarcely older than Vera Jackman herself; for some this was their first murder enquiry. But they were, in common, eager to be getting on with it.

Photocopies of maps of the locality were handed out. Already pinned up on the hall noticeboard was a three-inch-to-the-mile Ordnance Survey map of Cort Abbas and its surroundings. Roper slashed a line with a felt tipped pen at the halfway mark of the single main street. The teams under Detective Sergeant Makins would work from the north of the village to that line and the teams under DI Price would work from the south. Roper circled Jackman's garage, Church Lane, where the body had been found, and the Cort Arms. If anyone uncovered anything relevant, it was to be radioed in at once and Roper himself would follow it up.

'And we're looking for the girl's purse; it's white, with a wrist strap. And her wristwatch: a cheap one, gilt, built into a bracelet. Ask everyone if they've seen it—and if anyone has, I want to know. And keep as low a profile as you can. Right?'

A few more nods. Notebooks and pencils were tucked away.

'Your deadline is four o'clock,' said Roper. 'Back here. We should have the post-mortem report by nine o'clock this evening and I want an arrest within forty-eight hours. Off you go.'

The hubbub rose again as the teams headed for the door. Outside car doors slammed and engines were started. The official machinery was at last in motion.

SERGEANT JOLLYBOY canted the Metro half on to the grass verge outside the dilapidated little cottage at the western end of Church Lane. It was a typical turn-of-the-century labourer's cottage—brick, slate-roofed, one of a terrace of four of which three were already boarded up and heavily overgrown with shrubbery. Several slates were missing from the roof; one lay balanced precariously on the broken rainwater guttering above the front door. The gate lay rotting in the grass of the untidy front garden and the green paint on the front door was faded and pocked with sun-blisters.

'What's the best approach?' asked Roper.

'Softly,' said Jollyboy. 'He's not a bad lad and finding the girl's body this morning scared the hell out of him. And the mother's a bit of an old tartar. The father did a bunk about twenty-five years ago. So it's all very fraught.'

So softly it would be. Roper climbed out on to the grass and Jollyboy followed him up the uneven stone path. Closer to, the cottage looked even more decrepit than it had from the car.

Jollyboy rapped his knuckles on the scabrous green door with its single lozenge-pane of dirty glass. A few seconds afterwards, from the tail of his eye, Roper saw the net curtains in the front window being lifted covertly to one side. A wide crack in the brickwork above the front door went all the way up to the window above it.

'Condemned,' muttered Jollyboy, under his breath. 'Have been for the last couple of years. Subsidence, dry rot. They shouldn't be living here at all, to be honest.' He raised his knuckles again, but the door was opened a few inches against a chain so that his fist stopped in mid-fall.

A solitary eye peered warily around the edge of the door. A woman. Elderly. Untidy grey hair tied back. Waspish little mouth. The eye fixed on Jollyboy. 'He don't want to see you, Sergeant Jollyboy. He's all upset. You're to go away, see. You come back tomorrow, see.' The door was already closing. Jollyboy shoved the flat of his hand against it and pushed it open again against the chain.

'Sorry, Lizzi,' he said firmly. 'We're here on police business. This gentleman is a superintendent and he wants to talk to your Wally. We either come in or Wally comes out. Take your pick.'

The one eye took in Roper suspiciously.

'My name's Roper, Mrs Tupper.' He showed the eye his warrant card and smiled encouragingly. 'All we want to do is talk to your son. It's important, Mrs Tupper.'

'You ain't taking him away, see. Talk all you want, but you ain't taking him away.'

'Nobody's taking him anywhere, Lizzie,' said Jollyboy. 'Now let us in, eh? Twenty minutes and we'll be gone again.'

'And you just make sure you are, see.'

At long last the door was closed an inch so that the chain could be taken off.

The narrow little hall was dark and musty. It was floored with linoleum from which most of the pattern had long since been worn away and here and there the hessian backing was showing through. Down by the skirting boards the cheap brown wallpaper was blotched with damp.

Mrs Tupper shuffled ahead of them in her carpet slippers. The back room was a kitchen-cum-parlour. Two bagged-out and not very clean armchairs sat on either side of an antiquated cast-iron range, and in one of them, tightly huddled, facing the door, sat a shivering Wally Tupper. His fearful, slack-mouthed gaze followed them in.

'I don't know no more, Mr Jollyboy. If you've come back about Vera, I don't know no more.'

'Of course you don't, Wally,' said Jollyboy. 'We've only come so that you can tell Mr Roper here what you told me this morning. Do you mind if we sit down, Lizzie?'

'Aye, so long as it's not too permanent.'

Jollyboy pulled out a wooden wheel-backed chair from beneath the table that stood between the range and the dresser, while Roper perched himself on the arm of the chair opposite Wally Tupper. Jollyboy took out his notebook from his shirt pocket and opened it on the tasselled tablecloth.

'My name's Roper, son,' said Roper to Tupper. Tupper was about thirty, lean and dark-haired—hair with a curious touch of redness in it here and there— with irregularly spaced teeth, narrowed vacuous eyes and what seemed to be a chronic nervous tic twitching every now and then at his right cheek.

'You a policeman . . . like Mr Jollyboy?'

'Yes, son, that's right. I'm a detective superintendent. County CID. And your name's Wally, so they tell me.'

Tupper nodded. He seemed to have calmed a little.

'And you're the chap who found Vera.'

Tupper nodded vaguely. Then he said: 'I couldn't wake her up, see...That's how I knew she was dead...Her face were all covered in leaves.'

'What did you do?'

'I ran...I ran all the way to Mr Jollyboy's house...Didn't I, Mr Jollyboy? I ran.'

'And you did right, son,' said Roper. At the chipped china sink by the window Mrs Tupper was filling a white-enamelled kettle and pretending not to be listening. 'Can you remember what the time was?'

'Church clock was striking.'

'He can't tell the time,' Mrs Tupper broke in tartly. 'But he left here at quarter past nine.'

'I was going to work,' said Tupper. 'Second time.'

'Second time?'

'He goes out twice,' interpreted Mrs Tupper. 'First time's six till eight. Creed's Farm. He mucks out the cows and pigs.' She rattled crockery noisily as she set out cups and saucers on the draining board.

'You didn't see Miss Jackman's body when you went out the first time?'

Wally Tupper shook his head.

'Why was that?'

'I goes cemetery way first time,' said Tupper. 'Comes back cemetery way, too.'

Mrs Tupper skirted the end of the table, the enamelled kettle in one hand, a battered aluminium teapot in the other. She set down both on top of the range and opened a trap at the front to let a draught into the glowing coke. More heat blasted out into the room that was already hot and airless, and rank with the smells of yesterday's cooking, and perhaps even the cooking of the day before that.

'So when you *did* see Miss Jackman in the ditch, it was quarter past nine and you were going to work for the second time; that right?'

Tupper nodded. The patchy redness in his hair looked as if he had made a clumsy attempt to dye it. Then Roper noticed a similar peppery redness on Tupper's grubby white plimsolls and naked insteps; and concluded that it was some kind of dust.

'This second time you went out, where were you going exactly?'

'Miss Sutton's house,' said Tupper. 'I sweeps for her.'

'He means Cort Place,' explained Jollyboy. 'It's the local manor house. Miss Sutton and her brother run it. It's open to the public in the season.'

'When you found her, Wally,' asked Roper, 'did you touch her? Did you move her?'

'He *wouldn't* have touched her,' broke in Mrs Tupper with a new and unexpected vehemence. 'Not my Wally. He's a good boy, my Wally. She was a bad 'un, that Vera Jackman. A proper little tart that one was.'

'When you found her, son,' repeated Roper, ignoring Mrs Tupper's outburst, 'did you touch her? Try and remember. It's important.'

Tupper shook his head and averted his eyes.

'But you said her face was covered in leaves,' insisted Roper. 'And when I saw her it wasn't. So who cleared the leaves away?'

Tupper didn't answer.

'He *wouldn't* have touched her,' snapped Mrs Tupper again. 'Dead or alive, my Wally wouldn't have touched her. A lad can catch nasty things from a girl like that. Ain't that right, Wally?'

And Wally didn't answer her either; and Roper guessed that his earlier answer had been a lie.

'Look, son,' he said patiently, 'I'm not suggesting you hurt her. I'm only asking if you touched her. Did you touch her?'

Tupper glanced guiltily across at his mother, then nodded glumly. 'I called,' he mumbled. '"Vera," I said, "What you doing down there, Vera?" But she didn't answer.'

'And when she didn't answer? What did you do, Wally?'

'I thought she couldn't breathe. 'Cause of the leaves, see.'

'So you climbed down into the ditch and brushed them away. Is that what you did, son?'

Tupper's hanging head rocked up and down.

'You little bugger,' snapped his mother. 'I *told* you, didn't I? I told you what'd happen to you, didn't I?'

She might have gone on, but a sudden warning glance from Roper quelled her to silence. Ill-temperedly she came between Roper and her son and filled the teapot from the boiling kettle. She took the teapot back to the draining board and slapped a woolly patchwork cosy over it.

'I thought she was asleep, see?' said Tupper. 'Until I got the leaves off. Her eyes were *all* funny. And her face was *all* blue.'

'Did you move her?'

Tupper shook his head again. 'She didn't look right, see. I seen dead things afore.'

'She had a purse, son. A white purse. With a strap. Did you see it—in the ditch—or on the grass? Anywhere about?'

'He wouldn't have touched it,' protested Mrs Tupper. 'You wouldn't have touched it, would you, Wally? Not my Wally.'

'Did you see it, son?' persisted Roper, ignoring her. 'A white purse.'

Tupper shrank deeper into the frayed armchair and turned his face away. The sleeves of his blue-and-white chequered shirt were rolled up above his elbows. For all his sinewy leanness he did not lack physical strength and he could have strangled Vera Jackman with comparative ease. And he was distinctly uneasy about that purse.

'Look, Wally,' said Roper reassuringly. 'If you did find it, and picked it up—'

'I told you he didn't,' snapped Mrs Tupper. 'He'd have told you else. Wouldn't you, Wally?'

'Shut up, Lizzie,' broke in Jollyboy tiredly. 'The Superintendent's asking the lad'

'There was a wristwatch, too, son,' said Roper. 'Did you see that?'

Tupper's vacuous gaze locked guiltily on to Roper's waiting one. 'Told you,' he said pettishly. 'I didn't see no purse. Nor no watch.'

And Roper, with one of the best reasons a policeman has—the intuition born of many years raking through the human race's refuse heaps—did not quite believe him.

TUPPER HAD LEFT the Cort Arms last night about ten minutes after Vera Jackman.

'So you got back here when?'

His mother answered again for him. She was pouring the tea from the battered aluminium pot. 'I can tell you,' she said. A cup of tea that he didn't want was grudgingly held out to Roper. Roper took it and put it on top of the range. 'It was quarter past eleven. He was late. And I had a go at him, didn't I, Wally? Don't like him being late, do I, son?'

'I got fish and chips,' said Tupper sullenly. 'Had to queue up. Made me late.'

'And where's the fish-and-chip shop?'

'Not a shop. A van.'

'Comes down from Dorchester,' explained Jolly-boy. 'Tuesdays, Thursdays and Fridays. Italian bloke; name of Cominetti. He parks on the green near the war memorial.'

Roper jotted another brief note to himself:

Check with Cominetti. What time did he shut up shop last night? Did he see Tupper?

The Italian just might have seen something; the war memorial was on the green, a scant few yards from the bottom of Church Lane.

'Did he have any fish and chips when he got home, Mrs Tupper?'

'Yes. Always saves some for his mother, don't you, Wally?'

Tupper nodded. 'Yeah. Always.' Then he added, 'But she still told me off for being late.'

'Did you see Vera Jackman again last night, Wally?' asked Roper. 'After you left the Cort Arms?'

Tupper shook his head.

'And did you go out again—after you got home?'

'*She* wouldn't let me.' He jerked his head defiantly sideways in the direction of his mother. '*She* never does.'

'No, I don't either,' she said. 'I like him here. Where I can keep an eye on him.'

Mrs Tupper's tea had the consistency of engine oil. Through the back-door cat flap came an obese ginger cat. It stretched itself languorously on the rag rug at Wally Tupper's feet then launched itself up to his lap.

'This Cort Place,' said Roper, 'where you were going after breakfast—what do you do there?'

'Sweeping and gardening,' said Tupper. 'And I help Mr Huxley sometimes. I do sweeping and gardening for Miss Sutton. And I help Mr Thruxton sometimes too.'

'—And *they're* a funny lot, an' all,' Mrs Tupper interrupted yet again. 'Communists, that's what they are over Cort Place.'

'It's a *commune,* Lizzie,' said Jollyboy patiently. 'They aren't *Communists.* It's an arts and crafts commune,' he explained to Roper. 'When old man Sutton died his son and daughter turned it into a business. It's all on the up and up.'

'Vera works there, too,' volunteered Tupper. 'In the caff. Helps Miss Sutton.'

'And the rest,' added Mrs. Tupper weightily, patting her hair. 'Oh, yes, I could tell you a fair few things about Vera Jackman and Cort Place. Not that I'm one for gossip, mind. But I could if I wanted to, believe you me.'

'A few things like what, Mrs Tupper?'

She sniffed disapprovingly. 'Painting classes,' she said. 'And we all know about painting classes, don't we? My Wally's seen, haven't you, Wally?'

Wally Tupper's face slowly reddened. 'Yeah,' he said, shifting uncomfortably in his chair. 'Two times.'

Roper waited for him to expand on that, but Wally was clearly too embarrassed.

'She was *posing*,' explained Mrs Tupper, sniffing again. 'Naked. That's what you saw, wasn't it, Wally?'

'In the painting room,' said Tupper. 'Mr Sutton chased me off. But I'd seen.'

'There,' sneered Mrs Tupper triumphantly. 'What did I tell you. Fornicators. That's what they are at Cort Place.'

Such spurious accusations came thick and fast in any enquiry. More often than not they were spawned out of sheer vindictiveness, but Roper had learned over the years that in the muddy gumbo of evidence-gathering, facts, half-facts and fictions were so often intertwined that it was as well to listen to everything and cast aside nothing. Vera Jackman had been murdered. Vera Jackman had probably posed naked for painting classes in Cort Place. Instead of walking straight home last night, Vera Jackman had walked south. And Cort Place lay to the south of the Cort Arms. And Wally Tupper had arrived back at this shabby cottage later than usual last night.

These were facts.

Only intuition led him to think that Wally Tupper knew something about Vera Jackman's purse and wristwatch. Perhaps, like a jackdaw, he had only picked them up this morning in Church Lane because they had caught his eye. Equally possibly, Wally Tupper had killed Vera Jackman and taken both last night.

But these were early days. Wally Tupper was unlikely to wander far and Roper deemed it wise, at least for the moment, not to press him too hard. There was always tomorrow.

FOUR

IT WAS COMING UP for midday. Fred Jackman had re-opened his garage and was filling the petrol tank of a grey Renault estate car. Roper and Jollyboy waited for him to finish and bring back the driver's change.

He pushed back a cowlick of hanging hair as he approached them. 'I thought you said you were coming back at half past two,' he said.

'Yes, sir, we still are,' said Roper. 'But I wonder if you'd let us look at your sister's room in the meantime.' And when Jackman appeared reluctant, he said: 'I could get a warrant, of course, it that's what you'd prefer...'

'No,' said Jackman. 'It's OK. It's at the top of the stairs. First room on the right. Next door to the bathroom.'

And, no. He did not want to be up there with them.

'I don't want to know,' he said. 'You just find out who killed her, that's all I care about.'

The room was small and chintzy-pretty. A single bed covered with a floral-patterned duvet took up most of it. The white-painted built-in wardrobe beside the fireplace looked homemade. An old chest of drawers tarted up with white paint, and a low dressing table with a single mirror, took up most of the remaining floor space. Roper started looking through the wardrobe while Jollyboy went methodically through the chest of drawers.

Her clothes were cheap but smart, and, Roper supposed, trendy, mostly brightly coloured. Without exception, everything on a hanger was protected by a polythene bag. Blouses, skirts, jeans. Few dresses. The only expensive items seemed to be a well-cut barathea blazer with brass buttons and, on the same hanger, a white skirt. From the looks of both they had hardly been worn. She had had an extensive collection of shoes. All were in boxes, all were wrapped in tissue paper, but again they didn't look expensive—except one new white pair that looked as if they were meant to be worn with the blazer and white skirt. They were Italian. Roper was no expert, but they smelled like real leather. £30 or £40 worth of strappy nonsense, with heels like toy daggers. From the state of their soles and heels they too had rarely been worn.

The red photograph album was standing up against the wall at the back of the wardrobe and wedged upright by the shoe boxes. Not simply put there, but hidden there by the looks of it.

Roper stooped and lifted it out. He needed to turn only a few of its thick, black board pages to recognise it for what it was. A model's sample book. Glossy eight-by-tens, some in colour, some in black-and-white. Full-length shots, portraits, professional photographs all of them. And Vera Jackman looked equally professional smiling out of them. Vera Jackman dressed in the blazer and skirt and the strappy white shoes, Vera Jackman in a black bikini, pertly seductive in clinging white lingerie; and, finally, several shots of the top half of Vera Jackman in nothing at all.

This was another Vera Jackman, Vera Jackman the extrovert, full of life and zest, and doing her damnedest to get out of this cramped little village—and this cramped little room—and making a name for herself in the great beyond, wherever that happened to be. Probably London. And she might just have made it, Roper thought, even in London where pretty girls were ten a penny.

'Super—'

Jollyboy too had found something out of the ordinary, or certainly something very out of the ordinary to find in a room like this one. It was a building society deposit book. Jollyboy had found it under the lining paper in the bottom of the top drawer, and since it could never have got there by accident it had obviously been secreted there to keep it away from prying eyes. Probably her brother's. What made it out of the ordinary was the sum of money that had been deposited in it, and in a very short time: £1851 and a few pence; since last January. Only five and a half months. And folded into the book was a cheque waiting to be paid in. It was for the sum of £20 and the drawer was JM Sutton. A woman's handwriting.

'That'd be Miss Sutton,' said Jollyboy. 'Along at Cort Place. Could be wages.'

The date on the cheque was last Saturday's, and the dates in the deposit book showed that Jackman had put money into her account once a week with unfailing regularity, except last Saturday. Some weeks she had paid in £50, some weeks £60. On two occasions in March she had paid in over £100. Another £30, near enough, and Jackman would have saved £2000. And perhaps that had been her target, and perhaps when

she had gathered in those last few pounds she had intended breaking out of Cort Abbas once and for all.
The album of photographs wasn't more than a few
weeks old and was the sort of thing a girl wouldn't
have had prepared too long before she intended to use
it. So perhaps both the deposit book and the album
had pointed to Jackman's imminent departure.

Roper found the battery-operated tape recorder in
the bottom drawer of the white dressing table, buried
under a pile of flimsy underwear, hidden as the album and building society book had been hidden. It
was Japanese. A Sharp. There was a cassette already
in it, its tape half on one spool and half on the other.
Roper pressed the PLAY button.

Silence, just the occasional crackle as the empty tape
ran over the recording head. Roper pressed REWIND
and took the tape back to its beginning. He pressed
PLAY.

A throat was cleared. A moment of silence. 'My
name is Vera Jackman.' The tinny voice was shaky and
nervous. The throat was cleared again. 'My name is
Vera Jackman. I am eighteen years old.' Between pas-
sages of silence, this message was repeated over and
over like a litany, gradually becoming less self-con-
scious.

'That her?' asked Roper.

Jollyboy stood with his head tilted to one side and
frowning. 'Yes,' he said. 'Certainly sounds like her.'

'The rain in Spain falls mainly on the plain. My
name is Vera Jackman, I am eighteen years old and I
come from Cort Abbas in Dorset. My name is Vera
Jackman...'

The changes were gradual, subtle, but definitely there. Vera Jackman had spent a great deal of time practising her elocution and getting rid of much of her Dorset burr. And, it seemed, with considerable success.

'One two three vorr. Four! One two three *four*. *Four!*'

From time to time a small mistake made her angry with herself.

'My name is Vera Jackman ... *Jackman!*'

'A determined young woman,' said Roper, as he thumbed down the OFF button.

'Aye, she was,' said Jollyboy. 'She was going to get on was our Vera.'

Determined. And intelligent. And industrious. And yet not so bright; she had allowed herself to become pregnant. And that struck Roper as odd. Out of character. A girl planning her life for perhaps six months ahead, the kind of life that Vera Jackman had in mind, would surely never have allowed herself to become pregnant.

So who? *Cui bono?* Roper was sure that if he found the man he would be well on the way to winding up the business. Somewhere, perhaps not too far away, was a man who had been to bed with Vera Jackman. Six or seven weeks ago, if Dr Pedlar had been given the right dates. He would not be a yob. Vera Jackman had been too smart and too ambitious to fool around with pimpled boys with calloused hands and dirty fingernails.

Rape was a possibility.

'She'd have reported it,' said Jollyboy. 'And bloody nearly killed the bloke into the bargain.'

Between them, they painstakingly ransacked the rest of the chest of drawers and the dressing table. There were no contraceptive pills tucked away anywhere. Their absence proved nothing—except that Vera Jackman was probably not promiscuous. With a lively, pretty girl like that, that was usually the first accusation to be levelled, especially in a tightly knit little community like Cort Abbas. And if the newspapers were ever to get hold of that photograph album they'd have a field day. On hundreds of commuter trains tomorrow morning there would be the inevitable winks and nudges and the equally inevitable snide remarks that Vera Jackman had 'probably asked for it.'

THE ALBUM, the tape recorder, the building society deposit book, all clearly both mystified and hurt Fred Jackman. He had seen none of them before. He touched them and picked at them in puzzlement as they lay on the table in front of him. He, Roper and Jollyboy were downstairs in the neat little dining room at the back of the cottage.

'I don't get it,' he said. 'I just don't get it. It's like she was someone else I didn't know.'

'Did you get the feeling she was being secretive, Mr Jackman?'

'Well, we always kept ourselves to ourselves, like,' said Jackman. 'And she always said she was going to be a model—except I thought it was just a fantasy. I didn't realise she really meant it. And I didn't know it had gone *this* far.'

'And if you had known, would you have approved?'

'No,' said Jackman bluntly. 'It's a dodgy job, isn't it, modelling for pictures. Magazines and all that. I know. I've seen 'em. What bloke wants his sister posing for dirty pictures?'

'So you'd have tried to talk her out of it?'

'Christ, yes,' said Jackman, determinedly. 'I would have and all.'

Which left Roper in no doubt why Vera Jackman had secreted her other life so carefully away in her bedroom. And he wondered what Jackman's reaction was going to be when he finally found out that his sister was pregnant.

'How about your sister's boyfriends?'

'She didn't have one,' said Jackman. 'Not. since Christmas. Been too busy, hasn't she? Getting this little lot together.' He flapped a hand over his sister's deposit book with a gesture close to disgust.

'How did you get on with her?'

'Only so-so,' said Jackman. 'But then we lived on top of each other, didn't we? Always treading on each other's toes. And I had to keep an eye on her, didn't I? Sort of be her mother and father. And that wasn't easy, either.'

Their parents had been dead for six years. A traffic accident. Swift and sudden. Jackman had been twenty at the time, his sister twelve. There was an aunt down in Weymouth who had helped out for the first few years. Other than the aunt, Jackman had more or less raised his sister on his own.

'I'm sorry to have to ask you this, Mr Jackman,' said Roper. 'But the answer's important. Did you ever have any reason to think your sister might be promiscuous?'

'I was never sure,' said Jackman. 'I know I used to worry myself sick about her.'

'How do you mean *used* to, Mr Jackman?'

'Up to last Christmas, I used to,' said Jackman. 'There was always a bloke about; usually an older bloke; a bloke with cash. Different ones every week. Motor bikes and sports cars. I never knew where she was half the time. Some Saturday nights she wasn't home till two... three o'clock in the morning. One night, it was nearly four o'clock—I waited up for her. I really lost my rag that night—she used to round on me, tell me to mind my own bloody business. Well, that night I lost my temper. I thumped her—I broke one of her teeth. I didn't mean to, but I was that worked up, see.'

Roper could well imagine. The stolid, down-to-earth Jackman, the flighty, skittish younger sister who was too attractive for her own good and perhaps even beyond his control.

'Then she got the evening job across at the Arms,' Jackman continued. 'And a relief that was, I tell you. It meant I knew where she was six nights a week. Then mornings she found another job along at Creed's Farm, then another one across at the vet's, then another one along at Cort Place. So, like I say, I thought she'd pulled herself together and settled down. Only I'm getting married myself, soon, and Vera the way she was would have been a right millstone—' Jackman broke off as he realised the implications of what he had just said. 'I didn't mean that the way it sounded,' he said. 'It's just the way she used to be really got to me sometimes. Trying to run a business and look after Vera at the same time. It wasn't easy.'

'It's all right, Mr Jackman,' said Roper. 'I can guess how you feel. But what I'm interested in are *recent* boyfriends. Someone she might have quarrelled with. Someone who might even have killed her.'

Jackman thought about it again; but could only rock his head from side to side.

'Not since Christmas,' he said. 'She never had the time.'

AT FOUR O'CLOCK the door-to-door teams were straggling back to the church hall. The hall had now been taken over completely. The scene-of-crime photographs took up most of the wall at the far end. Along the side walls the trestle tables were ranged, a telephone switchboard on one, a VHF transceiver on another; a typewriter—a slick golf-ball affair—figured prominently on another, a desk-top photocopier, a micro-computer connected directly back to the mainframe machine at County Headquarters. To the crew that had been here since early this morning had been added three WPCs and a civilian typist.

Roper waited for the queue to diminish at the tea urn. A semicircle of folding chairs had been arranged around the table near the door that was serving as his office. If necessary, he would stay here all night. As old as he was he still had the stamina, more so at times like this when the adrenalin was flowing. In Roper's thinking, murder was still the ultimate crime. Murder was a word that stood alone. He had looked in many a thesaurus and never found a substitute with the same functional ring to it.

And he still remembered all too easily the expression of sickened horror on Jackman's face a couple of hours ago in the mortuary when the attendant had lifted aside the white sheet.

He sipped at his mug of tea. He was a patient man. He was patient most of the time. Anger was a waste of energy. Murder lent him a kind of anger, but it was of the chill kind, the kind that didn't raise the blood pressure. The lads were all talking together, comparing notes. A few of the older hands were lighting cigarettes. Roper himself puffed away quietly at a cheroot. The afternoon was even hotter than the morning had been; stickier too, storm weather. The last man in was Price, together with the cadet who had gone the rounds with him. He left the cadet at the urn and came across the parqueted floor—less shiny now than it had been earlier in the day—and joined Roper at his table.

'Any joy?' asked Roper.

'Some,' said Price. 'Not much to go on, but the two old ladies who run the local Post Office were walking their dog at about ten to eleven last night. They passed Vera Jackman.'

'Going which way?'

'She was still walking south. They were walking north. They passed each other a few yards north of the entrance to Cort Place.'

Price took out the by now crumpled Xeroxed copy of his map from his notebook and unfolded it. It was liberally marked with ballpointed red circles, each one with a number inside it. Where the Misses Butterworth remembered seeing Vera Jackman, the circle enclosed a figure 2. It was about thirty yards to the north of the entrance to Cort Place.

'Did they see if she turned in there?'

'No,' said Price. 'But I was talking to DS Makins about an hour ago. He'd been interviewing the vicar—Smallways.' One of Price's neatly manicured fingernails moved further south to circle 8, at the southernmost perimeter of the village. A small group of cottages, one of which was ringed in red. 'Every Tuesday night, Mr Smallways cycles here to play chess with a Mr Croker. Last night, Smallways left Croker's cottage on the dot of ten to eleven. He cycled north up the High Street.' Price's fingernail traced Smallways' route. 'Smallways told Makins that he passed the Butterworths and their dog here'—circle 9, about fifty yards north of the entrance to Cort Place—'and he knows it was exactly there because their dog had its hind leg up against the telephone box—this one. They called good night to each other.'

But the Reverend Mr Smallways did not remember passing anyone else at all except the Misses Butterworth and their dog. And he was sure about the time he had left Croker's cottage, and doubted that more than two minutes could have passed between then and the time he had cycled past the Butterworths.

So in the space of time during which the Misses Butterworth had walked some twenty or thirty yards, Vera Jackman had dropped from sight behind them. And south of Cort Place was only wall, wire-fencing and hedgerows all the way to Mr Croker's cottage.

Ergo, thought Roper: if Mr Smallways had had his eyes open last night, there was only one place into which Vera Jackman could have slipped away.

And that was into the grounds of Cort Place.

There had been other sightings of Vera Jackman on her way south late last night. Three customers of the

Cort Arms had stayed talking for several minutes on the floodlit forecourt. Vera Jackman had called good night to them over her shoulder. A Mr and Mrs Hardiman, who owned the newsagent's and wool shop halfway between the Arms and Cort Place, had also seen her pass by: they had been coming home from a cinema in Dorchester and at the time of seeing Vera had been unlocking their front door beside their shop. They were not sure of the time, however, but they suggested a few minutes either side of ten to eleven. Upstairs, Mrs Hardiman had made herself and her husband a pot of coffee and still had time to settle in an armchair and see the beginning of the news on BBC2 at eleven o'clock.

One of the uniformed constables had interviewed the few residents of Church Lane. A certain Tim Jackson, son of the couple who owned the smallholding beside which, in the ditch, Vera Jackman's body had been found that morning, had also seen Vera late last night. She had been standing at the entrance to Cort Place, one hand against the brick gatepost to keep her balance while she shook a stone out of her shoe. Of the time Mr Jackson was absolutely sure. Mr Jackson was in training for a marathon and had been running against the clock. A few seconds after passing Vera Jackman with her shoe off, he had glanced at his wristwatch.

It had been ten-fifty-one, exactly. Nine minutes to eleven.

And in common with everyone else who had seen her, Tim Jackson was sure that the flash of white in her hand had been either a purse or a small handbag.

And, of course, there had been the inevitable vilifications.

Lips had curled. 'Well, of *course*. Asked for it, didn't she? Flaunting about the way she did.'

'Flaunting about, madam?'

'Short skirts, blouses you could see through. Practically naked half the time. Disgusting, that girl. A proper hussy.'

'When you say hussy, madam . . . ?'

'I mean what I say. Hussy. Rolled in the grass with anything in trousers. You take my word for it. Never was any good, that one wasn't.'

From the tenants of Creed's Farm had come only praise. And from Warboy's Farm. And from Mrs Blattner, wife of the local vet for whom Vera also worked an hour each morning.

And, naturally enough, in a small place like Curt Abbas where people lived almost in each other's pockets, there had been the occasional whispered confidence and pointed finger.

The Tuppers. That Wally. Not right in the head, that boy. Ought to be locked away somewhere. Institution material was Wally Tupper.

'Why d'you say that, sir?'

'Oh, for God's *sake*, officer. Ask anyone. Do you know what he does? What his *hobby* is? He scours the countryside for dead animals. *That's* what *he* does.'

'And—?'

'He takes them home and *buries* them, in his mother's back garden. That's what he does, officer. Look for yourself. You'll see the garden's *full* of brick tombstones. The boy's an absolute menace.' Then, the informant leaning closer and dropping his voice to a confidential mutter: 'Do you know, officer, I've lived in Cort Abbas for the last fifteen years—and I've only seen one dead rabbit, outside of the butcher's shop, in all that time.'

'I don't follow you, sir.'

'Snares, man! He *snares* them. He kills the damned things himself. An absolute *menace,* that boy. And one thing leads to another, doesn't it? If you take my point.'

'No, sir. I don't quite.'

'Killing animals, killing people. Follow now? Who's to say he didn't kill that poor girl? I ask you. Eh? Eh? Snares and strangling by rope? Very little difference. Eh? Eh?'

There had been several accusations like that, most of them against Wally Tupper. One informant had assured DS Makins that he had, on one occasion, seen Wally Tupper with a *twelve-bore shotgun.* And a licence? Was an idiot like Wally Tupper even *likely* to have a gun licence? Well, I *ask* you, Sergeant.

These truths, half-truths and suspicions, and permutations of them made up most of the statements to date. But amongst all the chaff were sufficient grains of wheat to have made the tedious door-to-door exercise worthwhile. For a whole hour Roper listened, made notes, asked questions, prodded memories.

IT WAS FIVE-FIFTEEN and the weather had become even muggier and stickier. The westering sun was shining in through the windows behind Roper as he scribbled on the blackboard on the hall wall.

'...Summarising, then.' He tossed the cylinder of white chalk an inch and caught it again as he turned to face his audience. 'I think we can safely say that Vera Jackman was alive at nine minutes to eleven last night. At that time, she was seen by a reliable witness outside the gates of Cort Place. But if the vicar's right and this jogger—Jackson is also right, then Jackman seems to have gone into the grounds of Cort Place. She might have gone in there to meet somebody, stayed a short while, then come out again unobserved. It could be that she went off with whoever it was, and perhaps he—or she—killed her.

'She *might* have been murdered in Church Lane; but, if she was, nobody apparently saw or heard anything. So odds are the girl was murdered somewhere else and the body dumped in that ditch beside the Jacksons' smallholding—Yes, son?'

One of the cadets who had been working with the forensic team in the lane had raised a tentative hand.

'I found a valve cap this afternoon, sir. On the verge. A brass one. Looked fairly new, sir.'

'On the verge where?'

'By the ditch where the body was, sir.' The boy was embarrassed. He had a professional audience; and his dealings with detective superintendents were rare. 'It was a cap off a car tyre, sir. I was thinking . . . if Vera Jackman had been murdered somewhere else, sir . . .' His voice tailed away coyly as a couple of dozen pairs of eyes turned attentively towards him.

'The valve cap could have fallen from the vehicle that brought her body there—right?'

'Yes, sir.' Clearly relieved at Roper's helpful intervention, the cadet gratefully resumed his chair.

'Good thinking, son,' said Roper. It might be wrong thinking, but it meant that the lad had used his imagination. And if it was right thinking it was the nearest thing to evidence that had come in all day.

The valve cap was fetched from the trestle table that was the workbench of the young woman on loan from the forensic laboratory at HQ. It was sealed in a polythene bag. There was nothing extraordinary about it, except that it was made of brass, and most modern valve caps were plastic, which meant that, as valve caps went, it was an upmarket valve cap. Its outside was grimy with road dust. But its internal thread was bright and shiny and it showed no signs of having been run over by another vehicle. So it had not lain long in Church Lane. A day. Two at most. Or perhaps, hopefully, only a few hours.

The plastic envelope was passed from hand to hand.

'That's the next job,' said Roper. 'Before dark.' There were a few murmurs of discontent. Some of the uniformed men had been due to go off duty at midday. 'Door-to-door again. Ask to look at everyone's car, but don't tell anyone what you're looking for in case they've got a spare tucked away somewhere. Cars, tractors, vans, caravans and trailers. If it's got tyres, look at it. And when you find anything with a missing valve cap, you come away quietly and report to DI Price here. Have you all got that?'

To speed things along they could all go out singly. DI Price would slice up the village like an orange. A small sector for each man. Garages, barns, outhouses, anything that was big enough to house a vehicle or trailer was to be checked over.

'You tell 'em it's all part of our routine enquiries. And if anyone asks you to get a search warrant, I want to know about it. Right?'

THE WEATHER began to change for the worse soon after six o'clock. There was a clammy sultriness in the air now and sullen green clouds with bright copper edges and hanging black underbellies were rolling up from the south-west. Roper and Price were out of their jackets and neckties, sipping at mugs of too hot tea. One of the WPCs had driven across to the Cort Arms to drum up a supply of sandwiches and cold lagers. Over in the far corner the radio receiver occasionally crackled to life with a message from the County information room, but there was nothing for them.

This was the dead time, the waiting time, the hanging-about time. A lot of policing was spent poised in this kind of limbo. It was a period of helplessness, of bored irritation. It bred ulcers in some, impatience in the younger ones like Price who were eager to push on to higher things; but Roper had learned the value of relaxation. He smoked a cheroot and sipped his tea and occasionally plucked his sticking shirt away from his armpits and for a while cast his mind adrift from mayhem and murder. A fortnight ago he had ceased to be a lifetime bachelor; and this year, God willing, he was going to retire into the antiques business. He and Sheila already had their eye on a shop in Bournemouth with a nice little flat over the top, and enough pieces of porcelain and quality furniture to keep them for six months if they were able to sell it. She was at an auction today up at Salisbury. Some nineteenth-century watercolours—seascapes mostly. If it hadn't been for the murder of Vera Jackman, they would have been here together.

The hall darkened. Lightning flashed somewhere and a few seconds afterwards a roll of thunder followed it like a barrage of distant artillery. Rain was suddenly flung against the windows of the hall like an onslaught of lead shot.

Over in the corner the radio came to life again. The WPC operating it held up her hand. 'Sergeant Rodgers, sir,' she called across to Roper. 'He wants to speak to you.'

Roper slid back his folding chair and crossed the hall. The WPC pushed her microphone towards him.

'Roper, Sergeant. What have you got?'

'I think I've found the car, sir. Three brass valve caps—and one missing from the back near-side wheel. It's a white Range Rover—in Jackman's service station. I haven't asked who it belongs to yet. Shall I do that? Over.'

'No,' said Roper curtly. 'We don't want anyone knowing we might be on to them—and Jackman might just put two and two together and go and give the owner a bloody good hiding. You never know. But I'll have the registration number. Over.'

As Rodgers transmitted it Roper scribbled it on the radio operator's pad, ripped it off and waved it at the WPC who sat at the computer. 'DVLC, Swansea,' he said, as she came to collect it. 'And as quick as they like.' Then to Rodgers over the radio: 'Drive around and gather up the lads, Sergeant. Beer and sandwiches back at the centre. Over.'

They straggled back in twos and threes over the next ten minutes, most of them soaked to the skin. It had not looked like a day for wearing a raincoat and most of the uniformed men had gone out in their shirt-sleeves. The storm was right overhead now, the lightning followed almost immediately by a crack of thunder that seemed to shake the hall to its very foundations.

Roper waited by the computer, watching its blank green screen.

Then the information began to come up letter by letter as it was fed in from the computer at Swansea.

REGISTERED KEEPER: JENNIFER MARY SUTTON
ADDRESS: CORT PLACE
         CORT ABBAS
         DORSET
         ENGLAND

Then the word WAITING followed by a flashing question mark at the bottom left-hand corner of the screen.

'Tell 'em that's it,' said Roper. 'All we need for now.'

He ripped the tongue of paper bearing the information about the white Range Rover from the computer's printer with a feeling of satisfaction. He joined DI Price back at the table in the corner by the door and slapped the print-out down in front of him.

'When you've had your tea and dried out, my son,' he said, 'that's our next port of call.'

FIVE

WITH ROPER BESIDE HIM and Price in the back seat, Jollyboy drove through the ball-finialled gateway of Cort Place. A large signboard just inside proclaimed that this was Cort Place, built in 1602. Morning coffees and cream teas. Admission to the house was £1.50 and to the arts and crafts centres a further 50p. Over to the left were a couple of acres of gravelled car park and in it, despite the lateness of the hour, were still a couple of motor coaches and a private car.

The house was classical Tudor, the genuine article. Built of sandstone, with Portland-stone mullions framing leaded windows, it had already seen out a dozen generations of owners and looked more than capable of seeing out a dozen more. The several acres of mature lawn in front of it were as flat as a bowling green, with here and there a scattering of flowerbeds. Rain still dripped from the trees and shrubbery round about.

A man and a woman came out from the front porch and made their way towards the car park. The man carried a white plastic carrier bag with a print of the house on the side of it.

'And that's Jennifer Sutton,' said Jollyboy, as he hauled on the handbrake in front of the porch.

She had just come to stand in the doorway and was seeing out a crocodile of schoolchildren, most of whom were carrying one of the white plastic carrier bags. The four adults shepherding them brought up the rear, each of them shaking hands with her on their way out.

Her professional smile dissolved and gave way to a friendlier one as the noisy crocodile wended its way to the two motor coaches and she came down the single wide step towards the Metro. Coolly self-contained, she walked with that slight forward lean from the waist that is sometimes affected by the English ruling class.

Jollyboy touched the black visor of his cap, much as his ancestors might have touched their forelocks. 'Evening, Miss Sutton.'

'Good evening, Sergeant.' Her dark eyes took in Roper and Price. She was somewhere in her late thirties, high cheekboned, brisk and businesslike, her long black hair clipped back in a ponytail and her make-up sufficiently understated to show the healthy skin beneath it. 'And you two are policemen too, I take it?'

'The name's Roper, Miss Sutton.' He held out his warrant card. 'And this is Detective Inspector Price. We're County CID.'

'I suppose you've come about poor Vera Jackman?' she said.

Roper tucked his card away. 'I understand she worked here occasionally, Miss Sutton. We'd be grateful for anything you can tell us about her.'

'Yes, of course,' she said. 'Not that I know very much, frankly. You'd better come in. We're just shutting up shop for the day.'

The vast hall was like a film set for a Gothic melodrama. Stone-flagged, oak-panelled to shoulder height, its stone walls hung with massive paintings and tapestries, its high ceiling colourfully crowded with cherubim and seraphim and several mature-looking ladies in states of undress being hotly pursued by centaurs around the crystal chandeliers which looked as if they might weigh half a ton apiece. Chinese pots, roped off, stood all about the walls, together with chairs and settles that were certainly as old as the house. The only anachronism was a souvenir and postcard counter built into the corner to one side of the great stone fireplace. Behind the counter, two women were draping dustsheets over the items on display while another was cashing up.

Jennifer Sutton led them through a narrow oak door, down a short but precipitous flight of stone stairs and along a chill stone passage to what had probably been the pantry in the heyday of the house. It was now an office, small and cramped, with a single narrow, grimy window that looked over the grounds at the back of the house. From somewhere not too far away Roper heard the unmistakable shriek of a circular saw.

Jennifer Sutton wedged herself behind her cluttered desk, while Roper and Price lowered themselves to old wooden chairs. With little space left, Jollyboy was just able to manoeuvre himself between a filing cabinet and the door.

'We'll try not to take up too much of your time, Miss Sutton,' said Roper, as Price took out his notebook and flipped through it to an empty page.

'Rumour has it the poor girl was murdered,' she said. 'Is that true?'

'Possibly, Miss Sutton,' said Roper. 'She worked for you; so we hear.'

'Yes,' she said. 'Afternoons. Mostly across in the cafeteria.'

'How did you find her? Reliable?'

'Very. Not exactly punctual, mind. But she was prepared to turn her hand to practically anything. The souvenir shop, the cafeteria, anything.'

Roper chanced his arm a little, trusting that Wally Tupper had been telling the truth about the art classes. 'And she did a bit of modelling for Mr Sutton, I believe.'

Jennifer Sutton faltered slightly, as if the question had wrongfooted her. 'Yes, she did,' she said, after a moment or two. 'But that wasn't generally known. In a little village like this... well, you can imagine the gossip, can't you? And the poor girl didn't have much of a reputation to start with. Although,' she added hastily, 'I'm sure that half the stories about her were quite untrue.'

'Your brother runs art classes, that right?'

'Yes,' she said. 'In the season. April to September. The students come as boarders. It makes a few extra pounds.'

Her white silk shirt was beautifully tailored, several of her fingers were laden with expensive rings; so that Roper had due cause to wonder what a 'few more pounds' were in Jennifer Suttons' language. A damned sight more, he guessed, than they would have been in Vera Jackman's.

'Do you have any boarders now?'

'No,' she said. 'Not this week. We have them for a month at a time, then take a week off. It's terribly hard going otherwise.'

'When did you last see Vera Jackman, Miss Sutton?'

'Last night,' she said. 'In the Arms. I went along to see if Jack Crosby could lend me a couple of cases of canned drinks. We'd run out in the cafeteria.'

'Did you speak to her?'

'No,' she said. 'I don't think she saw me. I was in the saloon bar; she was serving in the public.'

No, she had not seen Vera Jackman with a boyfriend since last Christmas. Like Jack Crosby at the Cort Arms, Jennifer Sutton thought that something had caused Vera Jackman to undergo a sudden transformation at about that time. She had no idea what had caused it.

'When you say "a transformation", Miss Sutton...'

'Well, yes. That's the only word for it, really.' Jennifer Sutton smiled with, Roper thought, a hint of deprecation. 'I honestly think she was trying to change her image. Trying to be fearfully posh—you know? How now brown cow—and all that sort of thing.'

'Anything else, or was that it?'

'She also seemed to have a sudden need to make money.' Jennifer Sutton rubbed finger and thumb together in the age-old gesture of the market place. 'And this is none of my business—and I could be wrong—but I think she was trying to get out of this place. Cort Abbas. And gossip has it that she and her brother didn't get on. He's a bit of a stick-in-the-mud, but Vera...I'm *sure* she wanted to get out. She was always talking about London—although I don't think she'd ever been there. Fred Jackman's happy enough to tinker about with his motorcars.'

'How much a week did you pay her?'

'I can tell you exactly.' She fumbled about under her mess of papers and produced a cashbook. She licked a finger and flipped through the pages. 'Last week it was officially twenty pounds, plus another unofficial five for coming in on Sunday afternoon to help me paint one of the guest rooms. And sixteen pounds from Allan; that was for four hours modelling. We don't pay her that from our own takings, by the way. The students contribute for life classes separately.'

'And that would have been an average week's earnings for her, would it? Forty pounds odd?'

'Yes. But only from here. I know her brother kept her in pocket money—and that she did cleaning work for several farmers' wives round about. I wouldn't be surprised if she had doubled what Allan and I paid her.'

From somewhere out in the grounds the circular saw shrilled again.

'Can you think of anyone who'd have wanted to kill her, Miss Sutton?'

'No,' she replied emphatically, 'of course I can't. Certainly nobody around here.'

'How about this local gossip, Miss Sutton? Did you ever hear anything about Vera Jackman that could point us somewhere?'

'She was a pretty girl who didn't give a damn for anybody; in a place like this, someone like that generates all sorts of gossip. But not all of it was true, I'm absolutely sure of that. For one thing, she simply didn't have the time to get up to anything, and for another, she was too shrewd ever to get found out if she had.'

Like Crosby, Jennifer Sutton had nothing but praise for Vera Jackman when it came to her work. She would turn her hand to anything. She could be given a job and be safely left to get on with it. Cooking, cleaning, laundry-labelling, and even hanging wallpaper. So far as the Suttons were concerned, Vera Jackman was a gem. She would be greatly missed.

Roper changed his tack and came to the real point of his visit.

'Did Vera Jackman call here at the house last night, Miss Sutton? About eleven o'clock, or a few minutes before, perhaps?'

'No,' she said.

Roper raised an eyebrow. Rarely did an answer come that unequivocally. 'You sound very sure,' he said.

'I can be,' she said. 'Everyone was in; and at eleven I'd locked up and switched on the alarms. She could only have got in by ringing the doorbell.'

'And you didn't hear the doorbell?'

'No, I didn't.'

'Could someone else have heard the bell and let her in, without your knowing about it?'

She shook her head and smiled. 'Hardly. I take the keys upstairs with me. The entire place is closed like a fortress at night. Has to be. The insurance.'

'Could she have come into the grounds?'

'The main gates would have been padlocked; but yes, I suppose she could have come in through the tradesmen's gate beside. But on the other hand, why should she?'

'I've no idea, Miss Sutton,' said Roper. Nor, when it came to the point, had he. Although from any number of possible reasons the likeliest one was that she had been on her way to meet a man, perhaps even the father of her child.

'You run a white Range Rover, Miss Sutton?'

'I don't,' she said. 'At least not personally. It's communal property.'

'When was it last driven up Church Lane? Do you know?'

Her eyebrows came together. 'Church Lane? Isn't that where they found Vera's body? Well, I suppose Saturday morning was the last time, I drove it up there. I called in at the Jacksons' place for some fresh vegetables for the freezer.'

'Would you know if it had been up there since?'

Her eyebrows had stayed together. 'You surely can't think our Rover was somehow involved with that poor girl's murder? Good Heavens, that's preposterous.'

'At the moment I'm in the business of clearing away dead wood, Miss Sutton,' said Roper. 'We found a brass valve cap in the lane this afternoon, and the only vehicle in the village fitted with those seems to be yours.'

'Oh, I see.' Her eyebrows came apart at last. 'Perhaps it fell off when I drove the car up there on Saturday.'

And that, Roper had to admit, albeit reluctantly, was possible.

'How many people here *could* have driven it? Since Saturday?'

'Oh . . . four . . . five including myself. I took it into Dorchester yesterday afternoon; and again this morning. I drove my brother in to catch the early train to Waterloo. I dropped it into the garage on my way back—at about half-past nine. But apart from that I'm pretty sure that it hasn't been out; since Saturday, that is.'

'Your brother's out, then?'

'Yes,' she said. 'London. Bond Street. One of the big galleries is running a show for him. He's staying overnight. But if you want to see him, he ought to be back tomorrow morning.'

'How about the other people who drive the Range Rover?'

They were all scattered about in their various workshops.

'Would you like me to gather them in?'

'No. Later will do, Miss Sutton.' Later, when he was armed with the results of the post-mortem examination. Until he'd got that he was working with one arm more or less tied behind his back. 'About ten o'clock—or is that too late?'

'No, of course not. We keep late hours here. I'll make sure everyone's gathered together.'

'Thank you, Miss Sutton,' said Roper, rising from his chair. 'We'd be greatly obliged.'

THE STORM HAD MOVED ON in the direction of London and taken the false dusk with it. Proper dusk was still a couple of hours away, darkness nearer three. Tomorrow was Midsummer Day.

The incident room was back in limbo. A half-dozen cadets had gone back to Church Lane, prospecting for more evidence on the chance that the rain, which for a while had been violent, might have washed up something else; although after the combing the lane had had this morning that didn't seem likely. Solo

schools flourished at two of the trestle tables. A few
wiser men had their heads down on folded arms, cat-
napping. The WPC who was in charge of the computer was collecting dirty tea mugs for want of
something better to do.

A half-hour ago a television crew had arrived and
Roper had read them the brief statement that he had
concocted with the Assistant Chief Constable over the
telephone, together with a few words of his own. The
ACC had told him to keep it short, sharp and to the
point. And now, at half-past seven, the cameras, lights
and recording equipment were being stowed back into
the BBC van preparatory to taking a few shots of the
taped-off length of Church Lane. The pictures and
interview would appear on 'The Nine O'Clock News.'
At nine o'clock, Vera Jackman would be briefly fa-
mous.

Roper's glances at his wristwatch became more fre-
quent.

Time was pressing. The murder detail, sprawling,
sleeping, playing cards, could all too easily lose their
momentum. Boredom was the worst enemy. Roper
had looked the television camera squarely in its Cy-
clopean eye and hinted that investigations were pro-
gressing satisfactorily. If the camera had been allowed
inside the hall it would have thrown the lie back in his
teeth.

And there was the rule of thumb of which Roper
was all too acutely aware: the longer it takes to get the
first sniff of the villain, the further away the villain
gets. Not necessarily in terms of geography, but in
terms of human memory. There was a possibility,
however remote, that somebody last night just might

have witnessed *something*—something, on the face of it, totally irrelevant, so apparently unimportant that the witness had not even thought it worth reporting— a piece of trivia that could crack the enquiry wide open. By tomorrow, the potential witness might regard his information as even more irrelevant. By the day after that he might have forgotten about it altogether. So time was the other enemy.

Eight o'clock came and went. The stub of Roper's cheroot joined four others in a cracked china saucer that was serving as his ashtray.

Over in the far corner the radio stirred to life again. It was DS Makins calling in from Church Lane where he was acting as whipper-in to the posse of cadets quartering the verges.

Roper plucked his sticky shirt from the small of his back on his way across. Even after the storm the evening still had the damp heat of the jungle.

'Yes, Sergeant?'

Makins, with his hand-held walkie-talkie, was at the moment standing on the grass verge outside the Tuppers' cottage. 'I can see smoke rising from the back, Super. Looks like he's got a bonfire going—I'm wondering if I ought to take a closer dekko—only it looks from the smoke as if he's using paraffin on it. I was thinking—if he's just burning garden rubbish it'd be wet, wouldn't it? I mean, why not wait until tomorrow?'

More smart thinking. It could, of course, mean nothing at all. But Wally Tupper had found the body, and statistics showed that it was *often* the murderer who 'discovered' his victim. Ergo...

'Go in,' said Roper. 'Take a couple of cadets with you for witnesses. Find out what he's burning.'

More waiting. Another cheroot.

Makins again, his voice tinnily distorted over the loud-speaker, but Roper could still hear the excitement in it.

He had found a white purse. With a wrist strap. In the middle of Wally Tupper's smoking bonfire.

THE JUNK ROOM at the rear of the hall had been converted into an interview room, one of the local bridge club's baize-topped card tables pressed into service as a desk. On it was an A4 pad and a ballpoint pen; and on a polythene evidence bag the partially charred white snatch purse that had once belonged to Vera Jackman.

Roper sat at one side of the table, a handcuffed Wally Tupper on the other. Tupper had resisted arrest. In panic, most likely. He had kicked Detective Sergeant Makins in the shin sufficiently hard to draw blood, and one of the cadets had been driven off in haste to the cottage hospital to have a tetanus injection and stitches in both the back and front of his right hand. The cadet's wounds had been sustained when Wally Tupper had gone for him with the hayfork that he was using to turn over his bonfire. So Wally Tupper had been immobilised with the cuffs.

Roper was angry. Angry with Tupper for wasting his time, angry with Makins for making a mess of a simple search and seizure.

'The purse, son, where did you find it?'

Tupper didn't answer.

'In the lane? In the ditch? Somewhere else?'

Still no answer. Jollyboy stood behind Tupper's chair, Makins by the door.

'If you promise to behave yourself, I'll have Mr Jollyboy take those cuffs off,' said Roper.

Tupper nodded.

'You promise?' said Roper. 'No more nonsense?'

Tupper nodded again.

'Take 'em off, Sergeant.'

Jollyboy unlocked the handcuffs and passed them back to Makins.

Tupper rubbed his wrists. 'They hurt,' he grumbled.

'So does my young copper,' said Roper grimly. 'You've put the lad in hospital. You know that, don't you?'

'I was scared,' mumbled Tupper. 'They come at me. All of 'em.'

'We bloody didn't,' protested Makins. 'We were going for the purse in the fire. He was pushing it in deeper with that bloody pitchfork.'

With a sudden upward glance Roper threatened him to silence.

'They all come at me,' mumbled Tupper again. 'All of 'em.' His hair was still peppered with that peculiar red dust. There was some in his eyebrows too.

'Did you kill Vera Jackman, Wally?'

Tupper shook his head fiercely.

'Did you put her in that ditch?'

Tupper's head continued to shake.

'But this is her purse? Right?'

'It was in the ditch.'

'The purse was?'

'It was pretty. Got gold bits on it.'

Plated brass bits. Probably glittered in the sunlight and caught his eye. One corner of the purse had split open in the heat and the white plastic had curled away with charred edges. There were still water droplets on it—a cadet had hurled a bucket of water over the flames to douse them.

'So it *was* Vera Jackman's purse?'

Tupper nodded.

Roper lifted the purse with a fingertip and turned it over. The side now uppermost was covered with a greasy black soot. It still smelled faintly of paraffin. 'Where did you find it?'

Another silence. Tupper's gaze slowly lifted, met Roper's, dropped again. 'Ditch.'

'In her hand?'

Tupper's head shook. 'By her feet.'

'Did your mother know you had it when Mr Jolly-boy and I called this morning?'

Tupper shook his head with renewed vigour. He was probably more frightened of his mother than he was of Roper. 'She'd have hit me.'

'And when we asked you about the purse this morning, you knew where it was?'

'I was sitting on it. Got it under the cushion.'

'Had you opened it? Taken anything out?'

Tupper shook his head.

Roper unfastened the brass catch and tipped out the purse's contents. A few coins, a diary, a crumpled paper handkerchief, a lipstick and a diminutive glass phial of *L'Air du Temps* perfume, a Yale doorkey. Roper flipped through the diary. There were no entries as such, just a pencilled cross every twenty-eight days. There was no cross for the month of May.

'Did you kill Vera Jackman, Wally?'

'Keep telling you, don't I? Never killed her. Liked her. She was pretty.'

'You liked her?'

'She didn't like me. But I liked her.' With his head hanging, Tupper pressed the palms of his hands together and rubbed the ball of one thumb against the ball of the other. 'Seen her *without* clothes on too. Up Cort place.'

'How about her wristwatch? When did you last see that?'

Tupper blinked, frowned. 'Keep telling you,' he grumbled. 'I never seen no bloody wristwatch.'

Roper sat back tiredly. It had been a long hot day and there was still a lot to do before it was finished. 'I'm keeping you here for a while,' he said. 'You took Vera Jackman's purse, and you didn't tell me. That was naughty; right? And I want you to think about anything else you might have done. Something you might not have told us about yet. Do you follow me?'

Tupper nodded sullenly. 'Yeah,' he mumbled. 'I'll try…But I didn't see no wristwatch. And if that's what you want me to say, I ain't going to.'

'The truth, son,' said Roper; although his intuition told him that he had probably already got it. 'That's all I want to hear.'

As he rose and slid back his chair a brisk rap sounded at the door. It was Price. Wilson was outside. He had finished his post-mortem examination on Vera Jackman.

'YOUR COPY,' he said. 'The original's with the district coroner.'

One of the WPCs came over and put two mugs of steaming tea between them on the trestle table.

Roper sipped and read by turns; whatever he was able to read, that is. The draft was in Wilson's childishly wayward handwriting and Roper, not for the first time, wondered how pharmacists ever managed to put doctor's prescriptions together without poisoning half their customers. He plucked out the salient words, however. Strangulation. Ligature. Pregnant. The victim had been attacked from behind. Grains of black dust impressed into the groove left by the ligature.

'Could the body have been moved after death? Do you know?'

'If it was, it would have to have been pretty *soon* afterwards.'

'So it could have been.'

Wilson remained cautious. 'It's possible,' he agreed.

'And what about this black dust?'

'*Predominantly* black,' said Wilson. 'Quite large grains. And a few grains of red dust; rather like coarsely ground red pepper.'

Roper's ears pricked at that. 'What's the red stuff? Any thoughts?'

'None yet,' said Wilson. 'But her right fist was clutching about a teaspoonful of it. I've sent a sample of it along to the lab; and brought a few grains with me in case you might recognise it from around here.'

Balancing his document case on his knees, Wilson lifted the lid and reached inside. He brought out a diminutive polythene envelope which he put on the table in front of Roper. Tucked into one corner was the sample of the dust. It did indeed look like red pepper, but only at first glance. Its colour was too consistent for pepper.

Roper beckoned over one of the cadets. 'Cut cross to the shops, son. I want a comb, preferably a white one. The finest teeth you can find. If the shop's shut, knock 'em up.'

'This dust, Mr Wilson,' he said, as the cadet hurried out. 'How important is it?'

'Vital, so far as you people are concerned,' said Wilson. He demonstrated with his own right hand. 'When she first struggled, she clawed at her throat to try and grip the ligature. Natural reflex. But then, as she began to lose consciousness her arms would have flailed everywhere, trying to get a purchase on something. Then, in the moment of death'—Wilson closed his fist dramatically, ivory knuckled, his fingertips grinding into the palm—'but even *tighter* than *that*. That's the cadaveric spasm I mentioned this morning. Now when that fist is shut, believe me, it stays shut until rigor mortis begins to diminish. I had to open that poor young woman's fist with a dental retractor. That dust is the last thing Vera Jackman got hold of. Find the source, and that's where she was strangled.'

Roper felt his skin prickling, his pulse quickening.

'And she was also clutching a single blade of grass. I've sent that along to the lab too.'

But for the moment Roper was content to settle for the red dust.

'How about the weapon—the ligature?'

'Smooth and cylindrical,' said Wilson. 'Nothing like a cord. Could have been some kind of plastic.'

'When did she die?'

'Between ten and midnight last night.'

'She was seen by three people round about ten to eleven.'

Wilson spread a hand. 'So she died between eleven and midnight. I'm sorry; I can't do better than that. Scientifically I can only spread the time over two hours.'

'How about the stomach contents? Didn't they help?'

Wilson smiled thinly. 'Like the stomachs of most figure-conscious eighteen-year-old girls, Superintendent, hers was very nearly empty. I'd say she'd eaten nothing since yesterday's breakfast.'

'Anything under her fingernails?'

'Fragments of skin—and blood. Both hers. She clawed her throat horribly, poor child.'

'That red dust,' ventured Roper—although he'd already guessed the answer; 'couldn't be *sawdust,* could it?'

'It's possible,' agreed Wilson, still with his infuriating caution.

But whether it was sawdust or not, Roper guessed that if anyone knew where it had come from that person would be Wally Tupper.

Two GLASS SLIDES. Between one pair of them a few grains of the red dust that Wilson had brought in; between the other the scrapings from the comb with which Wally Tupper, a few moments ago, had combed his hair.

Mrs Greenaway, the young woman on loan from the forensic laboratory, fed the first slide into her microscope. Her equipment was, of necessity, basic: a high-powered comparison microscope, a case of glass phials containing sufficient solutions for crude chemical analyses, a small box of electronic tricks for equally crude spectral analyses.

'It looks fibrous,' she said, focusing the twin eye-pieces.

It certainly wasn't pepper. But it looked cellular, organic... woody.

'Try the other one,' said Roper.

Mrs Greenaway took out the first slide and sprang in the other beneath the stage clips. 'This one's greasy,' she said. That sample was from the comb.

'But is it the same stuff?'

She focused more tightly, took out the second slide and replaced it with the first. Then replaced the first with the second again. 'I can't be absolutely sure...'

'As sure as you can be. That'll do for now,' said Roper.

Mrs Greenaway sat back in her chair and hooked down her spectacles from her hair to her nose.

Roper waited, still with prickling skin and the feeling that at last he might be on to something, that the last couple of hours' hanging about had not been a waste of time after all, but merely a quiet interlude between one act and the next.

'Yes,' she said at last. 'I think it is.'

'Could it be sawdust?'

'Yes,' she agreed cautiously, 'it could be.'

'Is, or could be, Mrs Greenaway?'

But Mrs Greenaway would not commit herself. Roper, however, could. And if he was right, and it was sawdust, then it was yet another road that could lead back to Cort Place.

SIX

THE MEMBERS of the commune sat around the scrubbed whitewood table in the basement kitchen at the back of Cort Place. Apart from Jennifer Sutton they were all still in their working clothes.

'We'd like all your names first, please,' said Roper. 'Starting with you, sir.'

'Thruxton,' the man said. He sat with his back to the open kitchen door. Beyond the door a flight of walled-in stone steps led up to the garden. The moon was full and cast a pale-blue glow over them.

'And you do what here, sir?'

'Sculptor,' said Thruxton. He was rising forty, fair-haired, lean and brown and sinewy. Clean shaven. A woman might have thought him too attractive to be trusted, too cleanly hewn, too sure of himself.

'And you, madam?'

'Susan Thruxton. Mrs. I'm Bill's wife.' Mrs Thruxton was a pale, washed-out little blonde with a birdlike eagerness. Her hands were clasped on the table in front of her. She wore no wedding ring and had the protuberant eyes of the hyperthyroid. She was a weaver and textile designer.

'And you, sir?'

'Huxley,' he said. 'Lewis. I do antique furniture.'

Early thirties, Roper thought. Red-bearded. Chunkily built with thick, tanned forearms. The cigarette he was smoking was homemade and sparsely filled with a particularly pungent tobacco. Where his mouth had touched it, the paper was moist with an unpleasant brown stain. The straggling beard could have done with a trim.

'Madam?'

'Haldane, Carol Haldane.' Middle to late twenties. Dark hair dragged back and held in place with a black plastic clip. The sort of skin that looks as if it has been sandpapered, and faintly sweaty. 'I paint,' she said, although Roper had already guessed that. It looked as if she wiped surplus colours from her brushes straight on to the front of her skirt. She was smoking a Gauloise. A crumpled blue packet of them and a cheap plastic lighter sat on the table in front of her.

'And you, sir?'

'Taunton. Michael.'

Taunton was the youngest. Early twenties, slim and gaunt, with a shock of dark hair. He was the only member of the coven around the table who looked ill at ease.

'And what do you do here, Mr Taunton?'

'I help Lewis.' Taunton jerked his head in the direction of Huxley. 'Staining. French polishing. All that.'

'Londoner?'

'Yes,' said Taunton. 'Greenwich.' For some reason best known to himself he kept his eyes averted from Roper. The fingertips and nails of his left hand were blotched with reddish-brown stains; French polish, most likely.

'And you, sir?'

The last man at the table. Built like a tug-of-war anchor man. Thickly spectacled, and bearded; and almost bald.

'Dance,' he said. 'Adrian. Glassworker.'

'Madam?'

'Rachael Dance,' she said. Her head tilted sideways. 'His wife. We work together.' Mrs Dance, built on the same heroic scale as her husband, was a smooth-faced blonde and, like him, was probably in her early forties.

An evening breeze from the garden blew the scent of flowers and damp grass down the steps. Roper cast his gaze slowly around the table. All met it, except Michael Taunton, who was absorbedly cleaning one fingernail with a corner of another. Carol Haldane dragged on her cigarette and blew a horizontal column of smoke.

Roper came to the point quickly. 'Vera Jackman,' he said; 'did any of you see her in the grounds here last night? About eleven o'clock?'

A few heads were shaken, a few shoulders shrugged. No one spoke. Roper tried again. 'She was seen at the gateway at about ten to eleven.'

'Who's to say she came in?' This from Thruxton, the matinée-idol sculptor.

'No one, Mr Thruxton,' said Roper. 'I'm asking.'

Thruxton hitched a shoulder. 'In which case you've got your answer. She must have gone on by.'

'She vanished, Mr Thruxton. Like a hole in the ground. One minute she was there and the next she wasn't.'

There was no response.

'She was a little slag.' This contemptuously delivered utterance came abruptly from Carol Haldane. 'Perhaps she came into the grounds for a bit of nookie behind the wall. Who knows?'

'Carol, for God's sake...' The chide came from Jennifer Sutton, but only for form's sake because Roper was there.

There was no concern here, Roper felt. Vera Jackman had worked here, had been seen outside late last night; everyone around the table, with the exception of himself and Price, had known her. And no one cared. A girl was dead and no one cared.

He looked around the table with a distaste he took no trouble to disguise, stared at each of the virtuous disinterested faces. He settled finally on Lewis Huxley.

'I heard a circular saw running this afternoon, Mr Huxley. Yours, was it?'

'Yes,' said Huxley.

'Do you use it often?'

Huxley nodded. 'Yes. Often. Why?'

'Have you cut up any mahogany lately? Or any other kind of red wood?'

'Yesterday. Mike did.'

Roper turned to Michael Taunton. 'What happened to the sawdust, Mr Taunton?'

'It got sucked up,' said Taunton.

'The circular saw's fitted with a vacuum extractor,' explained Lewis Huxley.

'And where does it finish up?'

'In a canvas bag,' said Huxley. 'Like a vacuum cleaner. And when the canvas bag is full, we empty it into plastic bags. Then we sell it. It's used for chip-board filler.'

'Anyone else in the village do similar work?'

'No,' said Huxley. 'At least, not that I know of.'

'Perhaps later we could have a look at this work-shop of yours, Mr Huxley?'

'Sure,' said Huxley. 'Not that it'll help you any.'

Roper's gaze slowly raked around the table again in the ensuing silence. Somewhere a clock chimed once for the quarter after ten o'clock. It sounded like a quality clock. It was followed shortly afterwards by the chimes of several others around the house.

'What I'd like to do now,' he said, 'is to establish where everyone was between, say, ten-forty-five last night and one o'clock this morning.'

'I was in bed.' This, her nervous second contribution, came from the ringless Mrs Thruxton.

'How about you, Mr Thruxton?'

'Working,' said Thruxton.

'Where?'

'Up in our quarters,' said Thruxton. 'I was sketch-ing.'

'Mr Dance?'

Dance peered out myopically from behind his peb-ble-lensed spectacles. Broken at some time or an-other, the bridge was held together by a few turns of grubby Elastoplast. 'Upstairs in our room. Both of us.'

'Mr Huxley?'

'Likewise,' said Huxley. His forearms and the backs of his hands were overgrown with ginger hairs a few shades lighter than the beard.

'Doing what, sir?'

'Reading,' said Huxley.

'From then till when?'

'From about half-past nine; until I turned in just after midnight.'

'You didn't come downstairs at all during that time?'

Once. At about five past eleven, Huxley had come down to fill his vacuum flask from the percolator that was kept bubbling more or less all the time in the kitchen.

'Anyone see you?'

'Jenny—Miss Sutton. She was in the recess under the stairs; switching on the burglar alarm.'

'That right, Miss Sutton?

She nodded. 'Yes, I think so.'

'You'd locked the house up by this time?'

'Yes,' she said.

'How did you know that everyone was in? Did you check?'

'I don't have to,' she said. 'Everyone knows that they have to be in by eleven. It's our only house rule.'

'When you've locked up—can anyone get in or out?'

'No,' she said. 'Everyone here only has a key to the back door—here.' She pointed to the door to the garden. 'That one. But at night, I turn the mortice lock on it. And the alarm's connected to it.'

'And what if there was a fire?'

'There's a fire escape. End of the house. The doors are opened by a special key in glass-fronted boxes; and the only way into those is by breaking the glass.'

'How about the windows?'

'They're all wired into the alarm system.'

'Without exception?'

'Yes.'

'So no one can get in or out—after you've locked up—without activating the alarm?'

'That's right.'

'Supposing,' said Roper, 'that you'd forgotten to lock one of the doors or windows connected to the alarm system?'

'I can't,' she said. 'If I did, the alarms would ring when I switched them on.'

'Can anyone else switch them off?'

'No one. There are only two keys. I keep both of them.'

Roper sat back. Vera Jackman had last been seen alive at a few minutes to eleven. At eleven, on the dot, if Jennifer Sutton was telling the truth, and there was no reason to believe that she was not, Cort Place had been sealed to the world. Like a fortress; her words.

'Miss Haldane? Where were you late last night?'

Tobacco smoke surged between her teeth like water through a sluice gate. 'It's Ms,' she said coolly. 'My marital state or otherwise is none of your business. I was upstairs. All evening. Painting.'

'Mr Taunton?'

'I got back here at quarter to eleven,' said Taunton grudgingly. 'I got myself a mug of coffee from the kitchen. Then joined Carol upstairs.'

'Back from where, Mr Taunton?'

'Cort Arms,' said Taunton.

'So you must have seen Vera Jackman there.'

'Sure,' said Taunton, with a shrug. 'Why not?'

'Did you speak to her?'

'Only to order a beer.'

'When did you leave the Cort Arms, Mr Taunton?' This was from Price.

'A few minutes after the second bell,' said Taunton. He was careful not to look at Price either, Roper noticed.

'And you got back here when?'

'About a quarter to eleven.'

'But from here to the Arms is only five minutes' walk.'

'I stopped off at the fish-and-chip van,' said Taunton.

'Did you see Wally Tupper at all? At the fish-and-chip van?'

Taunton shook his head.

'How about when you got back here, Mr Taunton? Did anyone see you? Other than Miss Haldane?'

'Yes... I did.' Mrs Thruxton raised a timid hand. 'Or, rather, I heard him. I heard him knock on Carol's door and speak to her.'

'Did you go out again, Mr Taunton?' Roper took over the questioning again.

'Not out of the grounds, no.'

'So you did go out of the house.'

'Mike sleeps across at the lodge,' broke in Carol Haldane, around the new Gauloise she was lighting from the stub of the last. A yellow tar stain at one side of her mouth suggested an inveterate chain smoker. She pushed the crumpled packet and her plastic lighter towards Taunton.

Roper hooked her up on a cold hard stare. 'I'd prefer it if you let Mr Taunton speak for himself, Miss Haldane. Where's this lodge exactly, Mr Taunton?'

'The east gate,' mumbled Taunton, around the cigarette he had taken from Haldane's packet and was lighting with her lighter. He was the youngest at the table, in Jackman's age group, and had that pop star's bonyness of face that young women seemed to go for these days. Someone like Jackman might have found him attractive. And he was edgy, definitely edgy.

'So you don't sleep in the house?'

'I just told you, didn't I?'

'Mike acts as a sort of caretaker down there at night,' said Jennifer Sutton.

That figured. For all their hiding behind their working clothes the group around the table, except for Taunton, were definitely not hobbledehoys. Taunton was the odd man out here, the poor white. So *he* slept down at the lodge.

'What time did you leave the house, Mr Taunton—on your way to the lodge?'

'Eleven,' said Taunton.

'That's right,' said Jennifer Sutton. 'I saw him coming down the stairs as I was locking up in the hall.'

'And you went straight to the lodge?'

'Right.'

'And stayed there?'

Taunton nodded. 'Right.'

'Did you happen to see Vera Jackman in the grounds?'

Taunton shook his head.

Price took over the questioning again.

'Do you drive the Range Rover, Mr Taunton?'

'Sometimes,' said Taunton. He plucked a shred of tobacco from his underlip. 'Not all that often.'

'When was the last time?'

'Thursday. Last week.'

'Wednesday,' said Carol Haldane, correcting him. 'It was Wednesday. You drove me into Dorchester.'

Taunton's eyebrows came together. 'Yes,' he agreed eventually 'Wednesday. Right.'

'Who else drives it, other than Miss Sutton?' asked Roper.

Three hands rose. Thruxton's, Huxley's and Dance's. Of the three, it appeared that the last of them to have driven the Range Rover was Adrian Dance. On Monday morning. Two days ago.

'Where did you go, sir?'

'Salisbury,' said Dance. 'There's a dealer there who handles our glass work.'

'You didn't drive the Range Rover along Church Lane?'

'Wrong direction,' said Dance.

But someone had, Roper was sure of it. The finding of that brass valve cap in Church Lane—when the Cort Place Range Rover was missing one—was too much of a coincidence to be dismissed. It might— just—have fallen off on Saturday when Jennifer Sutton had called in at the Jacksons' smallholding. But if it had not . . .

'How about your brother, Miss Sutton? Where was he last night?'

'Up in our flat,' she said. 'He always has an early night before he goes up to town.'

'Does he ever drive the Rover?'

'He doesn't drive. Hasn't for years—about five. He ran a child down. It left him with a nervous breakdown. He never drove after that.'

'I see,' said Roper. 'Thank you.'

He turned to Huxley. It was time to establish the provenance of the red sawdust. 'Perhaps we might have a look at this workshop of yours now, Mr Huxley.'

Huxley's chair grated back on the red-tiled floor. He rose and took the few paces to the big oak dresser behind him. From one of the brass cuphooks he took down several bunches of keys, selected one on a ring and hooked the others back.

'Are the keys to the house up there as well?' asked Roper. 'Or just the workshops?'

'All the keys,' said Huxley.

'And they're always kept there, on that hook?'

'Only during the day,' said Huxley. 'Jenny collects them from there at night, when she locks up.'

'And who locks the workshops?'

'We all lock our own.'

'Do you check them?' asked Roper. 'Could anyone have hidden in one last night?'

'Certainly not mine,' said Huxley. 'I always check it. Or Mike does.'

'Nor ours,' said Dance.

'Mr Thruxton?'

'Mine was locked too,' said Thruxton. 'And I checked it.'

'Miss Haldane?'

'I've got a studio down at the lodge with Allan,' she said. 'He always locks it. But I wouldn't know about last night.'

'I'm sure he would have,' said Jennifer Sutton. 'My brother's very thorough about locking up. He has a horror of vandals. Someone got into the lodge last summer and slashed all his canvases. We reported it to Sergeant Jollyboy.'

ROPER AND PRICE followed Huxley up the stone steps and across the grass towards a stand of poplars that stood like black quills in the moonlight. The old stable, Huxley's workshop, was immediately in front of them.

Huxley fiddled a key into a padlock, unlocked it and flipped aside the hasp from the staple. The double doors were on runners. Huxley slid one open eighteen inches or so and then went inside to turn on the lights. Roper followed him in.

It was a ramshackle old place, almost as old as the house, part timber, part brick. The original stalls had been stripped out and what had been the hayloft was now a timber store. The uneven stone floor had been levelled off here and there with a fairly new screed of cement. In the middle was a carpenter's bench almost as large as a billiard table, and beyond that, beneath the hayloft, was a smaller bench fitted up with the circular saw that Roper had heard running that afternoon. Around the walls were several items of antiquated machinery: a pillar drill, a treadle-operated wood lathe, an electric planer, an electric ring upon which stood two old-fashioned glue pots. In a rack near the large bench was an array of tools, some modern, some old enough to be museum pieces. The smell of horses still lingered.

Roper walked slowly around, Huxley and Price watching him from just inside the doorway. Galvanised electrical trunking all around the outer walls showed that the workshop had been very recently rewired. Several items of antique furniture lay about in various states of repair—a Victorian tallboy stripped of its varnish, the mahogany carcass of a grandfather clock, an Edwardian occasional table minus a leg, an elegant dining chair—mid-eighteenth-century by the looks of it—had one of its back supports cramped and splinted.

But what inevitably caught Roper's eye was a massive Sheraton-style breakfront bookcase, some seven feet high and nine long, shrouded in a suspended polythene tent to keep the dust off it. Its four lower doors were decorated with painted Graces, in the Wedgwood manner and in intricate detail. Only the fact that its upper doors were still unglazed and showed raw wood gave the lie to the fact that it might be the genuine article.

'Are you making this, Mr Huxley?'

'Yes,' replied Huxley. 'Some American with more money than sense.'

'What's it worth?'

'To us... four and a half thousand. He could probably buy one cheaper in an auction room.'

If he could find one, thought Roper.

Carol Haldane had painted the Graces and ornate medallions on the door panels, Thruxton had cast the intricate brass doorpulls and key plates, Michael Taunton was doing the varnishing; the doors would have two more coats over the next week or so. In early July, it would be crated up and shipped to its buyer on Long Island.

Roper continued his tour and finished up beside the circular-saw bench under the hayloft. The loft was reached by way of a flight of new oak stairs, beautifully put together, probably by Huxley himself. Above the vicious-looking saw blade was an inverted metal horn, the apex of which terminated in a corrugated plastic pipe that went upward to one of the beams that supported the loft floor and thence out through a hole in the wall that looked as if it had once been fitted with an airbrick.

'This the sawdust extractor, Mr Huxley?'

Huxley came slowly from where he had been by the doorway. 'Yes,' he said. 'That's it. The fan unit's outside.'

'Efficient, is it?'

'Very,' said Huxley.

'But I've seen circular saws working,' said Roper. 'They chuck dust everywhere.'

'Well, yes,' agreed Huxley. 'But that's the best extractor on the market. I'd say ninety-five percent of all the dust finishes up in one of the bags outside.'

'And what about the odd five per cent that doesn't?'

'We put a broom to it, shovel it up and chuck it in the dustbins.'

'And who does that exactly? You? Mr Taunton? Who did it yesterday, for instance?'

'Wally Tupper,' replied Huxley.

Outside again, Huxley replaced the padlock and locked it. Roper and Price followed him to the back of the workshop. In the light from Price's pen-torch, Huxley showed them his black plastic sacks of sawdust, a dozen or more of them under a lightweight tarpaulin with puddles of rainwater trapped in pockets here and there between the bulges of the plastic bags underneath. The bags, those at the front at least, were intact and sealed. There was no spilled sawdust.

'Where are the dustbins kept?'

'Down by the front gate,' said Huxley.

Roper stood aside. 'Let's take a look, shall we, Mr Huxley?'

They retraced their steps to the kitchen end of the house, along the side of it, and down the long drive towards the gate, their path lit by the moon and what little light spilled from a couple of upstairs rooms at the front of the house. But as they drew closer to the gates there was only the moon. Looking back over his shoulder, Roper saw that the house was now lost to view behind the trees.

Access to the dustbins was by a flagged path leading off the drive between banks of shrubbery, near the tradesmen's gate, well out of sight even to the daytime visitors. Huxley stopped. Price's torch lit two giant communal dustbins on wheels and half a dozen domestic bins, two of which were plastic, one without a lid. Price rapped the two tall bins with his knuckles. They echoed hollowly.

'They were all emptied early this morning,' said Huxley, 'whatever it is you're looking for.'

Roper lifted the lids off the smaller dustbins and Price shone his torch into each of them. Huxley was right. They were all empty.

And so was the lidless one—at first glance. But Price took a second glance. 'Sir,' he said, 'look at this—down at the bottom.'

A gallon of rainwater. And floating on it, amongst the other debris that had drifted up from the bottom during the afternoon, were several sodden wet clumps of what looked like red sawdust.

And there was more on the ground not a foot away, like red dandruff, scattered on a patch of grass. Not much, but enough for a sample for the forensic people.

While Roper held out an evidence bag, Price dropped to a crouch and dug up a sample of it with the tail-end of his ballpoint: soil, grass, sawdust.

Huxley was watching all this with reluctant interest, his hands in his pockets, his shoulders hunched. He said gruffly: 'Can I ask what you're doing that for? Or is it all part of police mystique?'

'No mystique about it, Mr Huxley,' said Roper, as he opened the bag wider for Price to drop in the sample. 'Do you know what a cadaveric spasm is, sir?'

'No idea.'

So Roper told him. Sometimes a small and deliberate leak of information could flush a culprit from cover. 'And you see, Mr Huxley, young Miss Jackman was gripping a fistful of grass and sawdust.' He smiled companionably in the moonlight. 'Not a common mixture, sir—if you take my point.'

Huxley took the point. 'Christ,' he said softly. 'You mean she was murdered right here?'

'Could be, sir,' agreed Roper. 'It could very well be.'

SEVEN

IT WAS WINDING-DOWN TIME in the incident centre. A
few minutes to midnight. A uniformed sergeant and a
constable had just come on duty to act as nightwatch-
men until tomorrow morning. Price and Rodgers and
Makins and the rest of the crew that had been here all
day had gone home for a well-deserved sleep—and a
few to make peace with their wives, some of whom
hadn't seen them in almost twenty-four hours.

Roper smoked his last cheroot of the night while
across in the far corner the radio crackled from time
to time: a traffic accident, a break in, a domestic incident, the grist of most police work. Murder, blessedly, was the rarest occurrence.

He let smoke curl up beside his cheek as he considered motives. Strange things, motives. Difficult to
prove. A motive was born of a particular state of mind
at a particular period of time. A motive was rarely an
excuse. Sometimes it provided an extenuating circumstance, but that was all. And most motives were
so feeble that they extenuated nothing, especially
murder. The courts were rarely swayed by them and it
was not the job of the police to find out what they
were. But a good jack always looked for a motive. It
was the villain's most private piece of property, the
little phial of corrosive poison that had taken him off
the straight and narrow. Which is why now, at the hot
fag-end of Day One, Roper was giving it his relaxed

contemplation. Whether a jury would ever hear what the motive was was of little consequence. At some time around eleven o'clock last night a girl had been murdered in Cort Abbas. Whoever had killed her must have had a reason, however momentary. Find that motive, however insane it was, however half-cocked and irrational it might be to the rest of the human race, and Roper knew that he would be well on the way to nailing the villain.

Vera Jackman had been an exceptionally attractive young woman. Extrovert enough to pose in the nude for Allan Sutton's life class, to have her photographs taken in various states of undress. She had also been pregnant.

Ergo: Vera Jackman's sexual awareness of herself had to figure prominently on the list of motives. Somewhere, for a fact, there was a lover. Or an ex-lover.

And that was equally likely. An ex-lover. Some young lad recently given the old heave-ho. Or someone not so young. One of the strange crew at that commune across at Cort Place, even.

For the moment, Roper could still only commit himself to a few educated guesses, but over the years he had learned that the simplest explanations for the facts are usually the best explanation for the facts:

Vera Jackman, *in extremis,* had clutched at sawdust-strewn grass. There was a patch of sawdust-strewn grass near the dustbins at Cort Place.

Ergo: Jackman had more than likely been killed beside those dustbins.

Vera Jackman had been seven weeks pregnant. She had only been *clinically* sure about that yesterday. And if she had been strangled last night in the grounds of Cort Place, then—ergo: she may have been paying a visit to that lover—or ex-lover—to inform him. And, ergo: that lover was very likely a member of the commune. Not one of the art-student guests because, whoever that man was, he would have moved on by now.

Ergo: Vera Jackman's murderer had been one of the four men who had been sitting around that kitchen table tonight: Taunton; Huxley; Thruxton; Dance. Or the fifth man, as yet unseen: Allan Sutton.

Roper stubbed out his cheroot in the chipped white saucer and rose and put on his jacket. Tomorrow, he was going back to Cort Place. *And* he'd have another word with Wally Tupper.

THURSDAY. Day Two. Five past nine in the morning and Roper and Price were patiently trying to stir Wally Tupper's sluggish memory to life.

'I done it Tuesday,' said Wally. 'I didn't do it yesterday 'cause...' He shifted uncomfortably. 'Well... you know. Vera an' all that.'

'Definitely Tuesday?'

Wally nodded. His mother stood watchfully behind his chair in the back kitchen.

'Nice and slow, son,' said Roper. 'Tell us what you did. Don't hurry.'

Wally closed his eyes. Roper waited.

'Done the caff first,' said Wally. His eyes screwed tighter shut. 'I 'ave a sack, see. Miss Sutton always likes the caff done before the visitors come. I done the floor... and the tables... and the chairs... and the baskets... for the ice-cream papers.' Wally's eyes sprang open and he beamed at what was, for Wally, a prodigious feat of memory. 'That's what I done,' he burst out, triumphantly. 'That's what I done, Tuesday.'

'Good lad,' said Roper enthusiastically.

Wally's beam widened.

'Now, son...' said Roper, bringing Wally gently back to earth again. 'After you did the cafeteria—can you remember what you did then? Think hard. Take your time.'

Wally's head lolled to one side. His eyes rolled upward. Then abruptly he shot upright. 'I know—I remember. I done Mr Huxley's workshop. I done it special 'cause Mike was varnishing.'

'Good,' said Roper.

'Mustn't 'ave dust when Mike's varnishing.'

'No,' agreed Roper. 'Course you can't. Do you use a vacuum cleaner... or a broom?'

'An 'oover,' said Wally. 'Brooms make dust. 'oovers don't make dust. I only use a broom when Mike ain't varnishing. That's what Mr Huxley tells me to do.'

Roper smiled encouragingly. 'Then what? Can you remember?'

'I had to empty the 'oover,' said Wally. 'It wasn't workin' properly and I asked Mike and he said it was all full and it'd be all right if I emptied it.'

'And did you?'

Wally nodded.

'Where?' said Roper. 'Where, son?'

'Dustbins,' said Wally, to Roper's immense relief.

'One of the big ones or one of the little ones?'

Wally scowled. 'Little one,' he said, at last 'An' the wind blew it *all* over me!'

'So you spilled some as well,' said Roper.

'Lots,' said Wally. 'It was the wind, see? I couldn't 'elp it.'

'Good lad,' said Roper. He and Wally were friends today, the incident of yesterday forgotten.

THAT HAD BEEN at five past nine. Now it was half-past, of the same morning, twenty-four hours almost to the minute since Wally Tupper had found Vera Jackman's body in Church Lane, and the director of the Regional Forensic Laboratory was on the telephone.

The grass in Vera Jackman's hand was timothy grass.

'—*phleum pratense.*' The Latin tag rolled over the director's tongue like a rare wine. 'It's a farmers' grass apparently. Used for grazing. Not the sort of grass you'd find in a town as a rule.'

'And what about the sample I sent along this morning?'

'Oh, no doubt at all.' The director's voice lilted with professional assuredness. 'My tame expert tells me that that one's also timothy grass.'

'And the sawdust?'

'Definitely mahogany. If you can hang on until this afternoon I can even get the people at Kew to identify the source genus.'

'No, sir, thank you,' said Roper, before the director became too carried away on his scientific enthusiasm. 'You've given me enough to be getting on with. Much obliged.'

Roper no longer had any doubts. The brass valve cap, the fortuitous juxtaposition of mahogany sawdust and timothy grass had ceased to be coincidences the second he put down the telephone. They had become copper-bottomed evidence.

THE SAME MORNING. Eleven o'clock. Hot again, and humid; and Roper more in mufti than usual: short-sleeved shirt, lightweight slacks, gilt-framed Polaroids and only immediately recognisable as a policeman by the sureness of his tread, and perhaps only then by another policeman.

He joined the short queue in the porch. A plump, jolly woman with a lapful of knitting and an agricultural voice took his £1.50 and tore him off a yellow ticket.

'Would you like a guide, sir?'

'Please,' said Roper, handing over another 20p in exchange for a few Xeroxed sheets of blue paper stapled together with a woodcut print of the house on the cover. 'Thank you.'

It was cooler in the hall. As yet there weren't many visitors. A few picking over the goods on the souvenir counter; a man and a woman, heavy-looking and faintly Teutonic, trying to find the best angle to photograph the great stone fireplace; a man sitting on the bottom step of the left-hand staircase with a small boy on his knees.

Roper followed the cardboard arrows on their stalks—what the guidebook called the suggested route. They led him first through a wide stone arch to the left of the fireplace. The passage gave on to two rooms, one on the left and one on the right. Both were panelled. The morning sunlight streamed in through lattice windows. The room on the left was a drawing room, furnished in late Georgian and with enough Chinoiserie and pottery about to make Roper almost forget what he was here for. Tucked well out of sight behind the curtains were a pair of wires leading down from the alarm switches on the three sections of the windows that could be opened. A somewhat ineffectual daytime guard was another grey-haired lady of a similar stamp to the one who had taken his money in the porch. She smiled coyly at him as he went out and continued with her knitting.

The room opposite was a dining room, its centrepiece a great polished lake of a Jacobean refectory table. Glass-fronted cabinets displayed a glittering show of old Waterford crystal and several Chelsea dinner services, any one of which would have cost Roper a year's salary at auction. Leaded casement windows again. Wired up. When he trailed the heel of his shoe lightly across the carpet nearby he felt the edge of a pressure pad. Family portraits about the walls: Admiral Sir Henry Sutton and Lady Mildred, *circa* William the Fourth; Mr Clive Sutton (Gentleman), by— Roper let out a soft whistle between his teeth—Joshua Reynolds no less.

Roper stepped back into the passage. At its entrance Jennifer Sutton was talking to someone unseen in the hall. Roper turned on his heel and returned to the dining room. The lady doing guard duty smiled dutifully at him again, seemingly unaware that he had been in there before.

When the coast sounded clear, Roper returned to the passage. The window at the end overlooking the

garden was narrow and barred and the only way in and
out of it would be with a welding torch.

He retraced his steps to the hall and went up the left-
hand staircase. The man with the child had been
joined by his wife. As he reached the first landing he
saw Jennifer Sutton talking animatedly to Adrian
Dance by the souvenir counter down in the hall. The
window on the landing was open, but the wires connected to a micro-switch near the top of the frame
were clearly part of the burglar alarm circuitry. A
wooden gallery led across the top of the fireplace to
the other side of the house, doors leading off it to
bedrooms. A bulbously carved Jacobean four-poster
in one, testered with French tapestry and with a Jacobean blanket chest at its foot. The casement windows were both wired into the alarm. The adjacent
room was brighter, a woman's room, silver-backed
hairbrushes and silver candlesticks on its dressing table. Its doorway was roped off; and a few inches from
the floor a slender beam of bright light shone from one
jamb to the other where it lit the black disc of a photo-
electric cell, proclaiming yet another alarm. A little
below waist height was a similar beam. This, the guide
stated, had been the bedroom of Ann Sutton (1780—
1820), sister to the admiral and a putative mistress of
Beau Brummel.

The oak-panelled walls of the gallery were lined with
more portraits of the Suttons, each generation looking slightly less prosperous than the generation before. A mutton-chopped Alderman Sidney Sutton, a
Victorian. Mr and Mrs Claud Sutton, Edwardian, and
their two sons, and then the two sons again, older, one
of them in an officer's uniform of the Great War.

Another bedroom. Its two casement windows were wired into the alarm. The adjacent room was a sewing room, frozen at some time in the mid-nineteenth century. Its one long rectangle of casement windows was again wired into the alarm system.

Roper was now on the landing at the other side of the house and immediately over the souvenir counter. A flight of stairs going up was barred with a white nylon rope with a PRIVATE notice hanging from it.

The single large, bright room leading from the landing was a picture gallery. An island display at its centre carried pictures that were for sale. The signatures on them were Carol Haldane's and Allan Sutton's. Her line seemed to be miniature landscapes; his wildlife, with a leaning towards birds. The windows of this room were all alarmed.

Roper returned to the landing and went back downstairs. The room beneath the picture gallery was a miniature ballroom, red-velvet-upholstered Edwardian settles and chairs at the edges of the parquet floor, mirrors in ornate baroque frames hung about the walls. The rear wall overlooking the garden was almost entirely glazed. The two pairs of French windows were open against the heat of the morning. Both were connected into the alarm system.

He went back into the hall. An arrow beside the souvenir counter pointed along a passage towards an open door at the back of the house and bore the legend GARDEN CAFETERIA. The door, hooked back to the passage wall, was fitted with both a Yale and a stout Chubb mortice lock, and its two glass panes were protected by steel mesh panels both inside and out. At the right-hand top corner of the doorframe was a fur-

ther pair of micro-contacts like the ones on all the
windows.

So that was that. At night, provided the alarm system was switched on, Cort Place was near enough im-
pregnable. Eleven o'clock on the dot, so Jennifer
Sutton had said; although, Roper recalled, according
to Lewis Huxley, on Tuesday night it had been nearer
five past when he had seen Jennifer Sutton switching
it on beneath the stairs.

But, even given that extra few minutes, was it possible that Jackman's murderer could have met her,
killed her, taken her body across to Church Lane and
got back here again in fourteen minutes flat? Because
that is what he would have to have done if the jogging
Mr Jackson and Lewis Huxley were right about their
times.

The nub of the problem was the murderer's return
to the house. No one had heard—or they were all lying—the doorbell ringing late on Tuesday night. No
one had heard the burglar alarms. So either the murderer had got his work done by five past eleven, or he
had spent the night outside, in which case he would
have been missed by someone or other—except perhaps for Huxley or Michael Taunton who slept alone,
the one in the house, the other at the lodge.

'Superintendent?' The icy voice at his shoulder was
Jennifer Sutton's.

'Good morning, Miss Sutton.' Roper smiled as he
hooked off his Polaroids.

Jennifer Sutton's smile was made of glass this
morning. 'Blacking your nose, Superintendent?' she
enquired sweetly. 'Aren't you supposed to come armed

with a search warrant or something, to make it legal?'

'My visit's perfectly legal, Miss Sutton.' Roper took his entrance ticket out of his guide and showed it to her.

'Oh—I'm sorry.' The light of battle went out of her eyes and she relaxed a little. 'It's just that I've never thought of policemen as having an interest in history.'

'I'm interested in everything, Miss Sutton.'

'Yes.' She lifted her head and smiled lopsidedly. 'Quite. My brother's back, by the way, if you want to speak to him. He's down at the lodge. If you like, I'll show you the way. I've told him you want to see him.'

'Later, Miss Sutton. Early this afternoon, if that's all right? We've still got a few more things to sort out.'

'Fine,' she said, and started to walk with him towards the door. The hall was filling. It looked as if a coachload of pensioners had just arrived. 'We're all very concerned, you know, Superintendent. What you told Lewis Huxley last night—well—it's really quite horrendous. Do you really think it's possible that poor girl was murdered only a few yards away from us all?'

'More than possible, Miss Sutton,' said Roper. 'I'd say it was pretty definite.'

'Oh, dear,' she said. They had reached the porch and the bright sunshine. 'I hope that doesn't mean you suspect that any one here killed the poor girl—because that's quite impossible, you know. We've all known each other a long time—years.'

Roper could have pointed out that *most* murderers were known by someone for years; and that someone was always astonished when the dark side at last erupted to the surface. And, conditioned to cynicism

by too much experience, he knew all too well that nobody ever *knew* anybody.

ROPER WENT BACK to Cort Place in the afternoon, this
time without a ticket and accompanied by Price.

Jennifer Sutton was rushing about behind the souvenir counter. After a glance to acknowledge their arrival, she finished serving the elderly couple she was
dealing with and came across to where Roper and
Price were waiting by the fireplace.

'Sorry about that,' she said, a little breathlessly.
'We're as busy as hell today. Allan's still down at the
lodge. Take the door out to the cafeteria, bear right
then straight along the path to the old east gate. You
can't miss it.'

'I'm sure we'll find it, Miss Sutton,' said Roper.
'Thank you.'

Their route took them past Huxley's workshop and
thence down a wide winding path towards the far end
of the grounds, rockeries and shrubbery on one side
and dense woodland on the other. They passed the
Dances' workshop, a converted barn among the trees
with a fair-sized collection of visitors inside it watching the Dances at work. He was dexterously spinning
a huge balloon of red-hot glass at the end of a pipe and
his wife was drawing out the wing of a blue-glass ea-
gle over a Bunsen burner. Perspiration shone on both
of them.

A hundred yards or so further on another small
gathering stood outside the doorway of another out-
building. Built of brick within a timber frame, like
Huxley's stable, this workshop was the Thruxtons'.
What he was welding together with an oxyacetylene

torch looked like a massive mask of Christ in sheet steel with a disembodied right hand lifted in benediction beside it. From the upper floor came the steady clacking of a hand loom.

More trees, an ornamental lake with a wooden bridge over it and a couple of ducks drifting on its unruffled surface. A few golden carp swam idly in and out of the shadows of the water lilies.

And then, appearing suddenly, a startling *trompe d'oeil* at the end of a darkened arcade of trees, the East Lodge.

A miniature château, ivy clad, in slate and Portland stone, a spired tower at each corner, the illusion of grandeur spoiled only because the doorway and windows were not to scale; nor, for practical purposes, could they be. It looked like an early-nineteenth-century folly.

The front door was open, and held back against the wall of the narrow hall with a Victorian bootscraper. The hall was panelled, its floor dusty. Roper thought he smelled linseed oil.

He rapped smartly on the open door. Its oak panels were shivered and split here and there for lack of varnish, which the antique-buff in him considered unmitigated carelessness. And he wouldn't have been able to buy a 150-year-old bootscraper like that for much less than £30. It was damn near perfect . . .

'Yes?' The voice came from the dark end of the hall.

'The name's Roper, sir.' Roper held up his card to the shadowy figure who had come from a doorway on the left.

'Oh, yes.' The man limped slowly into the light, leaning on a stick. He wore a paint-stained brown smock over a pair of jeans, and a pair of white sneakers. He smiled quickly and shyly through a neatly trimmed black beard and transferred his stick from his right hand to his left in order to proffer his right hand. 'I'm Allan Sutton. Been expecting you. Good afternoon.'

Roper ignored the hand as courteously as he was able and made a great play of fiddling his card back into his wallet until the hand fell back to its owner's side. When he was on duty, Roper shook hands with no one who might, however remotely, belong to the opposition.

He smiled, however. 'A few words, sir, that's all. About the Jackman girl.'

'Yes, I've heard all about that from my sister. Do come in, won't you?'

Sutton transferred his stick back to his right hand, turned awkwardly in the narrow space and led the way to the room whence he had come. At every pace a metallic click came whenever he put his weight on his right leg.

The large, bright, cluttered room into which he ushered them was a studio. At an easel in the corner, Carol Haldane was working intently on a foolscap-sized canvas, one paint-charged brush in her hand, another clamped between her teeth and a few more clenched in the other hand that held her palette. A single abstracted glance was all she gave them.

'I'd hoped to talk to you privately, sir,' said Roper.

'Yes, of course,' said Sutton. 'Would you mind, Carol? For just a few minutes?'

'Sure,' Carol Haldane said, with a petulant shrug. 'Whatever you say.'

She put her palette down on a high stool beside her easel, climbed down from the one she was sitting on and went outside. When the slap of her sandals had receded Roper said:

'Won't keep you too long, Mr Sutton. Perhaps you'd like to sit down, sir.'

'Yes, I would rather,' said Sutton. 'And you, too?' He gestured to a wicker armchair that had seen better days, and an old kitchen chair with a perforated ply-wood seat that had been painted a particularly hideous pale green. With his stick, he hooked forward a student's donkey-stool from a half-dozen ranged along the wall beneath the window. Leaning heavily on his stick, he lowered himself to the stool with his game leg stretched out straight in front of him like a bow-sprit.

The wicker chair creaked as it took Roper's weight. 'Do you mind if I smoke?'

'Whatever you like, sir,' said Roper as he took out his notebook. He watched Sutton light an old briar pipe. Short, slim, softly spoken. As diffident as his sister was thrusting.

The studio was clean, but untidy. Good light from the north-facing windows. Stained oak floor. Very cool. An old marble-topped washstand serving as a table for a litter of pots and jars and paints. Two easels, both mahogany, both old and paint-spattered: one Haldane's with a miniature landscape on it, the other one Sutton's with a five-foot-by-three-foot canvas clamped to it, of which Roper only had the back view. Through the open window, he saw Carol Haldane pacing slowly up and down outside with a lit cigarette.

Allan Sutton's pipe was at last burning to his satisfaction. He shook out his match. 'Right, Superintendent,' he said, leaning back against the small, angled easel at the end of the donkey. 'How can I help?'

'Well, sir: Vera Jackman. What do you know about her?'

'Broad question,' said Sutton. 'So broad answer: Not a great deal. I've known *of* her for years, of course. Watched her grow up, loosely speaking. Seen her about since she was in her pram. Her brother owns the local garage. Hard-working chap.'

'She modelled for you, sir. That right?'

'Occasionally. All very proper. In here. That's what I'm working on now.' Suttons' pipe was pointed at the canvas on the easel behind him. 'Or, rather, I'm trying to. Not altogether sure I can finish it now the poor young woman's dead.'

The wicker creaked again as Roper eased himself out of the armchair.

The face and naked body on the canvas were Vera Jackman's. She was sitting in the wicker armchair that Roper had just vacated, but with a mirror and window behind her. More like than a photograph.

'This your usual sort of thing, sir?'

'No,' said Sutton. 'But it's what I'd prefer to do. I make a living knocking out bird studies.'

Not the Vera Jackman of the photographs. This one was staid and elegant—even a little prim. She was reading a letter.

'Pretty girl,' said Roper, to Sutton's back.

'Yes,' agreed Sutton, 'she was. A damned good sitter, too.'

Roper returned to the wicker chair. Sutton had soft, dark eyes, long flexile fingers. Between the top of his right sock and the bottom of his right trouser leg peeked a crescent of pink plastic of his artificial leg.

'Accident, sir?'

'A car accident,' said Sutton. 'Several years ago now. It's playing up a bit today. The heat.'

Roper hitched a trouser leg and rested the ankle of one leg on the knee of the other. 'When did you last see Vera Jackman, sir?'

Smoke momentarily veiled Suttons' eyes. He thought about it for a moment. 'Monday afternoon,' he said. He pointed at the wicker chair with the mouthpiece of his pipe. 'She was sitting for me.'

'Did she talk to you, sir?'

'No,' said Sutton. 'Not a great deal. It breaks the concentration.'

'Did you ever have *any* kind of conversation with her? At any time?'

'Well, yes, I suppose I did,' said Sutton. 'But never about anything memorable. She wasn't very deep, you know. Her education finished at the village school.'

'Did she ever mention boyfriends?'

Sutton considered that for a long time, and finally shook his head. 'No,' he said. 'I don't think so.'

'Did you ever see her with one?'

'No, I didn't. Certainly not around the house, anyway. I could be wrong, mind, but I don't think she had one. Except young Michael, of course; but I'm pretty sure that that was over and done with months ago.'

Roper's head lifted like a gundog's. Sutton's aside, so casually dropped, was caught before it even hit the ground.

'Michael *Taunton,* sir? The lad who works for Mr Huxley?'

'Yes—Mike.' Sutton gave a casual lift to his shoulders. 'But as I said, it *was* over months ago. In fact it was probably over before it even got started. The two things Vera liked her boyfriends to have was money and a fast car. Mike has neither.' Sutton sucked at his pipe, unaware, apparently, that he had said anything untoward.

'This . . . liaison . . . between Jackman and young Taunton; what do you know about it, Mr Sutton?'

'Nothing,' said Sutton. 'Hardly anything. I saw them together a couple of times, that's all.'

'Saw them together how, sir?'

Sutton began to look uncomfortable, perhaps realising that he might have said too much. 'Well . . . it's tales out of school . . . I wouldn't like you to quote me,' he began hesitantly, 'but I tended to think they might be having a tiff.'

'Tiff, sir? How do you define a tiff exactly?'

'Well, they weren't exactly *shouting* at each other. No. Nothing like that. Just softly hissing venom at one another from angry faces only a few inches apart. Bare-fanged. Like snakes. Jackman's back against the wall and Taunton's outstretched arms braced against the wall on either side of her to stop her getting away.' Sutton's brief sketch was graphic.

'Both times, sir—having one of these tiffs?'

'Of course, I could be wrong,' cautioned Sutton. 'What I'm saying is, I couldn't *swear* to it. I didn't *hear* anything—it was only what I *thought* I saw. But I'm sure that Mike was pretty keen on her—although I'm not so sure it was the other way about. Like I say, Mike wasn't exactly qualified.'

'But how do you know what these qualifications were, Mr Sutton?' asked Roper.

'Well . . . rumour, I suppose. Local gossip. Young Vera did have a certain reputation. You know?'

'Quite, sir,' said Roper, turning a fresh page of his notebook. Earlier in the afternoon, he and Price had toyed with a few names. The one that had surfaced most often had been Michael Taunton's, the one person at Cort Place who didn't sleep in the house, the only one who was out of it at about the time Vera Jackman had gone visiting, the only one who didn't have to return to the house after it had been locked up.

At long last, Roper sensed a break.

EIGHT

CAROL HALDANE was still pacing up and down outside and puffing at another cigarette.

'Can I ask what you were doing on Tuesday night, Mr Sutton? Between ten-thirty and about midnight?'

'Not very much,' said Sutton. 'I locked up here just as it was getting dark—about half-past nine. I went across to the house, cut myself some sandwiches and went upstairs to the flat. And that's where I stayed. At half-past eleven I was in bed. During the intervening couple of hours I was watching television.'

'Anyone with you?'

'My sister,' said Sutton. 'At least, she kept popping in and out.'

'Can you remember what time your sister locked up, sir?'

'About eleven,' said Sutton. 'Perhaps a few minutes either side. It's a clause in the insurance policy.'

'And after that, no one can either get in or out without the alarms being switched off?'

'Yes,' agreed Sutton. 'Quite right. It's damn nearly foolproof—or so we're told.'

They went back again to that question of time. Those vital few minutes between Jackman's arrival at the gates of Cort Place and her death.

'We think she was killed here in your grounds, Mr Sutton.'

'Yes, I know,' said Sutton. 'Jenny told me. But anyone can get into the grounds, you know. We leave the tradesmen's entrance gate open all night, the walls can be climbed if you know the right places—and even the east gate outside here. What I'm perfectly sure about, though, is that none of us killed her. None of us had a reason.'

'We also found a valve cap off a car tyre, sir—a brass one. In Church Lane. And your Range Rover's missing a brass valve cap.'

Sutton sketched a shrug with the hand that clutched his pipe. 'Look, Superintendent—believe me, we're not taking all this lightly, but if you think that one of our people murdered the poor girl then you're way adrift. We're artists. We create. We don't destroy.'

'I'm not saying anyone living here killed her, Mr Sutton'—although Roper was pretty sure now that someone here had; 'only that she was murdered in the grounds of your house—and that a brass valve cap, probably off your Range Rover, was found in Church Lane a few yards from Jackman's body. And according to everyone who drives the Rover, none of 'em's driven it up there, except your sister. And that was on Saturday.'

Sutton flourished his pipe. Well, the gesture said, we're both on the same wavelength, so what are we arguing about? 'Then the valve cap must have fallen off on Saturday. Or it must have dropped off someone else's vehicle. Or are brass valve caps that unique?'

'No, sir,' agreed Roper. 'They're not unique exactly. But they're certainly rare. Your Rover's the only vehicle in the village fitted with them.'

'Really?' said Sutton, raising his eyebrows. 'But the one you found *could* have dropped off a vehicle from somewhere else, couldn't it? We're in the tourist season, Superintendent. We get cars coming in from everywhere.'

'Jackman was still murdered in the grounds of your house, Mr Sutton,' Roper persisted. 'That's the real point.'

'I've already told you. No one here killed her. We're not that sort.'

Roper was tempted to comment that murderers were of *no* particular 'sort', but he didn't. 'Tuesday night, sir; did you hear anything? Sounds of a scuffle, a fight, raised voices even?'

'No,' replied Sutton. 'Nothing at all.'

'How about the Range Rover? Did you hear that?'

'No, of course I didn't. If I had, I'd have told you.'

'Where's the Range Rover usually kept, sir?' The question had come from Price.

'The garage.'

'More to the point, sir,' said Roper. 'Do you know where it was parked between eleven and midnight on Tuesday?'

'I couldn't swear where it was. But I imagine it was locked up in the garage.'

'And this garage is where, sir?' asked Roper.

'The old coachhouse,' said Sutton. 'Over by the north wing.'

'Perhaps we could take a look at it?'

'Yes. Of course. But I'm sure you'll be wasting your time.'

Roper closed his notebook and slipped it into his shirt pocket, as if the interview was over and anything further was of little consequence. 'Purely by the by, Mr Sutton, is it likely that any of the other men here could have had a close relationship with Vera Jackman without your knowing about it?'

'I've already told you. Only Mike Taunton—and that only perhaps.'

'How about yourself, sir?'

The question clearly struck Sutton as humorous. 'Me?' He loosed a short sharp sound that wasn't quite a laugh. 'I'm nearly forty, Superintendent. A bloody cripple. A bit past eighteen-year-old girls, don't you think?'

The wicker creaked again as Roper stood up. Price rose with him.

'When you took your paintings to London yesterday morning, your sister drove you down to the local station.'

'Yes, that's right.'

'And you don't drive?'

'Not don't. Daren't.'

'And when you got to the station, you had to handle your paintings on your own?'

'Yes,' agreed Sutton. 'But I don't see the point . . .'

'How many paintings?'

'Twelve.'

'How large were they?'

'Twenty-by-twelve,' said Sutton. 'I always use that size for my wildlife studies. People collect them as sets. I have a sort of following,' he added modestly.

'You work on board or canvas, sir?'

'Canvas.'

'So it would have been a chunky parcel?'

'Somewhat—yes.'

'And you were able to manage them alone?'

'I rely on the goodwill of taxi drivers and porters,' said Sutton. 'I can't carry any sort of weight.' He slapped his knee. It clicked metallically. 'This bloody thing.'

And thus, albeit convolutedly, Roper established that Allan Sutton could not have carried Vera Jackman's dead body either to the Range Rover or from it. Nor could he have driven it to Church Lane.

'PERHAPS NO ONE DID,' ventured Price, as he and Roper returned along the path towards the house. 'Maybe Sutton was right. Perhaps it *was* a valve cap from another vehicle.'

'Stretching the long arm of coincidence too far, old son,' said Roper. 'Have a think: when did you last have a valve cap drop off *your* car?'

'I don't think I ever have,' said Price.

'Right,' said Roper. 'And I don't think I ever have either. But here we are faced with a special sort of cap, together with a local vehicle that's missing one. It's too pat. Too much of a bloody coincidence. I'll stake my pension that Jack-the-lad, whoever he was, shifted Jackman's body from here to Church Lane in that bloody motor.'

They parted briefly about a small plump girl standing alone on the path and so assiduously devouring an ice cream that she didn't even notice them.

'Seemed like a decent bloke,' Price ventured again, as he and Roper banded up again behind the little girl. 'Seemed very keen to protect his little flock of arty-crafties though, didn't he?'

'I noticed,' said Roper. 'But it *was* one of his arty-crafties. Bet your life.'

But the biggest problem still was that of time. How could Jackman's murderer—unless it was Michael Taunton—have met her—at some time after nine minutes to eleven, strangled her, driven her body to Church Lane, dumped it in that ditch, and still got back to the house before Jennifer Sutton had locked it up and set the alarms. Even allowing for Huxley's statement that he had witnessed Jennifer Sutton switching on the alarms at five past eleven on Tuesday night, that would only have given the murderer another five minutes—which was still not long enough. And Huxley could easily be wrong about that time. Only the time stated by the jogging Mr Jackson was totally acceptable as evidence. Jackson had had reason to look at his watch. All the other times were guesses, and the one thing juries didn't like were guesses, and nor did Roper.

They reached the end of the path beside Huxley's workshop, and for the first time Roper took a good look at the back of the house from the outside. On the far left was the low wall of the stairs down to the kitchen. A few yards to the right of that was the solitary narrow window of Jennifer Sutton's office—like the kitchen, another semi-basement. To the right of that was a stone-balustraded terrace that stretched roughly from the middle of the house to the end of the ballroom. At the middle of the terrace a flight of stone steps led down to the lawn. His count of the first-floor windows tallied with the ones he had seen this morning, so he knew that they were all alarmed. The rooms above were dormers, set into the roof, some thirty-five to forty feet above the level of the terrace. All the windows up there were open and here and there a curtain hung out over a sill like a limp tongue.

They walked across the front of the terrace. A photographic flash flared briefly from somewhere inside the ballroom. In the last half-hour the weather had quickly deteriorated; what had been a transparent blue sky was rapidly clouding over and a stiff breeze from the west had already dropped the temperature by several degrees and was perceptibly stirring the trees.

The iron fire escape was at the north end of the house. It looked like a recent addition. Two doors gave egress to it, one set in a dormer at the end of the roof and one on the first floor. The doors were wooden, their upper halves glazed with wire-meshed glass.

The coachhouse was about fifty paces away along a tarmacadamed path cut through the trees. Its two tall doors were open and the white Range Rover stood inside among a clutter of gardening machinery: a petrol-driven motor mower, a rotavator, a huge roller that would probably need half a dozen men to pull it. Unlike Huxley's workshop, the coachhouse was still fitted out with horse stalls, most of which were filled with old bits and pieces of furniture and carpets and rusting garden tools. The roof was glazed and fitted with dirty fanlights. It smelled of damp earth and there was mildew staining the peeling whitewash on the brick walls.

The white Range Rover was definitely the one that Roper had glimpsed briefly yesterday in young Fred Jackman's garage—and now fitted with a plastic valve cap on its near-side rear wheel and a brass one on each of the other three.

Roper crouched by the off-side rear wheel and un-screwed the valve cap, a brass one. Like the one that the young cadet had found yesterday in the lane, its knurled outside was grimed with greasy road dust; but its threaded inside was as bright as the day the thread had come from the lathe that had turned it.

Still on his hunkers he passed it up to Price. 'What do you think?'

Price turned the knurled brass cylinder between his fingers and thumb and tipped it towards the light. 'I'd say it was an identical twin. Tenuous, though. As ev-idence. No maker's name. Could be hundreds of 'em about.'

He passed it back down to Roper, who slipped it carefully into his wallet. It wasn't legal. Strictly speaking it was theft; but, then, so in its way was murder.

With his hands on his knees, Roper levered himself up. The doors of the Range Rover were all locked. Its interior looked spotless.

'Worth giving it a once-over?' asked Price. 'Get the forensic people on to it?'

'Could be,' said Roper. 'Except that Vera Jackman probably had a ride or two in it when she was alive. But get it checked all the same...' Then suddenly Roper stilled, with his head cocked to one side, listen-ing, and a warning finger rising to his mouth.

The soft, slapping footfall outside on the path drew closer.

It was Michael Taunton, T-shirted, jeaned and sneakered, and with an unbroached can of lager in his hand. Unaware that he was being watched, he cast a quick glance back over his shoulder towards the house and was almost inside the coachhouse when he realised that he had walked into company. His jaw dropped. He looked at Roper, looked at Price, turned about.

'Good afternoon, Mr Taunton,' said Roper to Taunton's departing back.

Taunton stopped with slumped shoulders; then reluctantly turned about again.

'Join us, Mr Taunton, sir, if you wouldn't mind.'

Taunton came shuffling back to stand in the doorway.

'Were you going somewhere, Mr Taunton?' said Roper.

Taunton shrugged. 'Yeah,' he mumbled. His voice was slurred, his face sweaty. 'I was coming in here. Why? What's it to you?'

'It's just that you seemed in a bit of a hurry to go away again.'

'Well, I would, wouldn't I?' countered Taunton sullenly. 'You're the bloody Bill, aren't you?' His boozy gaze went warily to Price then slowly back again to Roper.

'And you don't like the Bill, Mr Taunton? Why's that?'

Taunton shifted uneasily from foot to foot. 'Look, I was coming in here for five minutes' mike and a can of beer. That's all. What's wrong with that?'

'By the looks of you, you've had a few cans already,' said Roper.

'And what if I have?'

'Relax, son,' said Roper. 'We'd just like a few words, that's all. Why don't you find yourself a spot to sit down? Won't keep you long.'

For a second or two, Taunton looked like doing battle; but then he obviously decided that it was a battle he had already lost and perched himself on a dusty bundle of old carpet, his lank hair falling forward over his cheeks and the can of lager pressed between his hands.

'You come over here often, do you, Mr Taunton? This place?'

'Sure.' Taunton looked up slowly. 'Jenny doesn't like us drinking in front of the grockles. Says it lowers the tone.'

'Grockles?'

'Visitors,' said Taunton. 'Day trippers.'

'Could there be something you might not have told us yet, Mr Taunton?' asked Roper.

Taunton swept a hand through his flowing black locks and scowled upward at Roper. 'Like what?'

'Like you might have been Vera Jackman's boyfriend,' hazarded Roper. 'Something of that sort.'

Taunton's gaze fell again. 'Boyfriend? Me? That's a laugh. She didn't even know I existed.'

'I've heard differently,' said Roper. 'You were seen with her several times. That's what I've heard.'

Taunton's head stayed down. He rolled the beer can backwards and forwards between his palms. He looked like a loser, probably always had been, one of the burgeoning breed of young drifters who finished up on the same scrap heap that they started on.

'I went to the pictures with her once, and a disco in Dorchester with her twice,' he eventually and grudgingly admitted. 'End of story.'

'When?' asked Roper.

'I don't remember—Christmas; a few weeks afterwards.'

'Just the three times?'

'Yeah. Right. It didn't even get off the ground. I guess I wasn't her type. Not enough bread. And no car.'

'And you fancied her more than she fancied you? Right?'

Taunton glanced up bitterly. 'Vera Jackman didn't fancy anybody—except her bloody self. She was a bloody tease.'

'And she teased you, did she?'

Taunton didn't answer.

'Perhaps you were still chasing after her,' Roper suggested. 'Perhaps on Tuesday night you had *another* quarrel—only this time you really lost your temper.'

Taunton's grip tightened on the beer can. 'I told you, didn't I? It was over. Months ago. I've had a thing going with a girl in the village since then.'

'Since when?'

'End of March—about.' At last, exasperated, or perhaps because he desperately needed a drink, Taunton hooked a polish-stained forefinger in the ring pull of his beer can and gave it a tug. 'But that's finished. We had a row. But I didn't have a row with Vera Jackman the other night. Ask Jack Crosby.'

'That was in the Arms,' said Roper. 'What happened afterwards?'

With foam spilling over his fingers Taunton took a mouthful of lager. The can went down again and he dragged the back of his wrist across his mouth. 'There was no bloody afterwards,' he flung back angrily. 'I told you.'

'You came back here, had a cup of coffee with Miss Haldane, then went across to the lodge to go to bed.'

'Right,' said Taunton. 'And that's all I did.'

'You didn't see Vera Jackman? Down by the front gate, say?'

'I went the other way, didn't I?'

'I don't know, Mr Taunton. Only got your word for it, haven't we?'

Taunton took down another slug of lager. 'I didn't kill her. You've only got my word for that, too, haven't you?'

'Did you ever go to bed with her?'

Taunton smiled leerily. 'Screw her, you mean? That's a laugh. I didn't even get near her. Couldn't afford it, could I?'

'But you still felt friendly enough towards her to chat with her in the Cort Arms on Tuesday night.'

'Look, we had to work together, didn't we?' retorted Taunton. 'And I'd had another bird in between, hadn't I? No point in bearing grudges, is there? I didn't and she didn't. Get it?' His bleary eyes blazed angrily upward at Roper and the hand that held his lager can looked imminently capable of crushing it.

'Did you ever buy Vera Jackman a present, Mr Taunton?'

Taunton's face twisted in mirth. 'You've got to be kidding,' he sneered. 'What would I have bought one with? I came here dead broke.'

'Jewellery,' Roper persisted. 'Like that Egyptian cross she wore round her neck.'

Into Taunton's eyes came a brief flicker of remembrance and his mood became suddenly less hostile. He took another sip of his lager. 'That bloody thing,' he said. 'Yeah, I remember that. It's what our last row was about.'

'You had a row about the cross?'

'Yeah...well...' Taunton mumbled, 'I'd still got the hots for her, hadn't I? I was jealous. Knew she'd got somebody else, didn't I?'

Roper's interest quickened. He dropped to a crouch with his back against the body of the Range Rover so that he and Taunton were eye to eye. 'Tell me about that last row, Mr Taunton. Can you remember *exactly* when it was? It's important.'

Taunton shook his head. 'I can't. It was about a month after Christmas.'

'Did she tell you where she'd got it from?'

Taunton shook his head. 'I asked her. She wouldn't tell me.'

'Can you get nearer than a month after Christmas?'

Taunton blew out a long tired breath. 'I only remember that when she turned up, she wasn't wearing the bloody thing. And after tea she was. But not *just* wearing it. Parading it about. Like a bloody prize she'd just won.'

'Hang on,' Roper interrupted. 'You're saying that when she arrived here that afternoon, she wasn't wearing that cross. But at some time later that *same* afternoon, she was. Is that right?'

Taunton nodded sullenly. The last of the lager was tipped down his throat, then the can was crushed in his left hand and placed between his feet.

'Do you know if Jackman stayed in the house that particular afternoon, or could she have gone out?'

Taunton shrugged. 'I wouldn't know,' he said. 'But I don't suppose so. It was snowing rotten; and bloody cold. If anything had been wanted, Jenny would have asked one of us blokes to go and fetch it in the motor—or gone for it herself.'

'Fair enough.' Roper slowly pushed himself up with his hands on his knees.

Taunton seemed surprised. 'Is that it?'

'Yes, that's it, Mr Taunton,' said Roper. 'For now.'

Taunton slowly rose. Price put away his notebook and stood aside for him to go out. Outside, the daylight had dulled and spots of rain were darkening the path and sounding on the glass fanlights of the coachhouse.

Roper and Price watched him go. At the end of the path he ducked his head against the rain and broke into a run.

'What do you think?' asked Price, as Taunton went from sight behind a box hedge.

'Did he kill Jackman, do you mean?' Roper went to stand in the doorway. The rain looked set in for the rest of the afternoon. Already the soil was beginning to smell wet again.

Price came to stand at Roper's shoulder, but his question stayed unanswered.

'See if forensic's still got that *ankh*. If they have, get 'em to see if it's worth anything. If it is, I want a photograph of it circulated to all the likely jewellers' shops in the county. Find out where it was sold—and who bought it.'

The *ankh* at Vera Jackman's throat, hitherto stuffed carelessly at the back of Roper's cerebral files, had suddenly taken on an unexpected importance. Somebody here had most likely bought it for her, and if they had then it was most likely the man who had murdered her.

All roads, it seemed now, led back to Cort Place.

NINE

ROPER AND SERGEANT Jollyboy shared a table in the fireplace corner of the Cort Arms. Each sat huddled over a pint tankard, Roper with a cheroot and Jollyboy with his pipe. At twenty-five to six, the pub had only been open a few minutes and the saloon bar was still quiet. Jack Crosby was fitting a new bottle of Gordon's gin into one of his optics.

'When I was a lad,' said Jollyboy, 'old man Sutton was the squire. Young Mr Allan's grandfather, that was. And a proper squire, I mean, not one of those jumped-up scrap merchants who buy up country estates so they can call themselves lords of the manor. I remember my old father standing aside and lifting his cap for old man Sutton when they passed in the street.

'He died the year the war ended, then his son came back from the army and took over—or rather took over what was left. The old man hadn't been able to handle money, so by the time the son inherited, the estate was nigh on bankrupt.'

Jollyboy broke off to take a sip of his beer. Even in a tweed jacket and grey slacks he could never be mistaken for anything but a policeman. He hunched back over his tankard and took a draw on his pipe.

'The son was John Sutton. He was the local MP for a while. He sold off two or three farms and all those cottages on the other side of the green. By the time he died in the late seventies, the estate was down to just

Cort Place. Then rumour had it that death duties were going to cause young Mr Allan to sell the place up altogether.

'Miss Jennifer came back from the States. Next thing we knew she had gone to law. Took on the Inland Revenue and the Probate people—even got all the county MPs to say a word or two for her with the Department of the Environment. Right fanatical she was about that house. Went all over the place getting names for petitions—and she won, too. Got a five-year delay from the tax people. Now, from what I hear, the duty's all paid up and she's making a profit. Smart lady. A worker, too. It was her who organised her brother's art classes, not him.'

'How about the commune?' said Roper. 'When did that start?'

'About four years ago,' said Jollyboy. 'That Huxley bloke came first—I remember him because of his red beard. He did a lot of restoration work in the house. Then he ripped out those old stables and turned them into his workshop. The Dances came along next, then the Thruxtons; about a year ago, they arrived.'

'How about young Taunton? When did he appear on the scene?'

'I don't know,' said Jollyboy. 'Not exactly. I first saw him in here'—Jollyboy pointed his pipe over his shoulder—'about last Christmas time. By the beginning of the year he was a familiar face around the village. Then a couple of times I saw him coming out of Cort Place and guessed he was shacked up there. He's in here a lot, I can tell you that; so could Jack. A right young boozer.'

'A villain, is he?'

'Don't think so,' said Jollyboy, taking up his jug again. 'Kept his nose clean in these parts, at least.'

Jollyboy's face went briefly behind his jug. Coins rattled on the counter and Jack Crosby came through the arch from the public bar. The new arrival was middle-aged and check-suited. An elderly, panting labrador slumped by his feet.

'Did you ever see Taunton with Vera Jackman?'

'Not that I remember,' said Jollyboy. 'Why? Reckon young Taunton did it?'

'Don't know,' said Roper. 'Wish I did.'

Crosby worked one of his pump handles. The bitter here was still from the wooden cask.

'Do you want another?' asked Roper.

Jollyboy settled for a top-up. Roper took their jugs to the end of the counter and waited while Crosby rang up his till and slapped the check-suited man's change on the counter.

'Same again?'

'Halves,' said Roper. 'Thanks.'

Crosby padded away. To his red shirt today he had added a vivid yellow bow tie. 'Any luck yet?' he asked, as he returned and deftly twisted the jug handles towards Roper.

'Some,' said Roper, 'but not a lot. Still early days.'

'There was something,' said Crosby, suddenly guarded. He glanced back over his shoulder, then leaned across the counter and dropped his voice a fraction. 'Of course, it could be nothing,' he said, leaning closer still and looking behind him again. 'But young Vera made a phone call from here on Tuesday evening. About half-past seven.'

'Do you know who to?' asked Roper.

Crosby lifted his broad shoulders. 'Sorry. She was in my office with the door shut. She was in there for about five minutes.'

'Had she ever used your telephone before?'

'No,' said Crosby. 'Not that I remember.'

Roper passed a £5 note across the counter. 'Could be useful, Mr Crosby,' he said. 'Thanks.'

He collected his change and returned to Jollyboy. As he settled himself into his chair and slid Jollyboy's jug across to him, he said: 'Crosby says Jackman made a telephone call from here on Tuesday night.'

Jollyboy glanced across sharply. 'Did she now. Who to?'

'He doesn't know,' said Roper, lifting his jug. Nor did Roper but he allowed himself a guess or two.

There was a telephone in Jackman's service station. But rather than use it, Vera Jackman had made her call from the privacy of Crosby's office here in the Arms. A call to a man, perhaps. One of the men at Cort Place. Perhaps to arrange a meeting. And perhaps, thereby, Vera Jackman might even have arranged the appointment for her own murder.

It was a theory that filled a few gaps in Roper's earlier suppositions. It had nagged him a little that Jackman had called in at Cort Place so late at night, because she would have known about the ritual of it being locked to the world after eleven o'clock. And which of its inhabitants—except Michael Taunton—would have been walking in the grounds at that same late hour? And would Jackman simply have trusted to luck that she would meet this man, this most particular man?

Roper thought not. If he was right, then that telephone call had been Jackman's first step on a path from which she would never come back.

AT HALF-PAST SIX Roper was back at the church hall.

'Anything new?' he asked Price, as he hung up his jacket.

'Nobody's come in and confessed, if that's what you mean.' Price squared up the ziggurat of paperwork he had been sifting through and set it to one side. 'But these arrived a few minutes ago. I've got lads tacking them up all over the village.' He pushed across a small poster with the word MURDER printed large in red across the top of it and a black-and-white picture of Vera Jackman from the waist up in her barathea blazer underneath. 'HQ's put them out all over the county. And we tracked down Cominetti—the fish-and-chip van feller. He remembers serving Wally Tupper the other night—about ten to eleven, he thinks. And he's pretty sure that Tupper was heading home up Church Lane when he left. He didn't remember seeing Taunton, though; not from the description we gave him.'

'Probably doesn't signify anything,' said Roper. 'Not exactly memorable, is he, our friend Taunton? What did forensic say about the *ankh?*'

'Definitely not English,' said Price. 'But it's gold all right. About eighteen carat. So's the chain. One of the women at the lab reckons it's probably North African. Probably Moroccan. A bazaar job... And the BBC's agreed to show a photograph of the *ankh* on "The Nine O'Clock News" if we can get them one in time. DS Makins is seeing to that now.'

'Pity,' said Roper. He had been hoping a local jeweller might recognise the cross and perhaps remember something about the customer he had sold it to. It had been a long shot, but who, at the moment, innocent or otherwise, was likely to own up to having been one of Vera Jackman's boyfriends, even if the question was asked directly of him?

'What about that valve cap?'

'Mrs Greenaway's had it up on her 'scope,' said Price. 'Reckons it's a twin like we thought. She's sent it to the lab for a second opinion. They'll ring back as soon as they can.'

BY NINE O'CLOCK, Roper, the night sergeant and a WPC had the hall to themselves. The overtime bill was high enough already without adding a night crew to it.

Roper had spent the last couple of hours drafting a summary of the evidence to date—not a great deal of evidence when it was committed to paper—and drawing up several permutations of a list of suspects. On the first occasion, he had included Wally Tupper's name, but had struck him out. Jackman had been killed in the grounds of Cort Place—that much was certain now—and her body had been transported to Church Lane in the Cort Place Range Rover—that was yet to be proved, but Roper's gut told him that it would be eventually—and Wally Tupper might be a bit on the slow side but he was also easily panicked, and if he *had* killed Vera Jackman he would have left the body where it was and run like hell. He certainly wouldn't have slung it over his shoulder and carried it to Church Lane.

And then there were five.

Huxley. Michael Taunton. It would be interesting to know what time Taunton had turned up in the Cort Arms on Tuesday night—before or after Jackman's phone call. The suave Mr Thruxton. Dance didn't fit the bill somehow; Roper couldn't imagine Jackman falling for anybody with a pot belly and his spectacles held together with sticking plaster. Allan Sutton, too, was a doubtful with that gammy leg; although not impossible. Roper had noticed the immaculate tidiness of Vera Jackman's bedroom, the way she had taken care of her clothes, the shining cleanliness of her hair as she had lain in that ditch. All pointed to a personal fastidiousness which discounted Jackman being drawn to any man who was even remotely disabled. But whichever one of them it was, he had probably given Jackman that *ankh.* And no man gave a young woman a present of that calibre unless he was either besotted or hell-bent on a spot of lechery.

The missing wristwatch was probably gone for ever. It may even have fallen into one of the dustbins and now be lying in one of the county's refuse department rubbish tips. A needle-in-a-haystack job, that.

The valve cap that Roper had illicitly borrowed this afternoon was now across at forensic. If it was a twin of the one found in Church Lane it would only substantiate what Roper already guessed. The purse, as evidence, was a write-off. Wally Tupper had seen to that.

Roper sat back in his uncomfortable chair and drew thumb and forefinger together across eyelids that prickled. Another half-hour and he'd call it a day. He felt that he had lost his momentum and was going round in circles, and when that happened he knew that it was time to knock off. And besides, these days he had a new allegiance—a wife and a home to go to. And tonight, four new pictures to gloat over. A bit of shrewd bidding on Sheila's part yesterday had got them for almost half what she and Roper had expected.

He tidied his table, got back into his jacket, then went across to the sergeant's table to sign off in the duty book.

'Good night, son.'

'Night, sir.'

Outside, the night air was cool and bracing and the last dregs of daylight were still in the sky to the west. A quiet drive home, a good supper, watch the telly, run a magnifying glass over those pictures perhaps and let the rest of the world go to hell till tomorrow morning.

He climbed into his new Sierra, started the engine and clipped his seat belt on—then in his driving mirror saw the WPC come dashing from the doorway of the hall and across the gravel. He treated himself to the luxury of a quietly mouthed obscenity, then hitched on a smile as he wound down his window. 'I'm wanted on the telephone. Right?'

'Yes, sir.' She smiled sympathetically. 'It's the director from Regional Forensic. Says it's important. Sorry, sir.'

'Not half as sorry as I am,' said Roper, unbuckling himself again. 'But thanks.'

The director, despite the late hour, was riding on another intellectual zenith. The valve cap found in Church Lane and the one Roper had purloined that afternoon were identical. Even from the same thread-cutting tool. And the particles of coarse black dust impressed into the groove of bruising around Vera Jackman's throat were grains of rubber.

'Perished rubber. Very old. We can't find any traces of modern additives—like butadiene—so it's probably pre-war or very shortly afterwards. Can't tell you what it's from yet, though.'

'Try electric cable,' said Roper. 'The old-fashioned stuff they used to call cab-tyre.'

There was a moment of surprised silence from the other end. 'Do you think it could be?'

'Tell you tomorrow, sir,' said Roper. 'I know just the gentleman to ask.'

Huxley. Who had had his workshop rewired but very recently. Roper guessed that some of the old ripped-out rubber cable had found its way into the Cort Place dustbins. And fortuitously provided the killer with his weapon. And completed the trio of circumstances which all murderers require and which finally take them over the brink. Motive. Opportunity. And the means to hand.

TEN

WALLY TUPPER slouched happily down the lane, off to work for what he called his second time. For Wally Tupper, the world was a beautiful place; little troubled him. In short, Wally was euphorically happy most of the time. His slouch was deceptive. It made him look hangdog, but Wally's eyes were fastened groundward because he was always looking for things—for pretty flowers, for caterpillars, for butterflies, for dead creatures lying in the grass and which had to be committed properly to the earth and given a memorial tombstone, or sometimes a wooden cross which Wally made from lolly sticks.

From time to time, Wally giggled. To an onlooker there was apparently nothing in sight to laugh at, and nor was there; but inside Wally's head was another world entirely. It was peopled with clowns in springy red braces—Wally had twice seen a circus—and springy red braces were the main touchstone of Wally's laughter—and Laurels and Hardys and Toms and Jerrys. Wally was only unhappy when he remembered nasty things.

Wally's smile abruptly died and his face crumpled sadly and his white-plimsolled feet stopped scuffing through the damp grass.

From his pocket he took a matchbox.

He dropped to his heels and tentatively prodded the brown-and-yellow hairy caterpillar. It stayed tightly curled up. With a little finger, and tenderly, Wally turned it over. It should have uncurled. But it didn't.

Tut-tutting softly to himself, Wally slid open the matchbox and with infinite delicacy, so as not to crush it, he picked up the dead caterpillar and laid it in the box that would later be its casket. He closed the box and tucked it inside his shirt. That afternoon he would bury it properly in the garden and give it a little cross.

He scuffed on down the lane towards the church. Then, just as one clown in red braces threw a bucket of water over another clown in red braces, Wally's burgeoning smile died again as he saw the man standing beside the dry ditch and looking down into it, the ditch where the other day Wally had found Vera.

Wally stopped, unsure whether to cross the lane or stay on the side he was on.

Wally didn't know the man's name—he had yesterday, but he'd forgotten—except that he was a policeman, but not a policeman like Sergeant Jollyboy. Sergeant Jollyboy was big and fat and happy and bulged over his black trousers. This man didn't want people to know he was a policeman because he didn't wear a uniform. And he had a face like a steel carving knife and a thin mouth and knowing eyes, like he knew what was going on inside your head. He probably even knew about the clowns in springy red braces; and even Wally's all-knowing Mum *didn't* know about those.

'Morning, Mr Tupper,' said the man, along his shoulder, with a friendly smile that took the edge off the carving knife.

Wally jerked his head. 'Mornin',' he said. It had been Wally's intention to sidle on by, but his curiosity got the better of him. He wondered if there was another body in the ditch, so he stopped, and, with some trepidation, he looked.

There was no body. They stayed side by side, looking down into the empty ditch.

Wally found the silence companionable. 'Nice morning, en' it?' he said.

The man turned his face up to the sky and looked all over it while he considered his answer. 'Aye,' he said, 'it's that, all right. Off to work, are we, son?'

Wally nodded. 'Going to Miss Sutton's,' he said. Then, in a sudden flush of confidence and because he liked sharing things, Wally reached inside his shirt and took out the matchbox. 'Found a caterpillar,' he said. He slid open the box. 'Dead. See?'

'You must have sharp eyes to have seen that.'

'I have,' said Wally proudly. 'I'm going to bury it. Make a little cross.'

The man looked suitably grave and solemn.

'I'm sending it to Jesus,' Wally confided.

The man nodded. 'Yes,' he agreed, still looking solemn. 'That's nice.'

Wally slid shut the matchbox and tucked it back inside his shirt.

'Your memory as good as your eyes, son?'

Wally pondered that. It wasn't that the question was complicated but, so far as Wally was concerned, the rest of the world spoke in a sort of code that took him a few moments to decipher. He blinked, frowning, his lips moving silently as he reworked the question until he understood it. ''Ave I got a good memory, you mean?'

'That's it. Have you?'

Wally wasn't sure. Sometimes he had and sometimes he hadn't. 'Sometimes, I have,' he said, at last. 'Depends.'

'Mr Huxley's workshop,' the man said.

Wally nodded. He knew Mr Huxley's workshop— was in there sweeping and vacuum cleaning almost every day.

'It was rewired. Electricity. New cable. Wire.'

Wally nodded eagerly. He had thought the game was going to be hard. 'I 'elped,' he said. 'Took all the wire and tube away. Put it in the van.'

The man laughed. 'Seems like you were having me on. I reckon you've got a *good* memory, m'self.'

Wally beamed. Flattery went a long way with Wally. 'Sometimes I 'ave,' he said. 'Easter, I went to the circus. I remember that all right. They had clowns.'

The man smiled. 'What...ladders and buckets of water and all that sort of thing?'

Wally beamed and nodded some more. He seemed to have found a fellow spirit. 'On the green. A big tent. They had red braces...I got wet—only it was little bits of paper.'

The man threw back his head and chuckled, and Wally chuckled too.

'I'll bet you enjoyed that.'

'I did,' said Wally. 'I did.'

Silence again.

The man took a brown packet from his pocket and lit a little cigar. He breathed in smoke leisurely and blew it out again. Wally watched the blue smoke drift upward in the warm morning air.

'This memory of yours; can we try it again?'

Wally nodded. He liked games. 'If you like,' he said.

'Those electric cables—those wires—and that tubing.'

Wally had to stop and think again. 'In Mr Huxley's workshop, you mean?'

'That's it. The bits you put in that van.'

Wally nodded. He was back on track and the man made it seem very important that Wally remembered.

'Did you put it *all* in the van? Or did some go somewhere else?'

Wally screwed up his face. Two men in a white van. Black, rusty tubing being levered off the wall. Old wires inside the tubing. The two men had given Wally a pound for pulling all the old wires out of the tubes. One had been called Arthur... and...

Wally had forgotten the question.

'Was any left lying about afterwards?' the man asked quietly and patiently. 'When the men had gone, did they leave any bits and pieces of wire behind?'

Wally beamed hugely. He remembered *that*. He nodded. 'Some,' he said. He held his hands apart like an angler describing his catch. 'Like that. Mr Huxley told me to put 'em in the dustbin.'

The man seemed to relax. He took a luxurious puff of his little cigar. 'You're sure, son?'

Wally nodded. The man had a light in his eyes that Wally recognised as appreciation.

'And when was that? D'you remember?'

Wally racked his memory. He could see the man was depending on him. He struggled, he wrestled. Then, triumphantly, he burst out: 'Sunday! Bells was ringing for church!'

'The Sunday just gone?'

The exhausted Wally nodded fervently. 'Sunday. Bells was ringing.'

The man clamped a hand on Wally's shoulder and squeezed it hard. 'Good lad,' he said, and squeezed again so that Wally felt all warm and comfortable inside. 'And you don't mention this conversation to anybody. Right?'

Wally nodded. He probably wouldn't remember it anyway, so it was a safe promise.

The man took his hand away and gave Wally another smile. 'You'd better buzz off now, eh? You'll be late for work.'

'Bees buzz,' said Wally.

'Right,' the man said, chuckling again. 'Go on. Hoppit.'

'Bye-bye,' said Wally.

'Take care, then.'

'Will,' said Wally. 'I always take care.' And, whistling tunelessly but happily, Wally once more slouched on his way.

ROPER WATCHED HIM RECEDE down the lane, pause once to kick a stone and send it winging over the hedge, then start across the village green.

So. Another piece of the jigsaw was slotted neatly into place. The chances of finding the weapon now were about as remote as Jackman's wristwatch turning up. Nil. But, if nothing else, there was at least some satisfaction in knowing what it had been and having his earlier guess confirmed, to be able to fill in the last few gaps of the probable scenario.

All he had to find now was the culprit. He dropped his cheroot on to the road, heeled it out, and retraced his steps across to the church hall.

'GOOD MORNING, Wally.'

'Morning, Miss Sutton,' said Wally. Wally was wary of Miss Sutton. She had moods. And when she flew off the handle, there was no stopping her. And this morning, by the looks of her and the no-nonsense gleam in her eye, Miss Sutton was in a mood.

This morning she wanted him to sweep out Mr Huxley's workshop and to wash down the chairs and tables in the cafeteria and to sweep the car park and spike up the litter on the lawn at the front of the house.

'...but Mr Huxley's workshop first because Mike's got to do some varnishing today. Do you understand?'

Wally nodded. He knew that when Mike was varnishing the smallest speck of dust could ruin a whole days' work. 'Yes, Miss Sutton. I'll 'oover and everything.'

'Yes, Wally. Thank you.'

The clowns were dismissed again and Wally brought his mind to bear on the real world. Down the steps to the kitchen. The key to Mr Huxley's workshop from the hook on the dresser. Back up the steps. Across the lawn. So much sun. He could feel it beating like a heart on his face. He clicked his tongue playfully at a fat wood pigeon. It tilted its head querulously at him, then flew off with a creaking of its wings and lofted over the trees. Wally felt he could fly sometimes, but he never had.

Key in the padlock. He slid the doors open wide to let in the sun and fresh air. He could smell wood—cedar and pine and mahogany—and his nostrils flared with pleasure. After the brightness outside he could hardly see. He trod carefully so as not to raise too much dust.

From a cupboard near the door he took out his battered vacuum cleaner and carefully assembled it. He plugged it in and switched it on. His way of cleaning Mr Huxley's workshop was always the same; long sweeps across the width of the floor, like mowing a lawn, working from the end nearest the door, towards the workbenches and finishing under the wood loft.

Occasionally he paused to cool off and dab a grubby handkerchief across his forehead, but not often and never for long. Tomorrow was payday, and when he was finished in here it would be time for a doughnut and a cup of tea at the back door of the caff.

He paid especial attention to corners, where the walls met the floor, around the legs of Mr Huxley's bench and underneath it, the big piece of furniture that Mr Huxley had made and Miss Haldane had painted and Mike was varnishing. Wally had watched it grow from rough planks of wood, and to Wally's untutored eye it had looked like a protracted conjuring trick. Sometimes, Mr Huxley gave him nice pieces of wood for his crosses, and when he wasn't too busy Mike ran them through the circular saw for him and turned them into manageable slivers that Wally could cut to length with a pair of scissors. Wally liked Mike.

The noise from the vacuum cleaner filled Wally's head. Sometimes Wally was an aeroplane and the vacuum cleaner his engine. Through the window he saw Miss Sutton crossing the lawn to open up the cafeteria, with her alsatian, Pete, leaping and bounding behind her.

Wally continued to work his way back down the workshop, sucking up the dust from one strip, then cleaning the strip beside it, then back-heeling the vacuum cleaner away behind him on its castors and cleaning the next swathe.

He stuck a foot out behind him and heeled the vacuum cleaner away again. As he straightened up he felt a tap on his shoulder, his left shoulder.

And Wally grinned. Mike was always doing that, tapping him on one shoulder while standing behind the other one, and Wally, not caught out for once, glanced quickly over his right shoulder and shouted, 'Boo!'

Only there was nobody there.

So Wally looked over his left shoulder.

The training shoes were Mike's. They swung gently in unison from side to side.

'SWITCH THAT bloody thing off,' bellowed Roper.

Price bent forward and flicked the switch of the vacuum cleaner. In the ensuing silence Roper turned and took in Mike Taunton's hanging body and the toppled step ladder beneath it. He put out a hand and felt one of Taunton's naked ankles. Its colour was a leaden pink. It was icy cold.

Price's face had gone a similar colour. He had seen a suicide before, but not a hanged one. The bloated purple face, the lolling, protruding tongue, the tightly clenched fists, the glazed, dead eyes.

Nor did Roper feel at his best. Violent death was always death at its most unpleasant and it was only with difficulty that he kept his own rising gorge at bay. Blood draining downward had swollen Taunton's ankles and insteps. His torso was naked. From the dirty canvas belt that held up his jeans the corner of a blue envelope protruded.

'Shouldn't we cut him down?' asked Price, at Roper's shoulder.

'No point,' said Roper. Nor was there, at this stage. At a guess, Taunton had been dead for eight or nine hours, perhaps more. 'Get one of the drivers to radio in for a photographer and a path-man.'

'Will do,' said Price, and was glad to be away.

Roper took a couple of paces back from the body. The rope was a new clothesline. Its top end was lashed to the handrail across the front of Huxley's wood loft, its bottom end tied around Taunton's throat with a simple running noose under Taunton's right ear. At a guess, the tips of Taunton's toes hung about five feet from the floor. His crumpled T-shirt lay beneath the fallen step ladder.

It looked, Roper had to admit, a more efficient than usual attempt at suicide. The envelope, tucked behind the belt, would contain the inevitable last note, either of explanation or expiation—or whatever.

The members of the commune stood in a knot just outside the doorway, each of them talking at once. Most vociferous was Carol Haldane. Wally Tupper, who had again had the misfortune to find the body, was sitting crosslegged on the lawn beside the wooden cafeteria. Jollyboy was crouched in front of him and doing his best to get some answers out of him as Wally, clasping his knees, rocked dazedly to and fro.

Roper walked slowly back to the door. The commune fell to silence.

'When did you last see him alive? Anybody?'

Carol Haldane stared back at him, white-faced but otherwise apparently in control of herself. 'Last night,' she said. 'When we came back from the pub.'

'He was drunk,' said Allan Sutton softly, from behind Haldane's back.

'Yes, he was drunk,' Haldane spat venomously, rounding on Sutton. 'But he wasn't *that* bloody drunk.'

Roper took her arm and turned her back to face him. She shook him off.

'He wasn't that drunk,' she hissed vehemently. 'He was pissed out of his mind. *Stupid* drunk. You know?'

Roper raised both hands placatingly. 'All right, Miss Haldane; let's take it easy, shall we? Can you remember what the time was?'

'Eleven—about.'

'It was twenty to,' Sutton broke in again. 'Exactly.'

'I can vouch for that.' The new voice was Huxley's. He was standing on Roper's left with Jennifer Sutton. The two Dances and Thruxton were ranged in a semicircle at the back. The heroically built Rachael Dance looked ready to pass out and her husband had a tight hold on her arm and was watching her anxiously.

'Do you mind if I take my wife back to the house?' he asked. 'The heat ... and all this ... horrible business.'

'No, sir,' said Roper. 'You do that.' And as Dance steered his wife back towards the house he said to the others: 'Apart from Mr Huxley, I'd prefer the rest of you to do the same. But stay within call, please.'

'I presume this means we don't open the house today?' said Jennifer Sutton. Her voice was testy, as if Taunton's death was yet another irritation in the day-to-day running of things.

'You presume correctly, Miss Sutton,' said Roper. 'And perhaps tomorrow as well. Sorry.'

More policemen were coming around the side of the house. At the rear was DI Price.

'And I'd be obliged if I could use one of your rooms, Miss Sutton,' said Roper. 'Somewhere I can talk to each of you, one at a time. Will you arrange that, please?'

'Yes, if that's what you have to do,' she replied, shrugging. 'You can use the downstairs drawing room. Will that do?'

'Admirably, Miss Sutton,' said Roper. 'Thank you.'

It took her a moment or two to realise that she had been dismissed, plainly a situation that was new to her. Then she pivoted on a heel and caught up with her brother who was limping back towards the house.

'WAS YOUR WORKSHOP LOCKED last night, Mr Huxley?'

'Yes.'

'You sure?'

'Positively,' said Huxley.

'And you say you saw Taunton at twenty to eleven last night?'

'I didn't see,' said Huxley. 'I heard. I only saw Carol. I was in the kitchen knocking up a sandwich when the two of them came back from the Arms.'

'You knew they'd been to the Arms?'

'I guessed,' said Huxley. 'They were both fiddler's-bitch tight; and the Arms is the only pub in the village. So...'

'Fair comment.' Roper moved a little deeper into the workshop. Huxley followed reluctantly, a few paces behind. 'What time did you lock up in here last night, Mr Huxley? D'you remember?'

'About half-ten,' said Huxley.

'Doors and windows?'

'Everything.'

'And if I remember, when you've locked up, you hang your keys on the dresser for Miss Sutton to collect when she shuts up the house—that right?'

'And I did,' said Huxley.

'So the only way Taunton could have got in here was through a window?'

'Yes,' agreed Huxley, with a shrug, 'I suppose so. But I'm sure I went around and checked them.'

'But there must be a spare key,' said Roper.

'Yes. Jenny Sutton keeps it,' said Huxley. 'But I've already asked her. Mike didn't ask her for it.'

'Do you know where he might have got the rope from, by any chance?'

Huxley sent a quick unwilling glance towards Taunton's hanging body 'Yes,' he said. 'He might have taken it out of the cupboard—over there.' Huxley pointed to a scarred green cupboard against the opposite wall. He kept several lengths of clothesline in there to use as Spanish windlasses. These, he explained, were used to cramp large wooden carcasses together while their glued joints were setting. The ropes were lashed around the carcasses, then tightened in the manner of a tourniquet with a gadget like a marlinspike.

'How about the step ladder?'

'Mine,' said Huxley.

'Kept in here?'

'Yes,' said Huxley. 'Regrettably.' He again glanced uncomfortably up at the body suspended from his wood loft. 'Do you have to leave the poor sod dangling like that? Can't you cut him down, for Christ's sake?'

'He can't feel a thing, Mr Huxley,' said Roper. 'Take my word for it.'

Huxley switched his gaze back to Roper, staring out from under his ginger eyebrows with something close to anger. 'Pretty much the cold-blooded bastards, aren't you?' he said softly.

'Yes, sir,' said Roper equably. 'Very likely. But that poor lad hanging up there is what we call evidence. He's got to be photographed, and pulled about, and cut up a bit and generally buggered around with. Thank God, I don't have to do that personally. But somebody does, you see, sir—or we don't know exactly how or why the poor lad topped himself, do we? Or even if he did? If you follow me. So you join your friends in the house, Mr Huxley, and let me and my unfeeling lads get on with the nasty side. Eh, sir?'

Huxley looked chastened. 'I'm sorry,' he said. 'It's just that I've never seen a suicide before.'

'Quite, sir,' said Roper. 'And each one I see is one too many, believe me. Go on, sir, please.'

PRICE DIRECTED the photographer, while two finger-
print crews did the rounds of the windows. Roper was
up in the wood loft looking down on it all. In a word,
it was what Roper called 'dodgy'. The suicide note
tucked behind Taunton's trouser belt, that was dodgy.

Dear Carol,

I expect Wally or Lewis will give you this in the
morning. I'm sorry to let you down, but I can't
go on with living with what I did. Sorry. Thanks
for everything.

                                        Love, Mike.

The confession of a suicide was always dodgy. And
both the letter and the envelope, with Carol Haldane's name on it, were typewritten. Which made it
even dodgier.

And what was Taunton confessing to?

If it was the murder of Vera Jackman, then that
would make it the ultimate in dodginess.

The rope that Taunton had used had been wound
several times around the guardrail before it had been
knotted. It was fairly new rope, waxed, good quality.
Nothing on the floor round about that could be defined as a footprint, although the fine film of sawdust had been disturbed here and there around the
vicinity of the ladder.

Down below, the workshop was a scene of quiet but
intensive activity. Four DCs were dusting the window
catches and ledges for prints; two more, working from
the entrance, were painstakingly quartering the stone

floor in case Wally Tupper's vacuum cleaner might have missed something. Sergeant Makins was making a handwritten copy of Taunton's letter on Huxley's workbench. From time to time came the soft plop of the photographer's flash.

'Sir?'

The call had come from one of the DCs dusting the windows. 'I've found a loose catch—and a shoeprint on the sill.'

Roper went down to join him. The casement window in question was on the side of the workshop furthest from the house. The window was closed but the catch hung loosely and the stay at the bottom was off its spigot.

And on the dull red tiles of the inside window ledge was a small but clear ellipse of a shoeprint, three bars of dried mud, the middle one poorly defined, the ones behind and in front of it slightly less so; and a similar mark on the stone floor immediately beneath it, but this second one was smudged, as if Taunton had jumped from the sill to the floor, skidded and twisted and perhaps lost his balance.

Delicately, the catch in one hand and the stay in the other, the DC opened the window. Immediately outside were the sacks of sawdust beneath their green tarpaulin. Where the tarpaulin had sagged was still a puddle of water left by the recent rains. And between the puddle and the sill was a perfect soleprint, an intact version of the ones on the sill and on the workshop floor.

'Get 'em photographed,' said Roper. 'All three.'

He joined Price and, while the photographer was slipping another cassette of film into the back of his camera, he crouched and examined the soles of Taunton's frayed and grubby white training shoes. The sole of the left one was dirtier than the right and its central bar of rubber was well worn, more so than the one on the right, which still bore part of the impress of the maker's name. It looked a perfect match to the muddy stains on the tarpaulin and the window sill.

Ergo: it was now looking likely that young Michael Taunton had, after all, done it all by himself, despite that questionable suicide note. And if that was so, then it was equally likely that the note was Taunton's confession to the murder of young Vera Jackman.

'And if it is, we can all pack up and go home,' said Price.

'And if it isn't,' said Roper, drawing himself upright, 'some fly bastard's moved the bloody goalposts. Right?'

WILSON, THE PATHOLOGIST, balanced precariously on a pair of aluminium steps while he carefully examined the rope and bruising about Taunton's neck.

'There's a contusion at the back of his head,' he called down. 'Did you notice that?' A plastic-sheathed thumb probed the spot under Taunton's hair. 'And a swelling—quite substantial. And by the smell, I'd say he'd been drinking. A beer man, was he?' He put his nose close to Taunton's gaping mouth and sniffed. He twitched his nose distastefully. 'Well, whatever his tipple was, last night it was *definitely* beer.'

Wilson came back down the steps. At the bottom he scrawled a few more hieroglyphs in his notebook. 'I can tell you better when we've cut him down, but at a rough guess, based on the state of rigor and lividity, I'd say he died sometime around midnight last night.'

'And he hanged *himself*? Or could he already have been dead and someone else have strung him up?'

Wilson puffed out his cheeks while he considered that. 'The former... I think,' he added cautiously. 'Can't tell you much else until I've had him on the table. I think we can take the poor lad down now.'

Four men took Taunton's weight while another cut through the washing line. As the rope parted the body buckled limply from the waist so that its discoloured distorted face finished up only a few inches from the face of one of the young uniformed men who was supporting it. He turned away and was promptly sick and had to be led outside.

The body was laid on a stretcher, the jeans unbelted and taken down to Taunton's meagre thighs, then turned on to its face for Wilson to slide in a greased rectal thermometer. While he was waiting for it to register he re-examined the bump and bruise on the back of Taunton's head.

'Quite a lump,' he observed. 'If the lad had been as drunk as I think he was, a knock like that could have laid him out cold.'

'So someone else *could* have strung him up?'

'While he was unconscious, you mean? It's possible, yes. But the eyes are partially open—and if you look at the hands, you'll see they're like the Jackman girl's hands. Clenched. Another example of cadaveric spasm. I'd say this lad had been aware of what was happening to him—perhaps he even changed his mind about what he was doing. Most suicides do, you know, when they choose a slow but violent way out—

like this one. He'd have done better to have jumped from up there'—Wilson pointed up to the wood loft—'eight or nine feet of jump. He'd have either broken the rope or his neck. Certainly a bloody sight quicker either way. Did he leave a note?'

'Yes.'

'Coherent?'

'It was typed. It was also by way of being a confession. Vera Jackman.'

Wilson crouched back on his heels. 'And you only found the single set of shoeprints?'

'That's all.'

'Then I think you're definitely looking at a suicide, Superintendent. And if you are, you could also be looking at Vera Jackman's murderer.'

Wilson withdrew the thermometer, tipped it towards the window, then compared it with another that was recording the ambient temperature on top of his instrument case. He tapped the readings into a pocket calculator, together with a couple of arithmetical constants.

'I wasn't far wrong,' he said. 'I'd say he died between eleven and midnight last night. If you can find out when he ate his last meal, I can get even closer.'

Roper levered himself up. 'All right if we keep his training shoes?' he said. 'I'd like to run a proper comparison-check against those prints by the window.'

'No objections at all,' said Wilson, as he packed his instruments back into their black case.

A DC carefully tugged off Taunton's training shoes and put each in a separate polythene bag. Then the body was turned on to its back and covered with a red blanket.

'When can you look him over?' asked Roper.

'This afternoon,' said Wilson, peeling off his plastic gloves. 'But I wouldn't waste too much time waiting for my findings. It's suicide, Superintendent. An absolute classic.'

ELEVEN

JOLLYBOY and a shivering Wally Tupper sat together on a Hepplewhite chaise-longue, Roper in a black japanned Regency armchair that was one of a set of four and was probably worth a small fortune.

'When you arrived for work this morning, son,' said Roper patiently, 'was the padlock on the workshop door locked or unlocked? Can you remember?'

'I do remember,' said Wally. 'It was locked.'

'You're sure?'

Wally nodded. 'I unlocked it, didn't I? 'Ad to get the key from the kitchen.'

'Then what?'

'I 'oovered. I always 'oover.' With his hands clasped tightly together Tupper started to rock backwards and forwards again.

'Did you touch anything—like the windows? Did you open one?'

Three questions at once were more than Wally could handle. Roper stifled his urgency and repeated them one at a time. Wally shook his head to each.

'Never touch nothing. Mr Huxley told me not to. I just 'oover.'

'Did you notice if a window was open?'

Wally shook his head.

Roper slowed down. Hustling Wally Tupper would lead nowhere. The lad's clasped knuckles were white and he was still shivering. But such was his memory that if he wasn't questioned now there was little point in questioning him at all.

'When you first went into the workshop, you didn't notice Mr Taunton—Mike—hanging up there?'

'Didn't look,' said Wally. 'Didn't see him till he touched me.'

Roper frowned. 'Mr Taunton touched you?'

'He touched me. With his foot.'

'But you didn't touch him?'

Tupper shook his head.

'Did you touch the step ladder? The one on the floor?'

'Didn't touch nothing. I ran. Got Mr Huxley.'

'And you're sure you didn't open a window?'

Tupper shook his head again.

'Supposing I asked you for your fingerprints,' said Roper. 'Would you let Mr Jollyboy do that? It's only to help us find out who opened that window. Then Mr Jollyboy'll take you home in his car. How about that?'

'I got to finish 'oovering.'

'Tomorrow,' said Roper. 'I'm sure Miss Sutton will let you finish hoovering tomorrow.'

ROPER OPENED the casement window and looked down. Immediately beneath him were the stone steps that led up from the kitchen to the garden. The room was small and cramped, but orderly. The bed was made, a single bed with a patchwork coverlet; a row of paperbacked novels stood on their shelf like a row of soldiers. A military chest and a narrow wardrobe filled most of the remaining space. A book on top of the chest was an expensive reproduction of Thomas Sheraton's original catalogue of furniture designs, a couple of paper flags in it for bookmarks. This was Lewis Huxley's room.

Jennifer Sutton stood aside as Roper and Price came out and locked the door after them. The adjacent room was Carol Haldane's. A double bed all but filled it. The bed was rumpled and unmade. And it looked as if she eschewed wardrobes, even though there was one jammed in the corner beside the window. There were clothes on the bed, under it, a few hanging on dry-cleaners' wire hangers from the picture rail. Partly hidden under the right-hand curtain were half a dozen of her landscape canvases leaning against the wall.

The window was closed and latched; perhaps why the room smelled so stale. Roper opened it wide on its stay. The view was almost identical to the one from Huxley's room, except that Roper had to look slightly to his right to see into the stairwell to the kitchen.

The Thruxton's room was opposite. It looked out over the front of the house. Very tidy. A place for everything and everything in its place. The curtains and the coverlet were both in a thick, chunky fabric—probably woven by Mrs Thruxton. Samples of similar fabrics were swatched into a book on top of a chest of drawers. On a drawing board leaning against the wall was a much smudged but still impressive charcoal sketch of the mask of Christ upon which Roper had seen Thruxton working yesterday in his workshop.

Jennifer Sutton's patience, Roper could feel, was almost at the end of its tether. He heard her sigh.

'This seems to be a terrible waste of time,' she said irritably. 'Or are you looking for something in particular?'

'No, Miss Sutton,' said Roper. 'Just getting the lie of the land, that's all.'

'But Mike hanged himself downstairs, for pity's sake. Not up here in the roof.'

Roper turned slowly to face her. Her face was very rigid, very pale. He gave her the benefit of the doubt and supposed her outburst was justified in the circumstances. To have someone murdered in your front garden and then have a suicide found only a few hours afterwards wasn't exactly a normal train of events.

'We're still investigating a murder, Miss Sutton,' Roper reminded her.

'Which we all know Mike did, don't we?' she countered. 'People don't hang themselves for nothing, do they?'

'You'd be surprised how many do, Miss Sutton,' Roper replied equably, skirting her to go back outside to the passage. Little old ladies who had stolen a tin of salmon from their local supermarket; teenage kids who couldn't face up to taking their exams. There was still a world that Jennifer Sutton and her ilk had never even glimpsed.

The adjacent room was the Dances'. A double bed, an ironing board standing by the window, a transistor radio on the chest of drawers. The room was small and cramped and it was difficult to imagine the two robustly built Dances both trying to move about in it at once. Its aura was one of battered homeliness.

They returned to the passage and Jennifer Sutton locked the door.

'Your brother's art students don't sleep here then, Miss Sutton?'

'No,' she said. 'The insurance company wouldn't allow it. We board them out in the lodge.'

At the far end of the passage a door blocked their way. Jennifer Sutton sorted out a Yale key from her bunch and opened it. She led the way in.

'This is your flat, is it, Miss Sutton?'

'And my brother's.'

They were in a continuation of the previous passage. There was a telephone on the left-hand wall, a message pad hanging beside it. Her bedroom was just beyond, her brother's opposite. At the far end, the remaining two rooms were a sitting room and a kitchen-diner. The large sitting room was comfortably furnished. The thick folk-weave curtains looked as if they had been made by Mrs Thruxton. A television, but no video recorder and no hi-fi. The faded carpet in front of the carved oak fireplace looked like a genuine piece of Persian and the few items of pottery about the room were eighteenth-century Chelsea. The window looked out towards the lawns at the front of the house, the driveway over on the left.

'Were you and your brother up here all last night, Miss Sutton?' Roper had walked to the other end of the room and lifted aside the net curtain. This view was over the garden, the cafeteria and the ornamental lake.

'Yes,' she said. Roper heard a cigarette case snap shut and the click of a lighter. 'Yes,' she said again. 'I was up here from eight until I went to bed. Allan came back from the studio at about nine.'

'And at eleven o'clock, you locked up as usual?'

'No. Allan did. I was very tired last night.'

Roper turned to face her. She was hugging herself with one arm across her, its hand trapped in the elbow of the arm that held her cigarette. She was shivering.

'Were the windows open?'

'Only those. Both of them.' She jerked her head towards the casement windows at the front of the house.

'Did you hear anything?'

She shook her head. 'No,' she said. 'Nothing.'

BY ELEVEN O'CLOCK Roper and Price and a WPC had established themselves in the drawing room. Outside, the sun was shining and the house was deathly quiet. Mike Taunton's body was now along at the mortuary.

'Do you want them separately or together?' asked Price, at the door.

'Separately,' said Roper. When he had interviewed them together the other day in the kitchen they had been merely witnesses. Now, if Michael Taunton's suicide was not what it seemed, they all had to be classified as suspects.

The first in was Adrian Dance, perspiring a little and tweaking at his broken spectacles. Very nervous; but Roper had been at his business long enough to know that most people were, the innocent ones usually more so.

'Take a chair, Mr Dance,' said Price.

'Thank you,' said Dance, trying on a smile and failing signally. He chose the raised end of the chaise-longue where Wally Tupper had sat earlier that morning. With some difficulty, Dance crossed his plump legs and did his best to look at ease. Unsure what to do with his hands, he settled for tucking them out of sight behind his raised knee. He blinked expectantly.

Roper glanced at his watch, and wrote the date and time in his notebook.

'Lousy business, Mr Dance.'

Dance nodded. 'Yes,' he said. 'Awful.'

'Know young Taunton well, did you?'

'Well…yes…I suppose so,' said Dance. One hand rose to his spectacles and made an unnecessary adjustment.

'Were you friends?'

'No…not exactly. But we saw him every day…we got on…you know?'

'Did it ever occur to you that he might be suicidally inclined?'

Dance shuddered. He was too nervous for it to have been an act. 'Lord, no,' he said. 'Never…He used to get pretty down sometimes…and we all know he drank too much…And he had been depressed lately…But not suicidally so, I'm sure.'

'Why was he depressed, sir?' asked Price. 'Do you know?'

'I think he thought he didn't fit in here,' said Dance. 'He didn't *make* anything…if you see what I mean. It made him the odd man out…He relied on all of us for his pocket money…I don't think he liked that. We all earn, you see. All chip into the common pot. Mike didn't.'

Which confirmed Roper's earlier diagnosis that Taunton hadn't slotted in here like the others, had been regarded as the outsider and was probably conscious of it.

'Did you ever see Taunton with Vera Jackman, Mr Dance?'

'Yes, I did,' he answered readily. 'Several times.'

'Doing what?'

'Talking…Arguing on one occasion…Quite some time ago, though. Not recently.'

'Close, were they, do you think?'

'I think they were, at one time. About Christmas, that was. I think Vera had Mike around her little finger in those days.'

'But not lately?'

'No,' said Dance. 'I don't think so.'

Dance had relaxed a little. He had sunk back deeper into the chaise-longue and stopped fiddling with his glasses.

'Can you remember what you were doing last night, Mr Dance? Between ten and midnight, say?'

'We were upstairs,' said Dance. 'Both of us. My wife was ironing and I was repairing a pair of shoes—these.' He lifted a foot with a heavy industrial boot on it. 'Although I did go downstairs at about ten o'clock to fill our flask with coffee. We went to bed at about eleven o'clock and listened to the radio. And that's about it.'

'Did you hear anything? Anything unusual?'

Dance thought for a while and then shook his head. 'No,' he said. 'Sorry. Nothing. Except that we thought that Carol made a lot of noise when she came back from the pub. Slammed her door and thumped about a lot. But then she often does that.'

'You say you heard Miss Haldane come up; how about Mr Taunton? Did he come up with her like he did the other night?'

'I don't know,' said Dance, having spent a moment or two thinking about it. 'Perhaps. Perhaps not. Although I don't recall hearing their voices.'

'Do you remember the time—when you heard Miss Haldane come back?'

'I honestly don't,' said Dance with an apologetic shrug. 'Except that Rachael and I hadn't gone to bed. So it must have been before eleven.'

RACHAEL DANCE was able to remember the hour more nearly. She had been ironing at the time and seen Haldane and Taunton returning along the drive from the front gates at half-past ten.

'It was dark,' said Roper. 'Are you sure it was them?'

'Yes,' she said. 'Mike stopped and lit a cigarette. I saw his face.'

Roper recalled that the Dances' bedroom looked out over the front of the house, so Mrs Dance could have seen Haldane and Taunton coming back from the Cort Arms.

'But both Mr Sutton and Mr Huxley say that they heard Miss Haldane and Mr Taunton in the garden later than that,' said Roper.

'Yes,' she said. 'I know.' She screwed and unscrewed a handkerchief between her large hands. Like her husband's, Mrs Dance's ample proportions were built to last. Since Roper had last seen her in the garden she had put on some lipstick and coloured her face. 'But I think when I saw them they were quarrelling. I'm sure I saw Mike give Carol a push—a hard one, I mean, as if he really wanted her to leave him alone. I know that quite ten minutes passed before

Carol came upstairs. Alone, I think. I remember saying to Adrian that Carol and Mike had been at it again.'

'It?'

'Rowing. Carol was always trying to get Mike to better himself and Mike didn't want to listen.'

'But you didn't hear Mr Taunton come upstairs last night?'

'No,' she said; then added sadly, 'But then he didn't *come* up, did he?'

'Did you ever see him with Vera Jackman, Mrs Dance?'

'Yes,' she said. 'They seemed very close at one time.'

'How about lately?'

'Well, of course, they were both working here, so they could hardly help seeing each other and talking to each other.'

Roper drew thumb and forefinger together across his underlip. It was tempting to believe that Taunton had hanged himself—*and* murdered Vera Jackman—and yet, somehow...

'An opinion, Mrs Dance: do you think young Taunton was still carrying a torch for Vera Jackman? Strictly off the record?'

She considered that at some length. 'Honestly,' she said. 'I really can't answer that. I know that round about Christmas, poor Mike was daft about her. If you wanted Mike, you found out where Vera was and Mike would be there. But lately...' She shrugged wearily. 'I'm sorry; I really don't know.'

'Mr Taunton a heavy drinker, was he?'

'Very,' she said. 'I know that sounds unkind. But he was.'

'Would you say that drink made him depressed?'

'Yes,' she said. 'Very. Either that or he wanted to fight everybody.'

'Did you ever think he might be suicidal?'

Rachael Dance shook her head. 'Not suicidal—but very unhappy. He didn't belong here, you see. Didn't fit in. I think in fact—oh, it's only a suggestion—but I think he was trying to get out of here. He wanted to go back to London, I'm sure of it.'

'Did he ever tell you that?'

Rachael Dance shook her head. 'But I'm sure the others will tell you the same.'

Mrs Dance's opinions and guesses were based, Roper had decided, on shrewd observation and were not to be lightly cast aside. She had a matriarchal stolidness and reticence, and in normal circumstances probably wasn't given to gossip.

Roper closed his notebook. 'That's it, then, Mrs Dance. You've been very helpful. Thank you. Perhaps you'd ask Mr Huxley to come in next.'

She rose with surprising ease, despite her girth, and sailed out. The door was scarcely closed behind her when, after a couple of brisk raps, it was opened again. Roper expected to see Lewis Huxley; but it was the face of DS Rodgers which appeared around the edge of it.

'If you've got a minute, sir; something's come up.'

It was Vera Jackman's wristwatch—or, more correctly, it was more likely Vera Jackman's wristwatch than not.

Roper turned the wristwatch in its polythene envelope. A cheap trinket, as Crosby had said. Gilt, with a clip-bracelet that hinged at the sides of the watch where a strap would normally be fitted. Even at £5, Roper thought, Crosby had been swindled.

'Where d'you find it?'

'In the garage,' said Rodgers. 'I was just sniffing about on the off-chance. It looked as if it had been kicked under a bale of old carpets.'

Which it probably had been. In the dark of Tuesday night. When the Range Rover had been driven back from Church Lane.

Roper passed the watch back to Rodgers. 'At least it supports what we've already guessed,' he said. 'But you'd better take it along to Crosby at the Cort Arms and get him to identify it for certain; and perhaps Jackman's brother. But don't tell either of 'em where it was found. Right?'

'Right, sir,' said Rodgers. 'And a message from George Makins. He thinks Taunton's suicide note was typed on the machine in Miss Sutton's office. He's checked with Miss Sutton—and she says that Taunton asked if he could use it yesterday evening. About seven o'clock. Before he and Miss Haldane went along to the Arms. Miss Haldane confirms that. He was in the office for half an hour, sir. They both heard him pecking away at the typewriter.'

Roper grimaced sourly. Professional he was, but human he also was, and as perverse and selective as the rest of the human race he *also* was. As a policeman his truths could only ever be based upon facts born of evidence—unequivocal evidence. As a plain human being he believed, as most of us do, in those things in which he wanted to believe. And he had wanted to believe that Michael Taunton was murdered—somehow or other—and that someone else had typed that suicide note because Taunton had been too dead to write it by hand. And that Taunton had not murdered Jackman—because that was too easy to believe. Roper believed in luck. Finding that valve cap, that had been luck. Vera Jackman's wristwatch turning up, that too was a stroke of luck. But a suicide note that was also tantamount to a confession of murder—to Roper that had a smell like a pair of old running shoes. In that kind of luck Roper could not believe—as a plain human being. As a policeman, it irked him that he might be forced to.

'Tell Makins to get the original letter and his copy across to forensic. And tell 'em we want priority on a check of typefaces and an answer by this afternoon.'

Makins had probably got it right—but, as the phrase had it, all reasonable doubt had to be removed. Because judges and juries didn't like typed suicide notes either.

TWELVE

HUXLEY LOWERED HIMSELF to the chaise-longue.

Roper wrote Huxley's name, the time and the date on a new page of his notebook.

'Perhaps we could start with your movements last night, Mr Huxley.'

Huxley shrugged impatiently. 'My movements?' he said. 'Frankly, I don't see what my movements have got to do with it. Mike committed suicide, didn't he? Hardly likely to have had an accomplice, was he?'

'It's been known, sir,' said Roper patiently. 'And I don't like asking questions twice, sir. Wastes your time, wastes my time, if you take my point.'

'All right,' Huxley conceded grudgingly. He leaned forward with his loosely clasped hands hanging between his knees. 'From six till seven—more or less—I was in the public bar of the Cort Arms. At about ten past seven I got back here and went straight out to the workshop—where I stayed till nearly half-past ten cutting glazing beads for that bookcase you saw. Then I came back to the house, cut myself some sandwiches and brewed up some coffee and took them upstairs—where I stayed until this morning.'

'And while you were cutting your sandwiches, I think you said, you heard Taunton and Carol Haldane coming back.'

'Couldn't miss hearing them,' said Huxley. 'They

were going hammer and tongs at each other. Ask Allan. He was down in the kitchen with me.'

'And you saw Carol Haldane come into the house?'

'No,' said Huxley. 'Not exactly. I caught a glimpse of her going into her room a few minutes afterwards. I was upstairs myself by then. I'd been for a pee.'

'But you didn't see Taunton?'

'No,' said Huxley. 'She was on her own.'

'Did you hear or see Taunton come up?'

Huxley shook his head. 'No,' he said. 'I don't think so. Not now you come to mention it.'

Which more or less corroborated the Dances' statements.

'And when you left your workshop last night, you'd left it secure—you think?'

'I thought I had,' said Huxley. 'But obviously I hadn't.'

'Taunton didn't have a key?'

'Jenny Sutton keeps all the spare keys on her own ring,' said Huxley. 'The only loose ones are the ones you've seen hanging up on the dresser in the kitchen. So I guess I must have left a window open.'

'I'd like to know more about Michael Taunton, Mr Huxley. Anything that comes to mind. No hurry.'

Huxley pondered that, still hunched forward. One powerful hand rose and scratched thoughtfully at his red beard. 'Jenny took him on a few weeks before Christmas. He was looking for work. Called here on the off-chance. I thought he was a dead-beat, but Jenny took pity on him. Put him to work tarting up a couple of the guest rooms down at the lodge. He did a pretty good job—and I was looking for some casual labour to give me a hand in the workshop round about that time. Varnish-stripping—knocking down cheap-jack old furniture for the wood. So I tried him out. He turned out to be a good worker—except when he was chasing about after Vera Jackman. I taught him how to stain and French polish—the old-fashioned way. He wasn't exactly over-endowed with grey matter, but he was patient—and good with his hands.'

'And he was a drinker,' said Roper 'Didn't that interfere with his work a bit?'

'More lately,' said Huxley. 'The last few months. He wasn't too bad before that. I told him a couple of days ago that if he didn't knock it off, I'd have him out on his ear.'

'We've heard he was moody. That right?'

'Up and down like a yo-yo,' said Huxley. 'One day he'd be all sweetness and light and the next day he'd hardly say a word to anybody.'

'And how long had he been behaving like that?'

'Since he really began to hit the bottle—a couple of months.'

'And before that he was reliable.'

'Yes,' said Huxley.

'How was he yesterday?'

'Fine in the morning. Touchy in the afternoon. I had a feeling he sloped off somewhere for a drink once or twice.'

'Do you know what could have caused all this, Mr Huxley? Did it ever occur to you that he might still be smitten by Vera Jackman?'

Huxley took longer to answer that. 'It's difficult to say,' he said. 'I got the impression it was more to do with this place. The commune. He only contributed with the sweat of his brow, if you know what I mean.

The rest of us can all help each other. Ideas, that sort of thing. Mike was the odd man out. Most of our conversations left him standing. I don't think he liked that.'

'You mean he didn't fit in?'

Huxley nodded. 'Exactly,' he said. 'We're a clique by the very nature of what we do here. But that isn't to say we cut Mike out. He did that all on his own.'

MRS THRUXTON THOUGHT the same. Michael Taunton had only ever been on the fringe of things here.

'Or, rather, that's what he thought, I think.' Away from her husband, the nervous Mrs Thruxton looked like becoming garrulous. 'But he was really very useful. He helped me repair my loom several times. But he did drink. Far too much. We all knew it.' Her pale moist eyes blinked earnestly. 'Such a silly boy...'

'Last night, Mrs Thruxton—did you hear anything? See anything?'

'Only Carol thumping up the stairs and barging into her room.'

'You didn't hear the rumpus in the garden?'

'No,' she said. 'I didn't. But then I wouldn't have. Our room is at the front of the house. But Bill—my husband—thought he saw Carol and Mike arguing in the driveway last night. At least it looked as if they were arguing, so he said. He said he thought they were having a proper fist-fight. Mike really had got moody and quarrelsome lately, we all saw it. I mean we could actually see him going downhill. Psychologically, I mean. I know for a fact that Lewis had already given him an ultimatum. But Bill had an idea that Mike was going to leave anyway—and that if it hadn't been for

Carol he would probably have left weeks ago.' She suddenly paused in mid-flow and looked apologetically at Roper, at Price, then back again to Roper.

'I'm sorry,' she said. 'I'm talking too much, aren't I? Bill's always saying how I talk too much. I think it's nerves.'

'It's all right, Mrs Thruxton,' Roper reassured her. 'You carry on. When you get to something we want to know more about, I'll stop you.' On balance, Roper reckoned that he had wrapped up as many cases by listening to gossip as he had by sifting through piles of evidence. And characters like Mrs Thruxton, the quiet, coy ones, the ones who lived on the sidelines, were usually the ones who saw the most. 'You were talking about Michael Taunton staying because of Miss Haldane.'

'Yes ... Of course, I don't know how true that was, but I do know that once or twice lately Mike met the postman at the gate. And once I saw him—from our window—sort through the letters and slip one inside his shirt. Of course, that probably didn't mean anything important, but at breakfast—the same morning—Carol asked him if he'd received any mail—and Mike said he hadn't—and I thought that was *very* odd, because he had, you see; or he had stolen somebody else's letter, which would have been worse, wouldn't it?

'But I think it was a letter he didn't want Carol to know about,' she hurried on. 'And when I told Bill, he told me it was best to mind my own business. "Hear all, see all and saw nowt," that's what Bill says. So I didn't say anything.'

'You seem to be bracketing Miss Haldane and Mr Taunton together a lot, Mrs Thruxton,' observed Price.

'Oh, there was *nothing* in it,' she protested. 'They were only friends. But Mike—well, he wasn't a mixer exactly; a bit of an outcast; and, well, Carol rather took him under her wing. She's like that. Very Left. Takes up *causes*.'

'You don't think that they might have been having an affair, Mrs Thruxton?' asked Roper. 'Taunton and Miss Haldane?'

'Oh, no. I wouldn't have thought so. Like I said, I think Mike was only one of Carol's causes.'

'I see,' said Roper, smiling, and closing his notebook. 'You've been very helpful, Mrs Thruxton. Thank you.'

She seemed disappointed that the interview was so suddenly over. 'Who shall I ask to come in next?' she asked helpfully.

'I think your husband, Mrs Thruxton,' said Roper. 'Thank you.'

PERHAPS BECAUSE HE HADN'T got his friends about him, Thruxton was far less sure of himself this morning than he had been in the kitchen on Wednesday evening. He sat uneasily on the edge of the chaise-longue while Roper made a deedy business of writing Thruxton's name in his notebook and an equally deedy business of looking at his wristwatch before he slowly wrote the time and the date. The silence was broken momentarily by Thruxton nervously cracking his knuckles.

Roper glanced up at last and weighed him speculatively. Yes, he thought, a young and impressionable girl might easily have fancied an older man like that, married or not; and perhaps she had.

'We understand that you saw Taunton and Miss Haldane quarrelling in the driveway last night, Mr Thruxton. That right?'

'Well,' Thruxton began cautiously. 'Yes. Perhaps. At least, that's what it looked like. I saw Mike give Carol a shove and Carol raise a fist to him. That's all. They could have just been fooling about, of course.'

'Did you think they'd been drinking?'

'Yes.'

'Then, later, you heard Carol Haldane come upstairs. That right?'

'Yes.'

'But not Taunton?'

'No,' said Thruxton. 'I don't think so. I imagine he'd gone straight down to the lodge.'

'We're told some time passed between Taunton and Miss Haldane being sighted in the drive and Miss Haldane coming upstairs.'

Thruxton nodded. 'Yes—about ten minutes.'

'How did you get on with Taunton, Mr Thruxton?'

Thruxton's nose and mouth twisted disparagingly. 'We suffered him. He was a bit of an oick. And when he was drunk he was stupid and offensive. Not my type at all.' Thruxton's interlaced knuckles cracked again; he glanced down in some surprise, as if he hadn't realised he was doing it, and coupled his hands more loosely on his knees.

'Getting back to Taunton, Mr Thruxton; what do you think made him hang himself like that? Did he have any problem you might have known about?'

Thruxton's lean shoulders rose, and fell again. 'Who knows?' he said. 'Could have been guilt, couldn't it? Or perhaps he was just brassed off with this place.'

'He wasn't happy here?'

'Damned right he wasn't,' said Thruxton.

'You mentioned guilt, Mr Thruxton. What d'you think young Taunton was guilty about?'

Thruxton's pale eyes lifted and locked on to Roper's. 'Bloody obvious, isn't it?' he said. 'He killed Vera Jackman.'

'You know that, do you, Mr Thruxton?'

'It's what we all think,' said Thruxton.

'And you subscribe to that idea, do you, sir?'

'I'm not saying anything,' said Thruxton. 'I don't know. But if Mike didn't kill her, I can't think who did.'

'Perhaps you did, Mr Thruxton,' Roper proposed, with a smile.

'Rubbish,' retorted Thruxton. 'I couldn't have. I was with my wife. And what reason would I have had? None.'

CAROL HALDANE was back to her old self, brittle and hostile and lighting yet another Gauloise from the stub of the last, a glass ashtray that she had brought in with her clutched in one upturned hand. Clamped between her fingers the glowing Gauloise was tapped against the rim of the ashtray while the end of the previous one still smouldered in it.

'I've told you before,' she said. 'Vera Jackman was a little slag.'

'I'm not sure what you mean, Miss Haldane,' said Roper. 'Are you saying she was immoral, amoral—or are you just being plain vindictive because you didn't like her?'

'The lot, sport,' she retorted. 'Immoral, amoral, and I couldn't stand the little bitch. Thought she was God's bloody gift to mankind.'

'That's not what we've been hearing,' said Roper. 'The general opinion seems to be that she was a hard-working young woman.'

'Oh, you've been listening to Jen,' she sneered airily. 'Not in our social stratum, is Jen; she didn't exactly see young Vera out of office hours, did she? Beneath her notice, you might say.'

'And Michael Taunton was once smitten with her,' said Roper; 'and you seemed rather tied up with Michael Taunton—from what we hear. Perhaps that's another reason you didn't like her?'

'I'm not that small-minded,' she said. 'And if Mike had decided to go back with her I couldn't have cared less.'

'Really?'

'Really,' she said. 'The world's in too much of a mess already. The one thing I don't need is emotional tangles. Life's too short. I've still got a couple of hundred pictures I want to paint.'

'So you weren't having an affair with Michael Taunton?'

'Affair?' She tilted her head incredulously to one side and looked at Roper as if she couldn't quite take in the enormity of the question. 'You must be from another planet, old chum. Or you're older than you look.'

If she had hoped to provoke a reaction, she failed.

'What exactly *was* your relationship with Michael Taunton, then, Miss Haldane?'

She expelled a stream of tobacco smoke. 'Earthmother,' she said. 'He was a lost soul who needed looking after.'

'I understand that you and Taunton quarrelled a lot.'

'Often,' she agreed. The Gauloise rose, glowed, was tapped again on the rim of the ashtray. 'It was the only way I could shake some life into him—get him to make something of himself.'

'What were you quarrelling about last night, exactly? D'you remember? Coming back from the Cort Arms.'

One side of her mouth lifted superciliously. 'My,' she said. 'They have been gossiping, haven't they?' The end of the second Gauloise followed the first into the ashtray, where it was tamped out with more violence than was strictly necessary, as if it were a substitute for the Cort Place gossips. 'Last night? . . . Well, he was being bloody pathetic again. Maudlin. He told me he was getting out. He'd had enough. Told me he was off back to London. Go back on the dole, if he had to. Anything was better than this place.'

'Suicidal, was he?'

'I wouldn't know what state his mind was in. But I'd have said he was physically incapable of tying that bloody knot. And that's for sure.'

'We understand he used Miss Sutton's typewriter early yesterday evening.'

'Yes.'

'Did he say why he wanted to use it?'

Carol Haldane shook her head. She had no idea.

'He had a bump on the back of his head, Miss Haldane. Looked like a recent one. Do you know if he took a fall last night?'

'Damned right, he did,' she retorted. 'It was home-truth night last night where Mike was concerned. Told me I was smothering him—amongst other things. And I was only trying to stop him scuttling himself, for God's sake. Twenty-five years old and he still couldn't tell his backside from his elbow. I just didn't want to know any more—I was pretty pissed myself. He was too much bother, you know? When we got round to the back of the house, I'd got so bloody angry with him that I clouted him and he fell over. That's when Allan came out to see what was up.'

'He fell over where, Miss Haldane?'

'On the grass.'

'It was a pretty sizeable bump, Miss Haldane. Could he have fallen on the concrete path?'

She shrugged. 'I wouldn't know. I told you, I was pretty far gone myself. I didn't notice where he fell. Could have been the grass, could have been the path.'

'Did you establish if he was hurt?'

'No.' For the first time she looked chagrined. 'I guess now I should have, but I was cheesed off with him. I don't think I even thought about it.'

Roper flipped back through a few pages of his notebook.

'Tuesday, Miss Haldane; do you know if Taunton received a phone call—sometime during the evening?'

She didn't know.

'Could he have?'

'Yes,' she said, with a little shrug. 'No reason why not.'

'How many telephones are there? What I'm getting at is, could he have received a phone call without anybody in the house knowing about it?'

'Yes,' she said. 'I suppose so. There's one telephone in the office and another one up in Jenny's flat. Two separate lines. And I know Mike was in the house early on. So perhaps he could have.'

'And do you know what time he went along to the Cort Arms that evening?'

'No,' she said, 'not exactly. But I think it was about eight o'clock. I saw his back view going down the drive.'

That fitted. Vera Jackman had made that call from Crosby's office some time around seven-thirty on Tuesday evening. Taunton had left the house half an hour afterwards. In answer to a summons, perhaps.

'That was his usual time for going out in the evenings, was it?'

'Not particularly,' she said. 'He went out any time.'

'Do you know what sort of mood he was in—when he came back, that is? Tight, was he?'

She plucked another Gauloise from her packet and treated Roper to a stare like a newly whetted flick knife. 'If you're asking me if I think he killed Vera Jackman, the answer's no.'

ROPER SAT ALONE in a corner of the Cort Arms. It was lunchtime. In front of him were two cheese rolls, liberally garnished with mustard pickle, and a jug of

Crosby's best bitter. Between bites at the former and sips of the latter, Roper scanned his current copy of the *Antique Collector*. About him was the buzz of half-heard conversations and the clatter of knives and forks. At the table next to him two locals were talking in undertones; Vera Jackman's name was prominent in their conversation.

'...if her brother ever gets a sniff of him, he'll do the bugger in.'

'...saw her in Dorchester last week...all legs and backside...if you ask me, she put it about once too often...'

'...my lad was at school with her...'

'...my daughter told me...and she was only thirteen then...'

At the bar a cadet and a WPC were filling a couple of cardboard cartons with wrapped sandwiches to take back to the church hall.

'...my missus saw her in Pedlar's surgery Tuesday morning...Didn't seem anything wrong with her, wife said...'

Roper took a bite out of his second roll and eyed the clock on the wall behind the bar. It was five to one. Another five minutes, then back to Cort Place to interview the two Suttons. To take a break for lunch was a rare event—almost a dereliction of duty—but he had needed to switch off for a while, to clear a mind that felt cluttered like an old attic with too much rubbish.

An hour ago Jack Crosby had formally identified the wristwatch that DS Rodgers had found in the coachhouse as having been Vera Jackman's. Without a doubt. Taunton had come down here the other evening *after* Jackman had made that telephone call from

Crosby's office. Two people, Jennifer Sutton and Carol Haldane, were prepared to swear that Taunton had used the typewriter in Jennifer Sutton's office early yesterday evening. Several sets of fingerprints had been found on the window catches of Huxley's workshop, among them Michael Taunton's—and his were on the catch of the window through which it could reasonably be supposed that he had gained entry last night. Wally Tupper's were not among them, so it was safe to assume that he had not opened that window this morning.

The bump on Taunton's head could now be accounted for. Foul play in that direction could therefore be ruled out. And Taunton was the only member of the commune who did not sleep in the house. Ergo: he could have murdered Vera Jackman on Tuesday night, driven her body along to Church Lane—assuming he had had access somehow to the Rover's keys—driven back again and gone to bed without anyone at Cort Place being any the wiser.

The dice, in law at least, certainly looked loaded against Taunton. And if Taunton had indeed committed suicide, then it was more than likely that he had also murdered Vera Jackman.

But what he had *not* done, Roper was certain, was to give Jackman that *ankh*. Someone else had given her that.

Who? Why? Did it matter? Or was it totally irrelevant? Taunton might have made a mistake—or was lying—when he told them that Jackman hadn't been wearing it when she had first come to the house that afternoon. If he had, then the *ankh* was just another red herring.

But if Taunton had not committed suicide, then the only other option was murder, and it would follow from that that he had *not* typed that note. Nor murdered Jackman.

Too many questions and too few answers.

Roper finished his beer and folded his magazine. Going outside was like stepping into a baker's oven. He turned left, across the forecourt and towards Cort Place.

Apart from the few cars parked along the street, the village had probably looked like this for the last fifty years, serene, apparently untouched. On the other side of the green, behind the school and the cottages, the slopes of the downs were awash with seas of ripening corn. It looked like being a good year for it. Past the Post Office, the newsagent's, a butcher's, a baker's—it smelled as if they made their own bread. A few hundred yards beyond Cort Place a herd of cows were being driven across the road by a couple of young lads. The heat rising from the ground made them shimmer and float like a mirage. From somewhere not too far away came the rhythmic to-and-fro clatter of a lawn mower that always reminded Roper of Sunday afternoons in London.

He approached the corner of the wall around the grounds of Cort Place, passed the telephone box where the Reverend Mr Smallways had seen the Misses Butterworths' dog squatting to drop his *crotte* late on Tuesday night—a few yards past the spot where the Misses Butterworth had seen Vera Jackman walking south...

Roper broke stride. Had he been the kind of man who was given to extravagant gestures, he would probably have smitten his forehead, flung up his arms and shouted, 'Eureka!' But Roper on duty was an undemonstrative man. His stride lengthened again and, secure behind his Polaroid sunglasses, his eyes were shrewdly narrowed.

If anything could tell a tale or two, it might just be that telephone box.

THIRTEEN

PRICE WAS HURRYING DOWN the drive towards him. He looked unusually eager about something. 'I was just coming along to the Arms to get you, Guv'nor,' he said.

'Something cropped up?'

'Could be,' said Price, turning and falling into step beside Roper. 'Mrs Greenaway's been checking Taunton's trainers against those soleprints. She says they match.'

'Bully for Mrs Greenaway,' said Roper.

'And forensic's certain that suicide note was typed on the machine in Jennifer Sutton's office. And Mrs Thruxton wants to see you. She thinks she remembers hearing something last night. Says it's important—or could be.'

'Like what?'

'She won't say—at least, not to me. I think she's scared about making a fool of herself in case she's got it wrong.'

Mrs Thruxton was sitting on a bench beneath the trees a few yards along the path from Huxley's workshop. She looked as if she had been sitting there for some time. She rose timidly as Roper approached her.

'I'm sorry...' Mrs Thruxton probably spent a great deal of time apologising for herself. 'I hope you don't mind my asking to speak to you especially... I feel silly, actually... But it might be important.'

Roper smiled down encouragingly at her. 'All's grist, Mrs Thruxton. And I'm a good listener. Let's sit down, shall we?'

She lowered herself back to the bench. Roper sat down beside her.

She clasped her hands tightly. 'You see,' she began hesitantly, 'I think I heard something last night. I don't think I was dreaming. Bill thinks I was; but I'm sure I wasn't.'

Roper waited patiently for her to gather herself again. It took some time.

'Peter'—her moist blue eyes under pale blond eyebrows swivelled to Roper—'that's Jenny's alsatian—I'm sure I heard him whining late last night.'

Roper smiled again to draw her out. 'I'd say that sounded *very* important, Mrs Thruxton. Tell me more. Can you remember what the time was, for instance?'

'Yes. It was twenty past eleven. We have a clock-radio beside the bed. I remember looking.'

'But your husband didn't hear it?'

'He was asleep. I tried to wake him, but he wasn't interested.'

'Does the dog often make a noise at night?'

'Hardly ever,' she said. 'But when he does, he barks—he *doesn't* whine.'

'Do you think the dog was upstairs or down?'

'Down,' she said. 'He was definitely downstairs. In the hall, I think. I think I heard scratching too.'

'Scratching at a door perhaps?'

'Yes,' she said, nodding. 'Now you come to mention it, I think perhaps he was.'

'So he could have been trying to get out. Maybe he was taken short.'

Her head rocked slowly from side to side. 'No,' she said. 'I don't think so. He's very well trained. And Allan always lets him out into the garden before Jenny locks up, you see.'

'And you think that this might have some bearing on the death of Mr Taunton?'

Mrs Thruxton drew back into her shell. 'I wouldn't have mentioned it,' she said timorously, 'I wouldn't have bothered you—except that I always feel that animals—dogs especially—have an extra sense about certain things. Like death. Psychic. You know?'

She looked hesitantly at Roper as if she expected him to laugh. 'I just thought...' Her voice tailed off.

'You thought that that might have been the time when Mr Taunton hanged himself. Right?'

'Yes,' she said. 'That's exactly what I think. I *do* believe that about dogs. They *know*. And that dog was very *attached* to Mike. He *knew*. That's why he was whining, I'm *sure*.'

Her earnest gaze fixed on Roper again. 'I'm right,' she said. 'You see if I'm not.'

FIRST INTO THE drawing room in the afternoon was Allan Sutton.

'You heard Taunton and Miss Haldane come back from the pub, you said?'

'I did.'

'What time?'

'Twenty to eleven. About. But I couldn't be sure to the minute.'

He had been in the kitchen, taking a bottle of milk from the refrigerator and decanting it into a jug—it had been Sutton's turn last night to supervise the communal coffee pot—and heard Taunton and Haldane arguing in the garden at the head of the outside steps.

'You sure they were arguing, Mr Sutton? Or were they just indulging in some high-spirited shouting?'

'They were arguing; I know the difference. The language was foul.'

But Sutton had not heard what the quarrel was about—although he thought that he'd heard Vera Jackman's name being bandied around.

'Anyway,' he went on, 'I went out and put a stop to it. Told them to come in and stop kicking up a racket.'

'And did they come in?'

'No,' said Sutton. 'At least, Carol did, but not Mike. Whatever had gone on I don't know, but Carol was absolutely livid, shaking. She called up to him that he could bloody well sod off—her words—and stormed off upstairs to bed.'

'And Taunton?'

'He stayed in the garden.'

'He didn't come in—that you know of?'

'I took Jenny up a cup of coffee. When I came back down, I went out to the garden to give the dog a run. I called Mike, but he didn't answer, so I concluded he'd gone on down to the lodge while I was taking up Jenny's coffee.'

'Who locked up last night?'

'I did,' said Sutton. My sister always takes Thursday evenings off.'

'And you locked up when?'

'Eleven—on the dot.'

'And what did you do when you'd locked up?'

'Nothing,' said Sutton. 'I went upstairs with Jenny and we watched the end of the late-night film on the television.'

'And what time did that finish?'

'About eleven-forty-five.'

'And where was your dog in the meantime?'

'Roving the house,' said Sutton. 'He could have been anywhere. Why?'

'Mrs Thruxton thinks she heard him whining at about twenty past eleven.'

Sutton shrugged. 'Perhaps. I wouldn't know. Perhaps we didn't hear him over the noise of the television.'

'Mrs Thruxton said the dog was whining—and he doesn't often whine.'

'That's true,' said Sutton. 'He doesn't. But, as I say, I didn't hear him at all last night.'

'Tell me about Taunton, Mr Sutton,' said Roper. 'Did he ever show signs of being suicidal? Depressed ever, was he?'

'I'm not a psychologist,' said Sutton, 'but one day he was up and the next one he was down. And more down the morning after he'd put a few pints down himself the night before.'

'This affair between Jackman and Taunton, sir,' said Roper; 'given a chance, do you think that Taunton might have gone back with her?'

'I can't speak for a dead man, Superintendent.'

'An opinion, sir. That's all.'

'I don't know,' said Sutton at some length. 'Mike was upset about the whole wretched business. No, I'm sure that he knew it was finished.'

'But from what you heard in the garden last night between Taunton and Miss Haldane, perhaps it wasn't,' suggested Roper.

'I didn't say that,' protested Sutton. 'I only said that I heard Vera Jackman's name mentioned.'

'Who mentioned it?'

'Carol Haldane,' replied Sutton.

'Can you remember any of the context, Mr Sutton?'

But on this issue Sutton insisted that his memory was vague regarding the *exact* words. Carol Haldane had shouted something like:

'Look, Vera Jackman's bloody *dead,* isn't she!'

And Taunton had replied, equally loudly: 'And better off if I was too. Eh? Is that what you bloody want?'

'Then Carol said: "What are you going to do then—effing join her in the Great Bloody Upstairs?" Then I heard a scuffle and Carol told him to "bloody well sod off". And that's when I went up to sort them out.'

'And what did you see?'

'Mike was just getting up off the ground,' said Sutton. 'I got the impression that Carol might have pushed him over. Mike was rubbing the back of his head. Mind you,' Sutton added cautiously, 'perhaps Carol hadn't pushed him, so I'd rather you didn't quote me on that. It *was* just an impression.'

After the altercation between Taunton and Haldane, Sutton returned to the kitchen. Haldane followed him after a minute or so, and that her argument with Taunton had continued in undertones during that time was evidenced by her parting shot back up the steps just before she entered the kitchen: 'I told you: sod off,' she had shouted.

'And that was the last you heard?'

'Yes,' said Sutton. 'She came in then. She was white and shaken. I asked if she wanted a coffee; she didn't answer. Just shook her head and went off upstairs. She was very drunk.'

'What then, sir?'

'I took up Jenny's coffee, came back with the dog and let him have his nightly wander in the garden.'

'You didn't hear him barking?'

'No,' said Sutton. 'Nothing at all. That's why I thought Mike had gone down the garden. Then I locked up and set the alarms. My sister and I watched the late film on the television and went to bed soon after midnight. And that's all I can tell you.'

It all sounded very plausible, and there was no real reason why it shouldn't be. Except that Roper's intuition still wouldn't bend to the idea that Michael Taunton had committed suicide. Not completely.

He turned back a few pages of his notebook, mulled over one or two earlier entries he had made.

'You said, Mr Sutton: "Mike was just getting up off the ground." Was that concrete ground, or grass ground?'

'I can't be sure,' replied Sutton. 'It was dark. But I think he was getting up from the edge of the lawn.'

'And you think Miss Haldane might have given him a shove?'

'Possibly,' said Sutton. 'But that's only an idea. Mind you, in the state Mike was in he wouldn't have taken much pushing over.'

'And he was rubbing the back of his head, you say.'

'Definitely,' said Sutton. 'And now I come to think about it, he looked a bit dazed.'

Roper wrote 'concrete'. That bump on Taunton's head had never been caused by falling backwards on to grass.

'SORRY,' said Jennifer Sutton, with a shrug. 'I honestly can't help you at all. I was upstairs all evening. I washed my hair, had a bath and watched the television. I take one evening off a week and I switch off completely.'

'And you didn't hear anything?'

'No,' she said, 'nothing—no, that's not quite true. I heard Carol Haldane come up. But I don't know what time that was. She slammed her door hard enough to jar the house.'

'You had no windows open?'

'Only at the front of the house. We can't have the windows at the back open on summer evenings because of the midges that come off the lake.'

'And your brother was up here with you?'

'Yes,' she agreed. 'From soon after ten o'clock. Although he did go down once or twice to the kitchen. He brought me up a cup of coffee at about ten to eleven and told me that there'd been a hell of a shindig down in the garden between Carol and Mike. I gave him the keys to lock up and he took the dog down with him.'

'What time did your brother come back upstairs, Miss Sutton?'

'Finally? ... Oh, about five past eleven, I suppose. As near as I remember.'

'And neither of you left your flat after that?'

She shook her head. 'No,' she said. 'Absolutely not.'

'And you had the keys back?'

'Yes,' she said.

Roper back-tracked. 'You told my sergeant that Mr Taunton used your typewriter yesterday evening. That right?'

'Yes,' she said, nodding.

'Did he say why?'

'No.'

Roper felt himself going up one dead end after another. Taunton *had* used the typewriter last night, ergo: he *had* typed that suicide note—as much as that idea was militated against by Roper's better judgement. The cause of that bump on his head was more than likely the shove that Haldane had given him. The shoeprints on the tarpaulin and the window sill matched the sole of Taunton's trainers. And if Wilson turned up later this afternoon and pronounced a finding of suicide, then Roper had no argument to counter him with. And yet Roper's gut told him all the time that something was way off target.

'What did you know about Michael Taunton, Miss Sutton? Do you know where he was living before he came here? When did you take him on?'

'He came here a few weeks before last Christmas. During the snow. He'd been working across at Southampton—a Wimpy bar, I think he said.'

'And you simply took him on?' Roper softly clicked finger and thumb. 'Just like that? No reference, no recommendations!'

'Yes,' she admitted. 'More or less. He looked exhausted—he'd been on the road for several days—and the weather was terrible. He was looking for work in exchange for bed and board.'

'You surprise me, Miss Sutton,' said Roper. 'A house like this, with a price tag hanging from practically everything—I'd say that very pocketable figurine on the shelf up there would be worth a month's wages to someone like Taunton.'

'It wasn't like that,' she said. 'Not for the first few weeks. The furthest he came into the house was the kitchen. He slept across at the lodge; we had him painting the inside woodwork over there.'

'Until you decided he was trustworthy? That it?'

'More or less. We had a meeting and decided to take him on permanently. Lewis found him particularly useful.'

'Did you know he was a drinker?'

She shook her head. 'No,' she said, 'certainly not. At least not at first.'

'But you kept him on—even when you knew about that?'

She made a small gesture with outspread hands. 'Yes,' she said, 'I suppose we did. But we were all he had. We could hardly turn him out—and he was useful. But he had become a *terrible* nuisance, just lately. We all thought so—except perhaps Carol.'

'When you say that you people here were all he had, Miss Sutton, is that a figure of speech—or what?'

'No,' she said. 'That's exactly how it was. He had no next of kin. No family.'

A suicide who conveniently had no next of kin. A typed confession written five or six hours before he had put the rope around his neck and kicked that ladder away. It didn't ring true; lacked—somehow—the hallmarks of authenticity.

'One last question, Miss Sutton: Is there any way young Taunton could have got hold of the keys to the Range Rover late on Tuesday night?'

'No,' she said. 'Definitely not. I distinctly remember taking them off the dresser hook when I locked up the kitchen.'

'Time?'

'A few minutes before eleven,' she said.

Roper sucked his breath in softly between his teeth. She sounded adamant. And if she was right...

'Oh, but wait a minute...' She was frowning, thinking, a fingertip pressed to her temple. 'No, it couldn't be...'

Roper leaned forward interestedly. '*What* couldn't be, Miss Sutton?'

'Well,' she said—but didn't sound too sure of herself, 'about three months ago, one of the car keys went missing. I never did find it. So I had another one cut. Probably doesn't mean anything, of course.'

'But Mr Taunton might just have found it and kept hold of it. Is that what you're saying?'

'Well...yes...That *is* just possible, isn't it?'

And Roper had to agree, grudgingly, that it was just possible.

ROPER, PRICE AND DS Makins, watched interestedly by Allan Sutton, spent the hour between two and three stripping Michael Taunton's room almost down to the floorboards. On the first floor of the lodge, the room was tatty and his possessions few. A cheap transistor radio, a quartz alarm clock, an electric shaver and a few grubby clothes in a scruffy wardrobe from which a door hung from one hinge and wouldn't stay shut. The only window looked out towards the east gateway. It seemed as if young Taunton had come from one slum to another.

Sutton watched from the only chair, an old kitchen chair, a clone to the green-painted one downstairs in his studio.

There was nothing of significance in any of Taunton's few pockets. His several pairs of frayed jeans were gone through, a scuffed fake-leather bomberjacket. There were no shoes in the wardrobe, so the only pair he had possessed were those trainers. A comb on the cabinet beside the bed was tangled with hairs. On the floor beside it was a plastic lemonade bottle half full of what turned out to be only water.

'Disgusting, isn't it?' commented Sutton from his perch on the chair. 'But it's all down to him. He promised to keep it tidy himself—but it looks as if he never did, doesn't it?'

'You and your sister never came up here to inspect it, sir?' asked Roper.

'Our interest stops at the guest rooms for the students,' said Sutton. 'We credited Mike with being able to keep this place tidy himself.'

Roper ran a finger along the window sill. It came away grey.

Price was putting Taunton's clothes back into the wardrobe.

'Might be worth looking behind it,' said Roper. 'You never know.'

Price and Makins shouldered one end of the wardrobe away from the wall. The dust of years clung to the floral-patterned wallpaper behind it.

'Nothing,' said Makins.

'Hang on,' said Price. With the toecap of his shoe, he was hooking forward something he had noticed sticking out *under* the wardrobe. It was an envelope. Roper crouched and picked it up. Postmarked in Southwark a month or so ago, it was addressed to Taunton.

'I wasn't aware that he ever received any letters,' observed Sutton.

'Obviously he did, sir,' said Roper, taking out the letter from the envelope.

Dear Mr Taunton[he read],

We thank you for your recent application for a post with our company, but regret that your lack of formal qualifications and the present economic climate . . .

The writer had been the personnel manager of a furniture manufacturers. It wasn't even worth putting aside as evidence. Just an inch-mark in a young man's life, that was all. Roper put it on the window sill.

All that remained was the unmade bed. It smelled of unwashed male.

'Strip it,' ordered Roper.

A stained coverlet, a reasonably clean blanket and sheet, an undersheet and another blanket. Nothing untoward tucked away out of sight. Makins peeled the cases off the two pillows, felt around the faded, striped ticking. 'Nothing,' he said.

Price lifted a corner of the blue-and-white striped mattress.

'What's that bit of wire?' said Roper, as it caught his eye—a small hook of galvanised iron wire hanging over one of the bedsprings, close to the head end of the bed. Price lifted the mattress higher while Makins unhooked it and passed it to Roper.

A short length of wire shaped like a butcher's hook. From its other end dangled a key.

An ignition key.

Allan Sutton confirmed that it was the long-lost key to the Range Rover.

'You're sure, sir?'

'Yes,' said Sutton, handing it back. 'Absolutely.'

THE FINAL NAIL was hammered into the coffin of Roper's theories soon after four o'clock that afternoon.

Wilson's voice crackled tinnily over a dozen miles of telephone line. 'I'd say the boy hanged himself, Mr Roper. That's *my* verdict—and I'm afraid it's the one I'll have to give the coroner. The bruising around his throat and neck is entirely consistent with his body weight—and so's the depth of bruising.' Wilson paused for Roper's reaction. And when none was evinced, he said, 'Am I right in assuming that the silence I detect is one of disappointment?'

'Could be,' said Roper. 'With respect to you, Mr Wilson, I've still got a few doubts. Something in my water tells me he didn't murder Vera Jackman. And if he didn't, what reason did he have for hanging himself?'

'Ah, now, that's up to you to work out,' said Wilson. 'My business is to find out the whats; not the whys. The only fishy item is that lump on his skull—but that certainly didn't kill him.'

'We already know how that happened,' said Roper. 'His lady-friend pushed him over and he hit his head.'

'And *that* wouldn't have been difficult for her,' said Wilson. 'If he'd been taken for a blood test last night the result would have been so many millilitres of blood in litres of alcohol. Frankly, I'm surprised that he managed to tie a decent knot without botching it.'

'*And* stand on a step ladder—and then kick it away,' Roper added with a touch of irony. 'Quite a balancing trick for a drunken young lad, don't you reckon?'

'True,' agreed Wilson. 'And don't think I don't see your point. But the facts say he did. Sorry. Can't twist the facts, can we, Mr Roper? I'll have a copy of my notes typed out and sent around to you tomorrow. All right?'

'Yes, Mr Wilson. Thanks,' said Roper, a gritty tiredness in his voice that made it plain he had wanted another conclusion entirely. 'Much obliged.'

He laid the telephone back on its rest, left his hand crabbed over it for a moment or two, then reached across the table for a new notepad and drew it in front of him. He uncapped his ballpoint pen, paused briefly to light a cheroot, let his mind go blank while he took the first few puffs, then began to write.

HE SLUMPED BACK tiredly in the chair and dragged finger and thumb together across leaden eyelids. It was eight-thirty. Friday night and the weekend looming up and a long way past the forty-eight hour deadline that he had demanded in here on Wednesday. Something, somewhere, was staring him in the face and he lacked the wit to see it; or perhaps, he told himself, he had failed to take that leap of the imagination that might turn the bizarre into the obvious.

Of the ten sheets of A4 notepaper that he had used, seven were balled in the wastepaper bin by his right foot. Of the three remaining sheets, one was headed MATERIAL EVIDENCE and twice underlined. The material evidence was pitifully scant: a valve cap, a handful of grass, a couple of soleprints, a typed suicide note, an open window that shouldn't have been. The window catch had borne—prodigally—Michael Taunton's fingerprints. But so had all the other window catches in Huxley's workshop—and the padlock on the door and the starter-button on the switch box of the circular saw and most of the tools besides. More to the point, half an hour ago Roper had learned that both the envelope and the note that Taunton had left behind had been subjected to an iodine-fume test. This had revealed that both bore, unmistakably, the forefinger and the thumbprints of his right hand. There had been no prints on the ignition key—but Taunton could have wiped them off.

In the face of that much evidence Roper knew that pretty soon he would have to shut the case up. Budgets were ruthlessly nit-picked these days. And when a mere gut feeling was outweighed by the cold facts, orders were to pull out. A gut feeling in those circumstances cost ratepayers good money.

It was up to the coroner's jury to decide whether or not young Taunton had hanged himself; Roper's job was only to warn them—or not—that foul play might be involved. And he could not. Like everyone else, he would have to settle for Taunton committing suicide, not so much because it could be proved but because it could not be proved that he had not. And if that happened, it would stick in Roper's craw for ever. Like most policemen, over the years he had trodden paths which were pocked with unsolved cases, but that wasn't the same as getting the answer wrong.

The second sheet of notepaper in front of Roper carried a tentative list of names: Allan Sutton, Lewis Huxley, Adrian Dance, Thruxton, Taunton.

The third sheet was the last remaining one of those that Roper had earlier crumpled and tossed into his waste bin. Whittled down from the others that had preceded it, it carried a tentative scenario for the events of Tuesday night. As yet the only name written was Vera Jackman's. Her killer was merely X, the algebraic cypher for the unknown, and for the time being would have to remain so. Roper could probably have labelled him Mr X, but forebore to as yet. And if Michael Taunton had indeed committed suicide, then that sheet of paper—the only plausible scenario left regarding the murder of Jackman, would have to follow its seven progenitors into the bin. That was the trouble with suicides—they usually took their motives with them.

Across the hall Price, who had been sifting through the typewritten transcriptions of the shorthand notes taken by the WPC during the day at Cort Place, leaned back in his chair and stretched and yawned. In the far corner, the WPC manning the radio and the switchboard was reading a paperback and doing her best to look awake. A cadet was gathering in the evening's harvest of plastic cups, in most of which lay a soggy cigarette end or two.

'Come up with anything?' asked Roper.

Price shook his head. His eyes were bloodshot from reading too long in the poor light.

'Not a dicky-bird,' he said. 'Wish I had. It all ties up.'

And that, Roper thought, was exactly the phrase that bothered him, the one that had crept into his own mind all too often during the course of the evening. Everything did, indeed, tie up.

Which was all very nice and cosy and kept the paperwork tidy. Except that Roper—who believed in luck and frequently prayed for it—was wary of it when it was heaped upon him in such fortuitous quantities.

That much luck was yet another suspicious circumstance.

FOURTEEN

ROPER PICKED UP his half of bitter and his change and
fought his way out of the rowdy press around the bar.
Friday night in the Cort Arms was obviously gala
night.

Holding his jug high, he wended his way between
the tables and round the end of the bar towards the
open doorway to the garden. Fairy lights hung from
the trees and the festive glow was reinforced by a couple of small floodlights. Leaving the noise behind him,
Roper started across the grass. She was sitting alone at
a white-painted wrought-iron table in the corner where
two walls met and was reading a paperback that she
held tipped towards the light from one of the floods.

'Do you mind if I join you, Miss Haldane?'

She glanced up at him with her usual inimitable
chill, saw who he was and looked even more glacial.
'I can't stop you, can I?' She flapped a hand towards
the bench on Roper's side of the table. 'Be my guest.'
The curt invitation delivered, she picked up her tumbler—it looked like whisky in it—and returned to the
company of her book.

Roper sipped the froth from his bitter. Carol Haldane put her tumbler down and, still reading, plucked
her last Gauloise from its packet on the table and then
reached for her lighter beside it. She seemed determined, having met Roper's eye the once, not to do it
again.

Roper lit a cheroot and from time to time took a swig of his beer. Haldane sipped, smoked and read as if he wasn't there. Her Gauloise burned down almost to her fingertips. Still concentrating on her book, her hand found the ashtray and crushed out the cigarette. Somewhere in the bar a glass was smashed and there was a brief moment of silence; but the hum of chatter soon started up again when everybody realised that it was only an accident and not a fight starting.

Carol Haldane's hand went to the Gauloise packet again. A quick grimace of irritation twitched her mouth as she realised it was empty. She glanced over her shoulder, as if she intended to go to the counter to buy some more. The crowd around the bar door obviously decided her to wait for a while until it thinned out.

Roper produced his cheroot packet, opened it and stretched his arm so that it was impossible for her to ignore it. Her eyelids lifted. Her gaze took in the packet, swung upward—and regarded Roper at some length while she resolved the deep inner conflict between her views about policemen and her craving for nicotine.

Grudgingly, at last, her hand rose and her finger and thumb made a beak around the end of a cheroot.

'Thanks,' she said.

Roper struck his lighter.

She leaned across towards the flame. 'Thanks,' she said again, exhaling smoke. She closed her book—*War and Peace,* Roper saw now—and picked up her tumbler. For a few seconds she went to cover behind it. Roper sipped at his beer. The hubbub from the bar rose and fell.

'You're on duty, I'll bet,' she said.

'Never off it,' said Roper, over the rim of his jug. 'One of the penalties of being a copper.'

'You're breaking my bloody heart.'

Roper smiled. 'I don't give a bugger what people think of me, Miss Haldane.'

'It's not just the Pigs I don't like,' she said. 'So it's nothing personal. I don't like authority *per se*.'

'Well, thank you for that at least, Miss Haldane,' said Roper. 'I presume by authority you mean people who want to know more about you than you're prepared to tell 'em.'

'Something like that.'

'And the folk who make the rules?'

'Right.'

Roper took a long sip of his bitter. 'And the odd body lying in the gutter never gets you thinking?'

'Of course it bloody does.'

'How about Vera Jackman's?'

She shrugged, unruffled. '*She* asked for it. *She* was stupid. You can push a guy so far—even the nice ones. She'd have done better to keep her knees together all the time instead of only part of it.'

'But you don't really *know* that she didn't.'

She narrowed her eyes against the pungent smoke of her cheroot and leaned closer. 'I'm not blind, sport. I've seen her stripped; remember? Bruises on her legs, love-bites on her neck, the odd scratch or two on her back.'

'Lately?'

'No. Not lately.'

'When?'

'A couple of months—about.'

A muted roar of triumph from the bar sounded like the darts team whooping it up.

'Taunton?' said Roper.

'He never got that close.'

'He told you that?'

'More or less.'

'Who then?'

She dragged in smoke and tapped her cheroot against the rim of the ashtray that advertised somebody's fruit juices. 'What do I get for guessing?' she said.

'A couple of Brownie points,' said Roper. 'That's the best I can do.'

For the first time Roper saw her smile and her hostile veneer crumbled a little. So she wasn't quite so tough after all. The smile died. She leaned close again. 'Mike didn't kill her,' she said. 'Mike couldn't have killed anybody. He was too bloody soft. And that's the God-honest truth.'

'Give me a name then. That guess you promised me.'

The forefinger of her left hand slowly circled the rim of her tumbler. 'I can't,' she said. 'Not in the particular. But *somebody* bought her a gold cross. One of the men at the house—and it couldn't have been Mike because he couldn't have afforded it. When she came to the house one afternoon she wasn't wearing it—a couple of hours later she was. If Mike was still here he'd tell you the same—she flashed it at him, you know? Just to let him know he was wasting his time crawling about after her.'

'I know about the cross, Miss Haldane. Taunton told me about it. It was shown on the television programmes last night. There's been no response.'

'Then I'm sorry,' she said. 'I can't help.'

'You had someone in mind, though, didn't you, Miss Haldane?' urged Roper.

She shook her head. 'No,' she said. 'Just whoever bought Vera that cross.'

'That note Taunton left; it was nigh on a confession.'

She picked up her glass and swirled the liquid in it, but didn't drink. Instead, she drew back into the shadows of the wall so that her face was only a grey oval in the dark. 'Then somebody else wrote it,' she said. 'It wasn't Mike.'

'But he used that typewriter. You and Miss Sutton both confirmed that.'

'He often used it.'

Roper's jug, rising to his mouth, paused at his chin. 'Often, Miss Haldane?'

'Fairly often. A couple of times a week he wrote for a job somewhere. I know because I helped him draft a standard letter a couple of months back. And he never got a single reply, poor little sod.'

'I think he did, Miss Haldane. I think he just didn't want you to see them, that's all. Pride, perhaps. We found a reply to one in his bedroom this afternoon.'

Roper sipped at his beer, Haldane at her whisky.

'Perhaps he used the typewriter to write for another job?' he said.

'Could be,' she said. 'But he was with me the rest of the evening, and he didn't post it. So it must still be about somewhere.'

'Or someone's destroyed it,' said Roper, sipping again.

'Well, whatever,' she said. 'But Mike didn't have *anything* to confess to, and you'd better believe it.'

'We found a spare key to the Rover in his room, too. One Miss Sutton reckons she lost a few weeks ago.'

She shrugged. 'So what?'

'Jackman's body was transported from Cort Place to Church Lane. Somehow. And Taunton was the only man who wouldn't be missed from the house for the hour or so after Jackman was murdered.'

'True,' she agreed. She slowly drained her tumbler, set it down, pushed it away. 'Case closed then. That it?'

'It looks that way.'

'Jenny won't be sorry. Cost her a few days' takings, all this business.'

'And she cares about that, does she?'

Her nose twitched. 'Damned right she does. The old ancestral home has to be kept going regardless. She's a right fanatic about that place, is our Jen. Bloody obsessed.'

'She can hardly complain, can she? All this free publicity she's getting in the dailies.'

'It's scandal, sport. She hates that. She doesn't even really approve of the tourists; but she needs 'em to bring in the cash. No cash, no Cort Place; savvy?'

Roper savvied.

'That row you and young Taunton had the other night...'

'What about it?'

'Something you said. Something about Taunton joining Vera Jackman in the Great Upstairs. Can you remember why you said that?'

'I told you. He was being stupid. He was beefing about being a jinx. Said he brought bad luck to everybody. Said if it hadn't been for him, Vera Jackman might still be alive.'

'Why would he say that, d'you reckon?'

'Nothing significant,' she said. 'It was Mike who put a word in for Vera with Jen. Got her the job at the house. You know? She was his girlfriend then or he thought she was. I think he chatted her up one night in the Cort Arms. Within a couple of days she was working for Jen. I think Mike thought that if Vera hadn't come to work at Cort Place . . . well, you know what I mean.'

'Nothing deeper than that, then?'

'No,' she said. 'I don't think so.'

Roper slowly finished his beer. 'You said that Jennifer Sutton was obsessed with Cort Place.'

'She is. Living there's like a cross between being in school and being in the nick. I'm getting out myself, soon. I've learned a lot off Allan, mind, he's a nice guy; but her, she's a cow. One of her precious bits of china gets moved a half-inch and she nearly hits the roof. When she thought Allan was going to sell up she came racing back from the States quicker than Concorde. She goes around with those keys each night like a bloody gaoler. The Dances aren't happy there, either. Rachael especially.'

'How about the Thruxtons?'

'She's a nice lady. He's a rat. He even tried to work his charm on me when I first came here.' She made a thumbs-down gesture. 'Zilch. He's a bloody good sculptor, maybe, but as a man he's bloody wet. Jenny, of course, thinks the sun shines out of him. He's upper crust. Ex-public-school, and his father owns a bloody great slab of Northumberland. When he gets within a couple of inches of Jenny, she goes all ga-ga. Simpers like a bloody schoolgirl.'

'And Lewis Huxley? What about him?'

She flapped a hand. 'He's OK. Lives for his work. A loner; you know?'

Roper finished his beer. She watched him. 'How did you know I'd be here?' she said.

'I was on my way for a crafty pint. I saw you come out of Cort Place. I followed you. I thought a quiet chat might be useful.'

'And was it?'

'Very,' he said.

'You know,' she said, 'copper or not, I reckon you're pretty shrewd. I reckon you know something you're not letting on about. Like, for instance, Mike didn't string himself up like that on his own. Like he didn't kill Vera Jackman. Like Mike was done in the way *she* was. I'm right, aren't I?'

'I can't answer that, Miss Haldane,' said Roper. 'Wish I could.'

'Come on,' she urged. She reached across the table and screwed up a handful of his jacket cuff. 'Restore some of my faith in human nature. Find out who killed Mike. The girl, I couldn't care less about. But find out who killed poor old Mike. Will you?'

ROPER WALKED BACK slowly across the green. If he went home now he knew that he would never sleep because something told him that he was getting close. The whys were obvious, the wheres were proven, the choices of the who had been pared down to four. He had asked all the right questions, but somewhere along the line he had been given a few wrong answers.

Jollyboy's Metro was parked on the grass beneath a street lamp a few yards beyond the gateway of the church hall. Jollyboy himself was in the hall, talking with Price down at the far end by the scene-of-crime photographs. Price had his jacket on as if he had been on the point of going home.

'Don't you ever sleep, Sergeant?'

'Just hanging about for the pubs to shut, sir,' said Jollyboy. 'Usual Friday night routine.'

A twenty-four-hour a day man was Jollyboy. Probably policed close to fifty square miles around these parts all on his own. It depressed Roper sometimes when he realised that all the old stalwarts like Jollyboy were slowly dying off and being replaced by young lads with GCEs, degrees and God knows what; and who were still wet behind the ears for all that.

'Mr Price here says you're wrapping it up,' said Jollyboy.

'Got to,' said Roper. 'Lack of evidence. But maybe we'll open up again after the inquest. Depends what the coroner says.'

'*You* don't reckon young Taunton's note was on the level, then?'

'Bloody right, I don't,' said Roper grimly.

THEN IT WAS NEARLY eleven o'clock. Jollyboy had gone to keep an eye on turning-out time and Price had signed off and gone home. Roper had stayed, sifting through statements, checking times, smoking a cheroot that at this time of a hot summer night tasted foul and metallic. He ground it out and promised himself that he would never light another—although of course he would, because he always did. The night sergeant brought him a cup of coffee and a couple of digestive biscuits on a saucer.

'Thanks,' said Roper. 'I'm looking for inspiration, son. Know where I can get some?'

'I read once that inspiration mostly comes from perspiration,' said the sergeant. He was a thin, dour young man, who had sought to make himself more impressive with a dense black beard and a pair of steel-framed spectacles. 'Perhaps you ought to sleep on it. Nothing much can be done before the morning, can it, sir?'

'It's all here, son,' grumbled Roper, between sips of coffee, angry with his own failure to put two and two together and make it come to four. 'Evidence. All we're likely to bloody get. And on Tuesday, I've got to prove to a coroner that young Taunton didn't do himself in when all the evidence says he did.'

A quarter of an hour later, fortified by the biscuits and revived by the coffee, Roper was standing in front of the photographs. A few feet away, the radio came sporadically to life. A stolen car or two, a knifing in a Cosmo café on the road to Charmouth—ambulance called—two arrests, a domestic—wife cracked late-returning husband over his head with a transistor radio—ambulance called, no further action; all the usual aggravation of late-night coppering.

These were the kind of photographs that the public never saw. Death in the most gruesome round, death with a dirty face. Roper had seen it all too often to let it haunt him, but it still didn't leave him cold. From kids to the old ones, all had an allotted span, however long or short that was, and nobody had a right to shorten it except as a kindness. But these two faces had been done a kindness by no one. Vera Jackman, whatever she might have done, hadn't deserved to die looking like that. And nor had young Taunton.

It was only Roper's job to bring villains to justice, not to mete it out, thank God, but there were times...

Taunton's jeans had been worn through at both knees. His feet had been turned inward, toes together, heels apart. The left training shoe, the one that had stepped in the puddle on the tarpaulin and left the prints behind, was coming apart at the toe. Both legs of the jeans were frayed where they had rubbed over Taunton's insteps. Sloppy, Roper thought. In his younger days, a lad would never go out with a girl in scruffy clobber like that, even to a pub. Nowadays it seemed to be the norm.

The shoes had been shot separately, in close-up, Taunton's swollen feet still inside them. From on top, and underneath. Beside the underneath views was a life-size enlargement of the soleprint on that window ledge in Huxley's workshop. A perfect match. Two peas from the same pod.

But the shoes weren't.

Roper bent closer to the photograph. Then closer still.

He clicked his finger and thumb loudly. 'Sergeant. Magnifying glass—got one? If you haven't there's one on Mrs Greenaway's table somewhere. Sharpish.'

The sergeant's chair scraped on the parquet. On the radio a foot patrolman was calling up the fire brigade—

'Here, sir.' A hefty reading glass was slapped into Roper's outstretched hand like a scalpel.

'Thanks.'

The photograph of Taunton's feet in their grubby trainers loomed larger. Roper peered. Left one. Right one.

Then he closed his eyes tightly and screwed up his face. Hell's bloody teeth! Fool he was! Blind! Woolly-minded!

'Sergeant!'

'Sir!'

Roper tossed him the keys to the interview-cum-junk room.

'Taunton's trainers—in the cupboard beside the radiator. Fetch 'em.'

Ten minutes later, Roper had roused the ACC from sleep, and five minutes after that there was no question of shutting-up shop tomorrow.

There were no two ways about it. Michael Taunton had *definitely* been murdered.

The knots on his trainer laces had been tied by two different hands.

FIFTEEN

SATURDAY MORNING. Half-past nine of Day Four. Hot again and muggy and not a breath of air stirring anywhere. Roper had been here since eight o'clock, writing steadily enough to have filled four sheets of A4 by nine o'clock. None of them, this time, had been consigned to his wastepaper bin, and only here and there had a word been crossed out in favour of an apter one.

Mr X was still Mr X, so it was still a lucky dip—only now the bran tub was smaller. Beside Roper on the table, perhaps as *aides-mémoire* or perhaps as macabre bringers of more good luck, lay Michael Taunton's insalubrious training shoes in their clear polythene bags.

Over in the far corner the switchboard chirruped. Makins answered it. The duty crew here this morning was down to the bare minimum: Roper, Price, Makins, a uniformed sergeant and a WPC.

'It's for you, Super,' called Makins. 'Miss Sutton. Shall I put her through? She wants to know if she can open the house to visitors today.'

'Tell her, yes. But not Huxley's workshop. And tell her we might be across later.'

Makins hunched back over the telephone, right hand gesticulating. All the wits back at County swore that if Makins' right hand was cut off he'd lose the gift of speech altogether. It was also said that Makins—

and Makins readily agreed—had power over women, that he could melt even the iciest ones with his rough-diamond charm. But his charm had obviously failed on Jennifer Sutton this morning; he winced dramatically and held the phone at arm's length before he let it clatter back on to its rest and shook his fingers to cool them.

'What did she say?' called Roper.

'She was not pleased, sir,' said Makins. 'Definitely on the tart side. Says if any of us turn up during opening hours, would we please not do so in uniform. I said we'd do our best, but you were busy so I couldn't promise anything. And that's when it sounded like she'd thrown her phone on the floor and stamped on it. I think her last word was "balls", sir—very genteely delivered.'

Nor was DI Price idle that Saturday morning. By ten o'clock, he too had come up with a theory or two of his own based upon Roper's chance discovery late last night.

'It's got to be Huxley,' said Price. 'If you think about it, he's the only one over there physically capable of stringing up Taunton on his own.'

And Roper had to agree with that. Huxley was certainly physically capable. 'I'm still listening.'

'Assuming he killed Jackman—just assuming,' Price ventured cautiously, 'he looks around for a scapegoat. He settles for Michael Taunton—because Taunton's a bit of an odd-ball anyway—and nobody's going to miss him except Carol Haldane, who's definitely another odd-ball. And Taunton had no next of kin to kick up a dust. On Thursday night, Huxley locks up his workshop as usual—but leaves that window open so that nobody has to see him take the keys off the dresser later on. He knows that Taunton is along at the Arms and likely to come back *non compos mentis*. He hangs about around the kitchen until Taunton comes back. He knows Taunton'll be with Haldane, so he waits for Haldane to come into the house, then goes after Taunton as Taunton goes down to the lodge. Huxley clouts Taunton over the back of the head, swings him over his shoulder and carries him across to the workshop. He fakes Taunton's suicide, opens that window, and as an afterthought decides to garnish the evidence a bit more by planting those shoeprints in a couple of likely places.'

'But how did he get back into the house without the others seeing him?' asked Roper. 'It would have been locked up by then, wouldn't it?'

'Simple,' said Price. 'He didn't.'

'You reckon he spent the night with Taunton's body dangling over his head?'

'Better than taking a chance of being seen sloping back to the house though, eh? And he could have slipped back into the house in the morning when nobody would have given him a second thought.'

Roper let smoke drift up beside his cheek. Price's scenario fitted in almost exactly with one of those that had finished up in Roper's wastepaper bin last night. It was close, but it wasn't right.

'And what about Tuesday night?'

'The same thing,' said Price. 'Jackman rings up Huxley. Tells him she wants to see him—perhaps even tells him she's pregnant—wants some help—some cash—something of that sort. And he either can't—or won't—and perhaps she threatens him. Perhaps they're along that path beside the dustbins. She upsets friend Huxley, the cable's lying on top of the rubbish, and it's the nearest thing to hand, so in temper he flings it around her neck and pulls it tight.

'And that's the point where it all breaks down,' Price admitted. 'He wouldn't have had the key to the Range Rover, would he?'

'Why not?' said Roper, willing to give Price his head even though the lad's theory might be wrong. 'Perhaps it was Huxley who had that spare key all the time. Perhaps it was Huxley who planted it under Taunton's bed.'

'Except,' said Price, retreating a little, 'we know that Huxley was back in the house at eleven o'clock on Tuesday because he and the Sutton woman saw each other when she was locking up. And she must have already locked up because she was switching on the alarm system.'

'She didn't exactly *say* she *saw* him, Dave,' Roper reminded him. 'She said, according to your notes: "I *think* so." She may not have seen him. Although he could have seen *her*. I mean he could have been outside the kitchen window, couldn't he? Seen her lock that back door and guessed how long it would have taken her to get back to the hall and switch on the alarm. He was pretty precise about the time, wasn't he?'

But Price was still in retreat. 'Problem,' he said. 'Taunton's note had his fingerprints on it, didn't it?'

'And it's very dodgy taking fingerprints from a corpse. Unless Huxley was very quick.'

Price brightened again. 'But if he'd got Taunton's fake suicide all mapped out, he *could* have been quick, couldn't he? He could have typed the note any time during the last couple of days and simply squeezed Taunton's finger and thumb on the paper and the envelope as soon as he'd killed him. The envelope was self-stick, so he wouldn't have had to worry about a saliva-test, would he?'

'True,' agreed Roper, again. But whereas Price had had only an hour or so to develop his possible scenario, Roper had slept on his. He turned his sheets of A4 round and slid them across to Price. 'As far as it goes. But try that on for size. I don't think you'll find it was friend Huxley—unless he bought Jackman that *ankh.*'

LUNCHTIME. And a kind of paralysis had set in. Roper had spent the morning pacing up and down outside the hall and smoking too much and swilling down more cups of coffee and tea than were good for him. Beyond the churchyard, in the real world, the sun was shining and on the green the Cort Abbas cricket team was measuring itself against another village and not giving a bad account of itself. When the breeze was in the right direction there came the occasional thunk of leather against willow and a desultory burst of hand-clapping. The grass was almost too green, the trees too full of leaf, the hedgerows too gaudily in flower. Across the green, the village shimmered in the heat of this quiet afternoon.

Price came out to stand at Roper's shoulder, at first screwing up his eyes at the bright sunshine. A ball was lofted skyward from the green and hung there for a seeming eternity.

'He's out,' said Price.

'It's a six,' said Roper.

A fielder at long-off made Price right and Roper wrong.

Another round of ragged applause saw that batsman off and greeted another one in.

'Sir?'

Roper looked along his shoulder. It was Sergeant Makins. A Sergeant Makins practically falling over himself with excitement.

'Telephone, sir. It's about that cross Vera Jackman was wearing. A lady up in Swindon reckons she's got one exactly like it. She's on the phone now, sir. Patched through from Swindon nick. Her name's Mrs Courtney.'

Roper strode back into the hall with Price and Makins hard on his heels.

'Which phone?' Roper felt the old familiar ripple of excitement. It was the last piece of the jigsaw, that *ankh.*

'Line One, sir. Beside the radio.'

Roper snatched it up. Plastered on a smile because even over the telephone a smile has a special sound and he could, if he wished, have been very angry with Mrs Courtney for wasting two days of his precious time...

'Good afternoon, Mrs Courtney. Superintendent Roper. What can I do for you?'

'Oh—er—good afternoon.' Mrs Courtney was nervous. In the background, her radio was playing and her dog was barking and somebody was ringing at her

doorbell. 'Excuse me a minute, will you? I'm so sorry.
There's someone at the door.'

Roper waited patiently while Mrs Courtney answered her summons and quietened her dog. There
was a rumble like thunder as she picked up her phone
again.

'Hello?' she said breathlessly. 'Are you still there?'

'I'm still here, Mrs Courtney.'

There was a long pause.

'Well...I was half watching the news the other
night...Wednesday, I think it was...or perhaps it was
Thursday...yes, it must have been Thursday because
I was leaving my daughter's...she lives in Winches-
ter...Well, my husband was bringing the car around
to the front of the house and I was just making sure
that we hadn't left anything behind...when I happened to notice what was on the television. The picture, I mean. And my daughter said, "Good Heavens,
Mummy, that looks just like yours,"—and do you
know, it *was*. Exactly!'

Roper, who had waited out stoically under the barrage of Mrs Courtney's circumlocution, took his
chance as she paused to draw breath. 'What was exactly like what, Mrs Courtney?'

'Oh...Didn't I say? The cross. The cross that they
showed on television. On Thursday. After the news.'

'And you have one like it, you say, Mrs Courtney?'

'Yes...Exactly...My husband bought it for me—
Our last fling.' She giggled nervously. 'He was made
redundant...his work...and we'd never been abroad
before and—'

'Mrs Courtney,' broke in Roper, and had to repeat
it twice more, the last time very firmly, before he fi-

nally reined her in. 'You said *abroad*, Mrs Courtney—whereabouts abroad?'

'Morocco,' she said. 'Tangier...We were in the Souk and there was this goldsmith...he was actually casting them, melting down little gold ingots, then chiselling the decoration into them...they're called *ankhs*, you know. They're supposed to be lucky. Like a charm.'

A pity it hadn't worked for Vera Jackman...

'How do you know that yours is exactly the same, Mrs Courtney? Is there some distinguishing mark that we haven't noticed? Something that might prove it had come from the same jeweller?'

'Oh, yes,' she said blithely. 'That little pattern on the bottom is his name. In Arabic. It looks like a pattern, only it isn't. If you look at it under a magnifying glass you'll see it's Arabic writing...very tiny...'

'Mrs Courtney, I want some photographs.'

'That's who I've just let in—a nice young man from our local police station. That's who was ringing the doorbell. *He's* come to photograph it.'

'Can you put him on the phone, Mrs Courtney, please? And before you go, do you mind telling me how much you paid for that cross?'

Mrs Courtney dithered. Two requests at once were obviously too many for her to deal with.

'How much, Mrs Courtney?'

'Well...we paid in dinars...but it was about £400.'

And he had thought it was just a cheap gewgaw. Ye gods!

'And now the officer who's just arrived, please, Mrs Courtney.'

DC Hoskins' brisk efficiency was like a breath of fresh air after the waffling Mrs Courtney. He had come armed with a Polaroid camera, a selection of close-up lenses, a small floodlight and a scale-rule.

'How soon? Sorry to push you.'

'About twenty minutes to take a decent set of pictures. My super says you're down at Cort Abbas, in Dorset—about fifty miles, say. I guess about two hours altogether. Motorcycle job.'

Roper shot his cuff. Twelve-thirty now. 'Do fine, old son. Much obliged. I'll expect your man about half-two.'

'Right, sir. Cheers.'

'Bye.'

Roper put the telephone down with a feeling of immeasurable relief. The *ankh* wasn't exactly unique, but there couldn't be all that many on mainland UK and few folk who went to Morocco were likely to blue £400 on something that looked like a piece of junk jewellery. But someone at Cort Place had—and it was the second worst mistake they were ever likely to make. Their ultimate one had been to leave it around Vera Jackman's neck after they had killed her.

IT WAS A FEW MINUTES after half-past two. Roper heard the motorcycle pull up in the lane, the harsh intrusive roar of its exhaust as its rider gave one last twist to his accelerator before he dismounted and kicked down the stand. His steel-shod footfall crunched up the gravel path. He paused in the doorway.

'Superintendent Roper?'

'That's me, son.'

From deep inside his blue waterproof the motorcyclist fished out a buff envelope.

'Superintendent Parker's compliments, sir.' Under his white helmet his face was beaded with perspiration. 'Sorry I'm a bit late: got held up in the holiday traffic.'

Roper was already ripping open the envelope. 'It's all right son. Relax a bit, get your gear off. See that WPC over there and she'll give you a cuppa.'

Roper shot the photographs out on to his table, turned them all up the right way and laid them out in a line. Mrs Greenaway, called in from a quiet Saturday afternoon in her garden, joined him and Price and Makins and Jollyboy with the artefact in question, drawn from the Regional Forensic Laboratory's safe on her way here. Roper poured cross and chain into his palm and laid them down carefully beneath the photographs.

'It's a dead ringer,' said Price.

Roper was less ready to commit himself. The time for guessing was past. DC Hoskins had laid a ruler alongside the *ankh* each time he had photographed it and the pictures were twice life size. Roper compared the arm and the looped upright of the cross with a plastic ruler. They appeared to be identical. And given that the two *ankhs* were crude castings, incised and finished by hand and probably several months apart, they were a remarkably good match. Under a magnifying glass, the Arabic hieroglyphs on the base of the upright of Vera Jackman's *ankh* were unmistakably the same as the ones on Mrs Courtney's. But Roper still had Mrs Greenaway check Jackman's *ankh* under her microscope before he was prepared to concede that the two crosses were made by one and the same hand.

And they were. Beyond all reasonable doubt.

SIXTEEN

CAROL HALDANE had a kettle on the boil and was spooning instant coffee into a mug. The rest of the commune were assembled around the scrubbed whitewood table in the kitchen and watching Roper thumb through their passports. It was five o'clock on that same Saturday evening.

'You don't have a passport, Miss Haldane?'

'I don't travel,' she said, over her shoulder. 'I've never been able to afford it.'

Roper stacked the seven passports and slid them sideways towards Price, who was sitting beside him, the most relevant passport on top. Roper's face gave nothing away.

'I presume you're worried that we might all leave the country,' said Thruxton loudly.

'Yes, sir,' said Roper. 'Something like that.' He took out his notebook and opened it at a fresh page. Adrian Dance fiddled with his spectacles. Allan Sutton chewed at the stem of his pipe. Thruxton, sprawled in his chair, drummed a persistent tattoo with his fingernails on the tabletop. His wife was her usual anxious self; Jennifer Sutton coolly self-contained and slightly superior.

Roper looked up with the air of a man who intends to draw everything to as swift a conclusion as possible.

'I'd better start by telling you that Michael Taunton was murdered,' he said.

The reaction was immediate. Some surprise. Some horror. Some doubt.

'Rubbish,' said Thruxton.

'He hanged himself,' said Huxley. 'We all saw him, for God's sake.'

'And his footprints were on the window ledge, weren't they?' came quietly but assuredly from Allan Sutton. 'Surely that indicates that he *must* have hanged *himself?*'

'Well, yes, sir, it would,' agreed Roper. 'But we didn't find any footprints—strictly speaking. Just a couple of soleprints from his left shoe.'

'Bloody semantics,' scoffed Thruxton. 'Footprints, soleprints—what the hell's the difference?'

'A lot of difference, Mr Thruxton,' said Roper. 'If it had been a footprint, then I'd have to agree that Taunton made it. But it was a shoeprint. And anybody can make a shoeprint.'

'Including Mike,' persisted Thruxton.

'Sir...' Roper hunched forward over the table. He definitely did not like William Thruxton. When Thruxton was in the offing Roper found it difficult to be impartial. Mrs Thruxton deserved better. And since Roper had already clocked up sixty hours on duty this week it needed little to take the edge off his patience. 'The prints were made with Taunton's left shoe—but Michael Taunton wasn't in it at the time. The laces were tied differently, you see, sir. The knots weren't the same.'

There was a moment of hubbub around the table. Carol Haldane, alone, was not party to it. She sat down with her mug of coffee and held her lighter to another Gauloise.

'Which means,' said Roper—and the silence did not so much fall again as come to meet him—'that Taunton was murdered.'

Carol Haldane's lighter snapped shut. Measured against the silence it sounded like a pistol shot.

'Perhaps he tied the knot differently because he was drunk,' Mrs Thruxton suggested helpfully.

'Hardly, Mrs Thruxton. We all learn to tie our shoelaces when we're youngsters. After that, whichever way we learned to do it, we're stuck with it—drunk or sober.'

'All right, so he was murdered.' This was from Lewis Huxley. 'But if he was, then somebody from outside did it. Has to be that way.'

'Taunton's note was typed on Miss Sutton's machine, Mr Huxley.'

'But Mike did type that note, Superintendent,' chimed in Jennifer Sutton.

'No, madam,' said Roper. 'He may have typed something—but it wasn't that note.'

'I agree with Lewis,' said Thruxton. 'It couldn't have been one of us. We can all account for each other.'

'No, sir,' said Roper. 'Nobody can account for Mr Huxley on Thursday night, for instance. Isn't that right, Mr Huxley?'

'Allan can,' snapped Huxley. 'He saw me in the kitchen on Thursday night a couple of minutes before I went up to bed. We spoke to each other.'

'But who went upstairs first, Mr Huxley? You or Mr Sutton?'

'He did. He took a tray up to his sister.'

'And you followed him?'

'Yes.'

'Or did you, Mr Huxley? *Did* you go upstairs after him, or did you go out to the garden instead? And perhaps hide yourself somewhere to see what developed between Taunton and Miss Haldane?'

'What the hell for?' snapped Huxley. 'Whatever they were quarrelling about was none of my business, was it?'

'Can you type, Mr Huxley?' asked Roper.

'With two fingers, yes,' said Huxley. 'Why?'

'Did you type anything on Thursday—or Wednesday even?'

'No,' said Huxley. 'Definitely not. Besides, if I want anything typed I usually get Mrs Thruxton to do it for me.'

'Where did you sleep on Tuesday night, sir?' asked Price.

'In my room.'

'Not in your workshop?'

'Certainly not.'

'Did you go *out* on *Tuesday* night—about ten to eleven?'

'I told you. No. Ask the others.'

'But they wouldn't know, would they? If you hadn't wanted them to.'

Huxley considered that, then with great patience asked: 'How long would I have been out—if I had been out?'

'About twenty minutes,' said Price. 'Perhaps half an hour. Perhaps even all night.'

'Then the others *would* know,' said Huxley. 'I would have had to ring the doorbell to get back in again. And that doorbell'd wake the bloody dead.'

'Not if you'd stayed out all night, sir.'

'Which I bloody didn't.'

'—Is that right, Mr Sutton?' broke in Roper. 'You and Mr Huxley saw each other in the kitchen on Thursday night?'

'Yes,' agreed Sutton.

'Did you see the going of him, sir? I mean, do you know if he went upstairs or out to the garden?'

'Well...' Sutton shifted uncomfortably on his chair, not quite sure where his loyalties ought to lie. 'When I came back down after taking up Jenny's tray, I didn't see the sandwiches Lewis had been cutting, so I assumed he'd gone upstairs.'

'You only assumed?'

Sutton looked across apologetically at Huxley. 'Yes,' he said. 'I *assumed.*'

'But *you* say, Mr Huxley, that later you saw Miss Haldane here going into her room—after you heard her and Taunton arguing in the garden. Did *you* see Mr Huxley on that occasion, Miss Haldane?'

'No,' she said. 'Sorry, Lewis, but I didn't.'

Huxley looked bemused. 'Look,' he railed. 'This is bloody madness. What would I have wanted to kill *either* of 'em for?' His beard jutted and his gaze went challengingly around the table. 'Well, say something, somebody, for Christ's sake.'

But none of them uttered a word.

'When you locked up your workshop on Thursday night, Mr Huxley, where did you leave the key?'

Huxley jerked a thumb towards the dresser.

'And *you* collected up the keys, Mr Sutton? The way your sister usually does?'

'Well...' Sutton slid another discomforted glance across at Huxley. 'Yes. I suppose I did.'

'You suppose? Does that mean you didn't check them?'

'No. There were several bunches on the same hook. I simply collected them up. I didn't exactly look to see what I'd got—except for the house keys, of course.'

'How about you, Miss Sutton?' asked Roper. 'Do you simply pick up whatever keys are there; or do you check them?'

'Only the house and car keys,' she said. 'I rely on the others to hang their keys on the dresser. But I think I'd notice if a set were missing.'

'But you didn't notice if the keys to Mr Huxley's workshop were hanging on the dresser on Thursday night or not, Mr Sutton?'

Sutton sent another sheepish apology across to Lewis Huxley. 'No,' he said. 'I'm afraid I didn't.'

Huxley started to rise, pale-faced and angry. Makins moved in quickly behind him.

'Will you sit down, please, Mr Huxley,' said Roper quietly. 'I haven't finished, sir.'

Huxley stared back balefully at him. 'What will you do if I don't?' he said. 'Bloody arrest me?'

Roper stared him out, four-squarely and for several long seconds. 'Yes, sir,' he said. 'I'd say that was very likely.'

'I didn't kill Vera Jackman. Nor Mike.'

An expectant silence had fallen over the table as all eyes turned to Lewis Huxley. A long cylinder of ash fell from Haldane's cigarette. Roper had never been quite sure what a basilisk stare was: until he saw the way Carol Haldane's dark eyes spiked up Huxley.

'I never said you did, sir,' said Roper. 'All I'm doing is marrying a few facts with some possibilities.'

Unwillingly, grudgingly, Huxley at last resumed his chair.

'Thank you, Mr Huxley,' said Roper. 'So somebody *could* have taken the keys to Mr Huxley's workshop on Thursday night. Whoever it was laid the poor lad out, strung him up, then took off his left shoe to dab a few soleprints about. And if only they'd taken the trouble to see how Taunton tied his shoelaces, then none of us would have been any the wiser. Right?'

There was no response.

From his jacket pocket, Roper fished out Vera Jackman's tawdry wristwatch in its polythene envelope and slid it to the middle of the table.

'Recognise that, Mr Huxley?'

'No,' said Huxley. 'Not particularly.'

'Anyone?'

Mrs Thruxton put up her hand. 'I do,' she said. 'I think Vera had one like that.'

'Yes,' agreed Rachael Dance. 'Sue's right. Vera did have one like that, I'm sure.'

Her husband leaned forward and gingerly picked it up. He lifted his spectacles up to his forehead and peered closely at the envelope.

'I think I saw her wearing one like that, too,' he said.

'It *was* Vera Jackman's,' said Roper. 'We've had it confirmed.' He held out his hand and Dance passed it back to him. 'One of my lads found it in the coach-house.'

'Perhaps she dropped it there,' suggested Jennifer Sutton.

'No, madam,' said Roper. 'I don't think Vera Jackman went anywhere near your coachhouse that night. In fact I don't think she got very far beyond your front gate. But she was wearing it in the Cort Arms on Tuesday night. And when her body was found in Church Lane on Wednesday morning this watch was nowhere in sight. Now, as I see it, the most likely explanation is that it was inadvertently kicked out of the Range Rover by the murderer when he'd driven back from Church Lane after dumping the body. Vera Jackman didn't come further into the grounds than the dustbins that night. Whoever killed her knew she was coming along here to see them as soon as she'd finished at the Arms. They didn't like what she had to tell them, so they killed her—with a length of cable that happened to be in one of the dustbins.'

'Just like that?'

'Yes, madam,' said Roper. 'Just like that. Now, nobody's going to cart a dead body from the dustbins to the coachhouse. It was easier to drive the Rover down to the gate, put Jackman's body aboard, dump her body in the ditch beside the Jacksons' smallholding, then drive back here. That's when whoever it was probably kicked the watch out. It most likely fell off while he was manoeuvring the body into the car. Difficult things to handle, corpses. They flop about all over the place.'

'I hate to say it,' said Jennifer Sutton, 'but if it happened the way you say, then it had to be Mike, didn't it? It *couldn't* have been any one else—because the house was locked up and we were all inside it.'

'But you *weren't* all inside it, madam,' said Roper. 'That's the point.'

He gave them a few moments to digest that, leaving what he had just proposed to float around the cheap parchment lampshade like a question mark. All he had to wait for now was what he always thought of as the magic moment.

He reached into another pocket and closed his fist about another polythene envelope. 'See any of these in Morocco, Mr Sutton?' he said, as the *ankh* and chain slid out of the envelope like a miniature golden river and settled on the table. 'They're called *ankhs*, sir.'

And Roper glanced along the table quickly enough to catch the brief flicker of recognition in Sutton's eyes, the momentary sag of his jaw, the tightening of his muscles as his adrenalin surged . . .

And that was the magic moment.

ROPER WATCHED THE OTHERS file out—Huxley, the Thruxtons, the Dances, Carol Haldane. Makins closed the kitchen door on them and stood with his back to it.

'May I have a cigarette?' asked Jennifer Sutton, of Price.

'I don't smoke, Miss Sutton,' said Price.

Makins came forward and proffered an open packet over her shoulder. She plucked out a cigarette and leaned sideways towards Makins' lighter flame.

'Thank you.'

Makins went back to his post by the door.

'So my brother gave her a present,' said Jennifer Sutton, shrugging and blowing out smoke. 'What the hell does that prove?'

'It's worth about four hundred pounds, Miss Sutton,' said Roper. 'That's right, isn't it, Mr Sutton?'

Isolated now at the far end of the table, Sutton nodded. His unlit pipe lay on its side on the table in front of him.

'Don't say anything, Alan,' warned his sister. 'I'm sure they can't prove a thing.'

'I've got all the evidence I need, Miss Sutton,' said Roper, not quite truthfully, but with sufficient assuredness to make both of them believe him. 'A valve cap off your car, a blade of grass from near your dustbins, a fistful of sawdust from Mr Huxley's workshop—and now this cross, which your brother admits to having bought in Morocco and given to Vera Jackman—perhaps in exchange for services rendered? Would that be right, Mr Sutton?'

'Yes,' agreed Sutton. 'I suppose so. But it—'

'Be quiet!' shouted his sister. 'Idiot! He's only *fishing*. He doesn't know a damned *thing*. In fact I don't think we even have to sit here and listen to him.'

'And *you* helped him, Miss Sutton, didn't you? Both times.'

Her pale eyes glittered malevolently at him. 'Utter nonsense. We'd have too much to lose.'

'Yes, you had, hadn't you, Miss Sutton,' agreed Roper. He folded his arms comfortably on the table. 'But all the same I suggest you did. I think Vera Jackman rang here on Tuesday evening—about seven-thirty—and told your brother that she was pregnant and wanted to see him. She came along after the pub

shut and met your brother down by the front gate.
Perhaps she asked him for money—I don't know—but
whatever she told him or asked him was enough to
make him lose his temper and slip a length of wire
around her neck—a piece of cable lying on top of one
of the dustbins. He held it there long enough to kill
her.'

'And then I suppose he drove the Range Rover
down to the gate,' sneered Jennifer Sutton, 'and
dumped her on the backseat.'

'No, Miss Sutton,' said Roper. '*You* drove the car
down to the gate. And the two of you, together, probably, put Jackman's body aboard and took it across to
Church Lane.'

'Couldn't have,' she said. 'I was here in the house
all the time. Lewis saw me locking up.'

'No, Miss Sutton,' countered Roper. 'I think you'd
already locked up. When Mr Huxley saw you under
the stairs on Tuesday night you weren't switching *on*
the alarms. You were switching them *off*. So that you
could go outside and help your brother.'

'And that's nonsense, too,' she said. 'How could I
have known what was happening, for God's sake?
There was no way he could have contacted me without the rest of the house knowing about it.'

'Easy, Miss Sutton,' said Roper. 'All he had to do
was to walk twenty yards out of the gate and use that
telephone box beside your wall. He *rang* you, Miss
Sutton. You've got a phone upstairs. Separate line.
Who would have heard it—except you? He could even
have reversed the charges. Isn't that right, Mr Sutton?'

And that was the second magic moment. Sutton didn't answer, but he didn't need to. His crumpled face said it all.

'I WAS CRAZY ABOUT HER,' mumbled Sutton. 'And she knew it. I thought I meant something to her, too. I gave her money for clothes—and whatever else she wanted. I let her bleed me white—and I didn't care.'

'And she was as common as dirt, you fool,' snapped his sister.

'And I didn't care about that either. But you wouldn't understand that, would you?' His eyes flared briefly along the table at her, then switched off again. His head fell forward and his shoulders slumped.

'About a month ago—out of the blue—she told me she was going up to London. She'd got a job modelling. She was leaving the village and wasn't coming back. I could go with her, she said; we could make our own way. Fool that I was, I said yes. I loathe this bloody place. She'd got like a drug, you see, and I couldn't do without her. She asked me for money: two hundred. Said she'd arranged a flat for us both in London. And like a sucker, I fell for it. It was advance rent, she said. A month. But then, during the next couple of weeks, she changed.

'Changed how, Mr Sutton?'

'She wouldn't let me touch her—made excuses. Said we'd get back to all that sort of thing when we got to London.'

'When you say touch her, Mr Sutton . . . ?'

'What the hell do you think I mean?' asked Sutton wearily. 'I thought she was playing the tease, winding me up—you know? A bloody game.'

'And when did you find out it wasn't?'

'On Tuesday evening,' said Sutton. 'She rang here—I forget the time—and told me she wanted to see me. Said she'd be along at about a quarter to eleven and I'd better be there. London was out. She wanted cash. A lot. She was pregnant, and it was mine. Said she'd tell her brother I'd got her drunk and taken advantage of her.'

'And had you—ever?'

'About seven or eight weeks ago,' said Sutton. 'No—I didn't take advantage. We were *both* tight. It was across at her place—her brother was out for the night. Only she was going to deny that and say it was down at the lodge.'

'But she could never have proved that, Mr Sutton. All you'd have needed was a good lawyer.'

'Oh, I knew that,' said Sutton. He looked very old, very tired, very small. 'It didn't bother me. I was angrier about the dance she'd led me. I said I'd meet her—but that I wasn't going to give her any money.'

'And what did she say to that?'

'"You want to bet?"—and laughed.'

'Was that when you decided to kill her?'

Sutton shook his head. 'God, no. I was angry. But I wasn't *that* angry.'

'So when did you?'

'I didn't *decide,*' said Sutton. 'It just *happened.* I don't think I even *meant* to do it until the very last moment.'

'And how *did* it happen, sir?'

Sutton pushed his fingers through his crisp, greying hair. 'It happened. She started to shout—called me a cripple—said what the hell did she want to go to London for with a bloody cripple. I *had* to shut her up, you see. I couldn't stand that. And she wouldn't shut up—so I lost my head. I honestly don't remember doing anything until I found myself standing over her with a length of old cable in my hand.

'For a couple of minutes, I must have stood there— I don't remember thinking anything except that I'd killed somebody and I could hardly breathe—I thought I was having a heart attack. And frankly I didn't care if I was. Then I pulled myself together. I knew I had to do something. I knew that Jonny would have locked the house by then—she didn't know I'd been outside, you see—and that I couldn't ring the doorbell because if any of the others heard it they might put two and two together if the police came.

'Then it occurred to me that I could ring her from the telephone box just outside the main gate. Contact her that way. No one else need ever know.'

'Did you tell her you'd killed Jackman?'

'No,' said Sutton. 'Just that I was in a hell of a lot of trouble.'

'Whose idea was it to drive the body across to Church Lane?'

'Mine,' said Sutton.

'Yours?' His sister sneered at him across the table. 'You were gibbering. *You* couldn't think of anything.'

'So it was your idea, Miss Sutton?'

'*He's* gutless—always has been.'

Roper rose slowly from his chair and took the few paces to the back door to stretch his legs. Out in the real world the sun shone and the birds twittered.

SEVENTEEN

'WE THOUGHT HE WAS DEAD, you see,' said Sutton, his quiet, diffident voice so soft now that Roper had to strain to hear it.

'That night...he came down the steps from the garden to the kitchen. He was tugging off his T-shirt on his way down—God knows why. He was terribly drunk...did I tell you that?...Anyway, I was at the sink...I heard him fall...I don't think he fell far...the second or third step perhaps...and I heard a thud. I think that must have been his head hitting the wall by the back door here. The T-shirt was over his face by this time...I suppose that was as far as he'd got taking it off. He didn't get up...I went out to help him.' Sutton's face lifted and he looked earnestly along the table.

'Honestly,' he said. 'I really *did* intend to help him...I pulled the T-shirt off his face. He was very pale. He wasn't breathing...or so I thought...and I couldn't feel his pulse...That's when I thought...well, I thought...' Sutton's voice finally tailed away altogether.

'That he'd do for a scapegoat?' prompted Roper, not even bothering to hide the contempt in his voice. 'Is that what you thought, Mr Sutton?'

With a tremendous effort, Sutton drew himself upright and twisted his chair to face the table again. He cleared his throat. 'I'm sorry,' he said. 'Sorry. Jenny came down... We talked about it. Decided we couldn't do much until we were sure all the others were in their rooms for the night. Between us, we managed to get Mike back up to the garden and laid him close to the wall by the steps where nobody could see him. After that... after that, I went through the motions of locking up... but I didn't switch on the alarms and I didn't lock this door here.' Sutton gestured absently towards the door to the steps beside him. 'While I was doing that, Jenny went to the office to type that note. We pressed his finger and thumb on it.'

'What happened to the letter that Taunton did type, Miss Sutton?' asked Roper.

'I burned them.'

'There were two letters,' said Allan Sutton. 'We found them down at the lodge on Thursday night. They looked like job-hunting letters... We'd gone to the lodge to hide that key to the Rover... But that was afterwards...

'We carried Mike between us across to the old stables... He was very heavy... We had to do it all by torchlight. Two step ladders side by side. I tied the rope around the handrail. Then we managed to get Mike more or less sitting on top of the steps. I tied the noose while Jenny held him upright... And that's when... that's when...' His voice faded away again.

'When what, Mr Sutton?' asked Price.

Sutton closed his eyes and shivered with horror. 'He half-opened his eyes and moaned... That's when we realised that he wasn't dead. Dear God... he wasn't dead... I started to untie him... but Jenny said, "Push him off, push him off." And she let him go... and he fell sideways... I went for a knife or something to cut him down. She told me not to be a fool, Mike was just a yob, and if you thought he'd killed Vera you'd all go away and leave us alone.'

'And all the while she was telling you this, Michael Taunton was swinging on the end of the rope?'

'Yes,' agreed Sutton. 'But it was quick. I don't think he really *knew* anything.'

'And whose idea were the shoeprints?'

Sutton jerked his head towards his sister. 'Hers,' he said. 'And leaving the window open. That was her idea too.'

'One last question, Mr Sutton: the time, when Taunton died—about twenty past eleven, was it? When Mrs Thruxton heard your dog whining?'

'Yes,' replied Sutton. 'About that.'

Roper leaned back in his chair, tired now himself, and more sickened than he had been in many a long year.

HANDCUFFED TO A WPC, Jennifer Sutton went down the step towards Jollyboy's Metro. Roper watched her duck and swing her legs in, then stood aside as Allan Sutton came across the hall manacled to Makins and leaning on his stick.

Sutton paused in the porch and took a deep breath of the late-afternoon air. 'You know, Superintendent,' he said, 'my sister's going to miss all this.'

'I'm sure she is, sir,' said Roper.

He watched Sutton climb into the car and Makins settle himself in beside him. For Roper there was no feeling of exhilaration, barely even satisfaction.

He cupped a hand around his lighter and lit a cheroot as he walked down the drive. The two cars overtook him and the small crowd at the gate parted like a wake to let them through. In the forefront of them was young Fred Jackman.

For a moment, Roper stood eye to eye with him. There was still one more piece of information about his sister that Jackman would have to know…and that wouldn't be a pleasant job either…

'Buy you a drink, son? Have a chat, shall we?'

Jackman thought about it. 'Sure,' he said. 'Thanks.'

Out here in the real world the sun still shone and the birds still twittered, and on the green the last man out was being noisily applauded.

'You got lucky, then,' said Jackman, as he fell into step beside him.

'Aye, son,' said Roper. 'We got lucky.'

The DOWN HOME *Heifer Heist*

First Time in Paperback

A Sam & Nicky Titus Mystery

THIN ICE

Rancher Joe Pilkington, neighbor to Sheriff Sam Titus and photographer wife Nicky, is run down when he interrupts rustlers during a heist. Aside from tire tracks in the snow, the only clue is the sound of Mozart heard playing from the killer's truck.

Two more grisly deaths follow, and it looks as if a beloved member of the Titus ranch may be accused of murder. Sam and Nicky grimly set out to corner a killer...before they become victims themselves.

"Sandstrom makes the most of her setting...."
—*Publishers Weekly*

Available in October at your favorite retail stores.

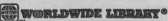

FOUR ON THE FLOOR

RALPH McINERNY

A Father Dowling Mystery Quartet

First Time in Paperback

THE FEROCIOUS FATHER
Mr. O'Halloran had lots of fund-raising ideas for St. Hilary's—plus an unidentified corpse in his car trunk. Had the Mob followed Mr. O'Halloran to town?

HEART OF COLD
Branded a thief, old Ray has paid his debt to society. But when he is abducted, Father Dowling must prove that crime is all in the family.

THE DEAD WEIGHT LIFTER
A body is deposited at St. Hilary's, and Father Dowling must find out who the man is and why he died.

THE DUTIFUL SON
Father Dowling agrees to help a man by exhuming and reburying the body of an infant who died years ago. But the body in question proves to be something quite different.

"Excellent short adventures, crisply written, with surprising twists." —*St. Louis Post-Dispatch*

Available in October at your favorite retail stores.

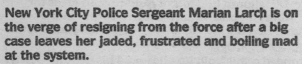
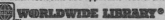